THE UNREPENTANT

THE UNREPENTANT

SKHARR DEATHEATER™ SERIES BOOK 06

MICHAEL ANDERLE

DISRUPTIVE IMAGINATION

LMBPN Publishing
PMB 196, 2540 South Maryland Pkwy
Las Vegas, NV 89109

Version 1.00 May 2021
ebook ISBN: 978-1-64971-772-6
Paperback ISBN: 978-1-64971-773-3

THE UNREPENTANT TEAM

Thanks to our JIT Team:

Dorothy Lloyd
Zacc Pelter
Peter Manis
Jackey Hankard-Brodie
John Ashmore
Rachel Beckford
Paul Westman
Diane L. Smith
Kelly O'Donnell
Jeff Goode
Angel LaVey

If I've missed anyone, please let me know!

Editor
SkyHunter Editing Team

To Family, Friends and
Those Who Love
To Read.
May We All Enjoy Grace
To Live The Life We Are
Called.

— Michael

CHAPTER ONE

I t unsettled Skharr to have to remain constantly alert in the
city. After all, he had begun to regard it as being as close to a
home as he'd ever had since leaving the DeathEater clan.

Still, it had been so many years since he left his true home
behind that he sometimes struggled to picture what it was like in
his quiet moments. The Clan would have changed entirely by the
time he decided to return—if he ever did.

This wasn't as likely a scenario as he had once thought.

Until that happened, Verenvan was where he spent most of
his time, and while it had irked him somewhat when he had first
arrived, there was something comforting about it now. Not that
he would ever feel homesick if he left. It wasn't the city itself that
appealed to him but the sense of familiarity it brought.

Despite this, he could still feel gazes following him as he
wandered through the streets. It was not an uncommon occur-
rence. A barbarian was an odd sight in most cities and towns of
the world, but there was a darker tone to the stares in Verenvan.
It hadn't been long since avarice had driven the desperate and the
violent of the city to try to kill him.

He had been assured that this was no longer the case, but it was never a good idea to assume there were no others who wanted him dead badly enough to pay for the effort required to accomplish it.

The barbarian slid his hand to the dagger he carried on his belt when he caught a glimpse of movement that suggested someone was following him through the narrow streets of the workshop section of the city. The buildings were taller and the streets were narrower, which thinned the crowd that moved through them and made it easier to detect any who might have dogged his footsteps.

Surprisingly, he soon identified what looked like a dwarf trailing him, and not with any kind of professionalism. In fact, it seemed as though he wanted to catch up to him without breaking out into a full sprint through the cramped streets.

After a few moments of thought, Skharr stopped completely and pretended he had paused to inspect his belt and adjust his clothes. He made sure his hand didn't stray far from his dagger and watched the cloaked figure cautiously as it closed the distance between the two of them without even a pretense of subterfuge.

"Heavens above, barbarian." The dwarf gasped as he approached and pulled his hood back. He looked out of breath, his skin pink and covered in sweat. "Your long legs are a true challenge to keep up with. I would have had to start running outright if you hadn't slowed. And you must know it is impolite to make a dwarf run after you."

"Hmm." The warrior grunted and narrowed his eyes. "Why?"

"Because dwarves don't like running. Our build is better suited to efficient, long-distance walking, not sprinting like a godsbedammed fucking elf."

"No," he interrupted before his pursuer could go off at a tangent. "Why following?" He was well aware that dwarves liked to walk at their own pace. They made a point of mentioning it to him and usually assured him that at a good pace, they could outlast almost any other species in the world. The problem was that they could not move quickly.

"Oh. Yes, well, Throk sent me. He asked me to mention to you that he would appreciate it if you used another route."

Skharr narrowed his eyes and inched forward. "What other route? And who are you?"

The dwarf opened his mouth to answer but the barbarian twisted sharply. Another hand was reaching for his coin purse and before he even fully registered it, he had grasped it in a vice-like hold and squeezed and twisted as hard as he could manage in his awkward position. He turned fully, expecting to find one of the local young pickpockets from the size of the hand.

Surprise registered on his face when he realized he had almost picked another dwarf up. He wore a heavy hood and cloak as well but looked leaner than most of his kind, although with his feet almost off the ground, he displayed no real sense of malice or danger.

The first dwarf did not look surprised. His eyes rolled and he drew a deep breath as if he tried to restrain himself.

"Throk would also appreciate if you stopped short of killing this little pest as well."

"Pest?" the smaller one retorted as Skharr lifted him fully off his feet. "I'll teach you to call me a pest—"

"If you don't snap your jaw shut, dwarf, I'll drop you on your head four or five times and see how well you talk then," he warned.

The hanging dwarf didn't answer and instead, reached up to try to pry his hand loose from the unyielding hold. His efforts were futile, and the barbarian simply studied the captive as he struggled.

A child would have been easy to hold up and the dwarf was considerably heavier than a child of roughly the same height, but he was not willing to drop the pest yet.

"Throk needs you to enter the warrens through another

route," the first dwarf continued and watched his kinsman's struggles with interest. "And since Brahgen is available, he will show you the way Throk wishes you to take."

"I take it Brahgen is the name of this sullen creature?" Skharr asked and raised an eyebrow.

"And I'm a creature now, am I?" Brahgen continued his fight to free himself.

"Aye," the other dwarf answered and ignored the protest. "Provided he ceases his difficult nature."

"I'm not difficult. I'm…adventurous."

"There's not much need for that in a city, ye little shit. Now stop being an adventurous pest and do as you're commanded. I won't return with news of how a barbarian was right to lop your arm off."

Brahgen stopped his struggles, looked around, and finally acknowledged the wisdom of this with a slow nod. Skharr smirked, opened his hand, and let the dwarf fall.

He was nimble and lithe and rolled smoothly over his shoulder to regain his feet before he brushed the dirt from the cobbles off his cloak.

"Right then," the younger dwarf muttered, straightened his clothes, and rubbed some feeling into his sore arm. "Follow me."

Skharr nodded and complied without comment. Their route branched off the thoroughfare he'd been on and proceeded along a handful of parallel streets through the sector until they reached what looked like a dead end.

His guide seemed undeterred, approached the wall at the far side of the alley, and rapped his knuckles against the stone in a quick code to whoever might have waited on the other side.

A few moments later, the sound of stone grinding on stone heralded a section of the wall being dragged clear. It moved along a meticulously dug rut in the ground that worked as a track to allow it to come free and be pushed into place again without too much difficulty. It would have been invisible to any eyes that weren't watching for it.

Not many in the world could work stone like dwarves could. The barbarian wondered if there was something innately magical in their blood that allowed for it, but those he'd questioned had all replied that it was merely due to skill and instruction.

The wall opened onto a narrow staircase leading into the earth. He needed to duck as he followed Brahgen into the Warrens.

That dwarves liked living underground was not new information, of course, but he wondered if even the city guard had been down there. It seemed to add a multitude of streets to Verenvan that were entirely populated by dwarves, kept secret and hidden, and allowed them some degree of autonomy in a city that was otherwise populated mainly by humans.

A few twists and turns through the well-lit tunnels came and went before there was any sign of other dwarves in the area. Skharr moved his hand immediately to his dagger when they turned a corner and came face to face with a half-dozen dwarves. These wore full armor and were armed with shields and spears.

All six were tense and lowered their weapons when they saw him and a swift shout stopped them short of attacking.

A woman pushed through the group, caught one of the guards by his shoulder pauldron, and shoved him roughly into the wall.

"*Voras wer* shit, you useless idiots," she snapped and mixed her native tongue with the common language spoken in the region. "And you, Brahgen—you and I will have words!"

His guide took a step back, which told Skharr that the nature of those words would not be pleasant. It was made worse when the woman boxed the young dwarf on the right ear and proceeded to grasp him by it as well.

"Throk has gone to great lengths so you don't have your *schion* chopped off for his sister's sake, but you'll find I lack his patience."

She dragged him between the six guards and toward another set of steps that appeared to open into a more spacious area underground. Unsure of what he should do next, the warrior looked at the guards.

They were similarly confused and simply shrugged and stepped aside to create a path for him to follow Brahgen and the woman who still had him by the ear.

No one stopped him as he advanced through their lines, down the steps, and into the Warrens.

In most ways, this could not have been more different than the previous council meeting Micah had attended. The members present were mostly human, for one thing, and all appeared to be from one noble house or the other. They spoke with perfect clarity and cultured intonations and called on the mighty names of the past to support their arguments and conclusions.

Oddly, however, they appeared to have the same greedy spirit to them as the old undercouncil had. While so dissimilar, it was all the same when it came to attitude and motivation.

She covered her grimace by sipping the goblet of pear juice that had been poured for her.

The count's council had been summoned, which included most of those who were involved in the running of the city. The Council of Verenvan had once been one of the most respected bodies of governance in the empire. Now, it had become little more than a cesspit of bureaucrats who were as willing to engage in criminal activity as their undercity counterparts. Those who were not were rotting in the swamps, far away from where curious eyes could find them—perhaps forever.

"What happened was an atrocity," one of the members stated and ran his fingers through his long, luxuriant golden locks. "There needs to be blame assigned to the responsible parties.

Many in the city would cause a greater disturbance if heads do not roll."

The man's hair was a point of some pride for him, which was why he avoided touching it with his right hand—the one crammed full of rings. Viscount Benning had the looks of an angel and the cunning mind to match, but he lacked the kind of willpower that would have elevated him to a higher standing in the empire. He was content to be the largest fish in a tiny pond.

It was why she was sickened by merely looking at him.

"Heads must roll," Baron Versan agreed and tugged his thick, grizzled beard gently. "The barbarian is the catalyst of the dangers that have befallen our beloved city. If none of you three will accept the blame, it must be passed to him."

Micah turned to look at her sister on her right—who had stopped mid-bite into a pastry—and then her left, where the Lady Svana sat. She was the Viscount's cousin and there was a certain family resemblance, although the lady had inherited all the willpower and courage in the family.

"I can tell you here and now that would create more problems than it would solve," Svana stated calmly and tilted her head while she inspected her reflection in the goblet in her hand.

"And you should know the emperor considers him a weapon in his arsenal," Sera added and swallowed the food she'd been chewing on before she continued. "I was there when a request was sent by the emperor's Falcons."

"I thought those were simply self-aggrandizing stories spread by the man himself," the baron retorted.

"I can't speak for all the stories," the guard captain snapped in return. "Only what I was present for."

The council members all exchanged a quick, nervous look. None had been happy with how power had changed hands, but the fact that it had happened so quickly and that no ripples had spread to the rest of the empire was a relief. Not only that, none of them had any inclination to range themselves against one of the new emperor's favorites.

"Even so," Benning continued, leaned forward, and spread his fingers over the table between them, "the vacuum of power left by those who were killed is not a problem to be ignored. It could result in violence on the streets and even the first skirmishes in a war. The city guard is not prepared for it."

Micah didn't want to tell him that the city guard was as likely to join the skirmishes as anyone else.

"I have worked hard to keep the fighting as minimal as possible," she stated and drew a deep breath. "Any who are found with innocent blood on their blades have seen swift and overwhelming retribution. Those who fight know to keep the underground…underground."

"And we are thankful for your efforts."

She turned to look at the one man she didn't understand among the group. He was slim and lean, with thinning hair and no beard, and wore simple clothes. No rings flashed ostentatiously on his fingers. He was the count's financial advisor and had an excellent mind for coin—the kind that few could match. And, oddly enough, the counting of coin was all he had any interest in. He had a simple home on the count's estate, no mistresses, no friends of note, and nothing she could use against him.

That said, he had a unique mind and she appreciated that. Sefor was an oddity and one she continued to study out of sheer curiosity.

"Sera's friendship with the barbarian is something to note," he continued. "Your shared relation to the emperor does not appear to have any influence on that. We cannot act against the man himself but the point remains that he cannot remain in Verenvan while there is still a vacuum of power to be addressed."

The other members of the council nodded. It was interesting

to see all of them listening calmly to a man who was raised in a fisherman's hut on the wharf.

"He is and will continue to be a problem," he continued, "as the city will turn itself into a hotbed of intrigue. Cloaks and daggers are all well and good, but the barbarian has a way of turning what should be a transition of power into a war. One we cannot afford."

Micah realized that all the members of the council were focused on her sister. Sera came to the same realization a few seconds later and looked around the room.

"What?" she asked, her eyes narrowed.

"We all think you must be the one to tell Skharr he has to leave the city," Micah admitted once it was clear that none of the other members were willing to state it in so many words.

"Where is everyone's sense of heroism now?" the guild captain asked. Her gaze swept around the table and met those of every member of the council. Each one looked away as she stared challengingly at them.

All but Sefor, who frowned a little and leaned forward.

Finally, she nodded. "Very well. I'll talk to him about leaving the city."

"Today," the viscount insisted.

Sera drew a deep breath and studied the man carefully. "I could always have him say goodbye to you first."

He shifted uncomfortably in his seat. "I suppose…tomorrow is soon enough."

She smirked, pushed up from her seat, rolled her shoulders, and stretched languidly. Something graceful always seemed to define her—as if she was perpetually in perfect balance and could snap into action from any position. It was intimidating, and Micah couldn't help but feel a little jealous of how the woman was able to carry herself.

"You finish your yammering," she said. "I have a barbarian to find."

She left quickly and her sister realized that the gazes now turned to her once she was gone.

"And if he refuses to leave?" Benning asked and raised an eyebrow.

Svana snorted. "I suggest we wait to confirm his plans before we consider what options we have available to us." Her gaze shifted to the Marchioness Edenine, who had dark, almond-shaped eyes and tanned skin that perfectly matched her short black hair and delicate features. "The man is known to be influenced by the wiles of the flesh when other considerations fail."

The marchioness narrowed her eyes. "I thought you had a predilection for barbarian flesh. Why would you pass the duties on to me?"

Of course, Svana's dalliances with the barbarian were an ill-kept secret. She had helped to spread the word as the man's physical attributes were likely to intimidate any lesser men who might try to court her.

The fact that it was her secret to share showed when she grinned impishly at the other woman. "I do have a taste for the man but for the moment, I am still...recovering. Besides, he would see any wiles of mine coming from a great distance. Someone new who he does not know would be a finer tool for the work at hand."

The marchioness leaned back in her seat and nodded acquiescence.

It was interesting that none of the men at the table feigned any kind of outrage at the impropriety under discussion. When they were all behind closed doors, none of them cared to maintain the pretenses that governed their society.

CHAPTER TWO

Skharr had only ever visited the outskirts of the Warren in the past and in reality, this was limited to Throk's forge. He had assumed, however, that the dwarves in the city had gathered in a small microcosm of their own.

They were notoriously fond of their own company, after all.

That said, he had no idea that the Warrens ran so deep under the city. What had been wide hallways had opened out and led deeper into the earth, carefully and lovingly crafted by skilled hands. They passed through a handful of water caverns, where he could see the water flowed clear and with no particular smell. This meant they had managed to tap a source from well below the city and far from the sewers and the swamps.

That alone was impressive. It was the type of productivity he had come to expect from the dwarves but it was one thing to hear of it and another to see it in action. He'd spent time with them before in their homelands and it was encouraging that they had retained these abilities so far from what they were familiar with.

Those who lived there had created a small city, complete with their own guards who patrolled through the Warrens. All studied

Skharr like they were trying to evaluate him and decide whether he posed a threat to them or not.

He could still hear Brahgen complaining to the woman for a good ten minutes after she had dragged him by the ear ahead of the group that escorted their visitor. In his mind, it likely meant some complaining had been earned. Even so, from the way the guards paid more mind to the youth than to him, he had a feeling the young dwarf had earned the treatment he was receiving as well.

"I would say this is a city in its own right," he said as they continued to move through what could only be described as streets beneath Verenvan. A short while later, their path wound toward a massive cavern lit by hundreds of fires and thousands of torches.

"I'd heard rumors of the Dwarven City under the City," Skharr continued and looked around the massive chamber. "I never dreamed that it was under Verenvan. Or that it would be so…large."

"Verenth var Chrondagh is a closely held secret among my kin," the woman answered and diverted her attention from the young dwarf for a moment. "I am surprised you heard of it. I suppose the dwarves in the mountains talk a little too much."

"DeathEaters and dwarves have a close bond in the mountains," he answered. "And even then, it was when we were all drunk that they told stories none were meant to speak of. I can see why, as you have hidden it under one of the empire's largest port cities."

She laughed, grasped Brahgen by the neck, and dragged him to where he could see rich fortifications, all marked with Anvil-Forged's sigil carved into the stone.

"If you wait at the fountain over there, I'll tell Throkrag you have arrived to speak to him," she said and shoved the younger dwarf forward and through the doors.

The barbarian nodded, moved to the fountain, and studied a

variety of markings in the stone. From what he could see, it looked like a story being told. Dwarves in full battle plate marched into combat and wound upward to the top of the fountain, where a carved dragon spewed the water that filled the fountain.

Perhaps it was a fictional battle against a dragon that was in the AnvilForged legends. It might not have been fictional, of course, but that was the most likely possibility.

"DeathEater! They told me that you were waiting for me out here."

He turned as a barrel-chested dwarf approached him. His eyes looked heavy and his steps weren't as sure as they usually were. Skharr was uncertain what to make of seeing him like this. There appeared to be something of a feast happening inside, and Throk motioned for the barbarian to join him at a nearby stone table where food and drink were being set out.

"I see fine stonework here," he noted as he sat across from the dwarf. "Your hands?"

"My grandfather's. He had a hand for stone, where my hand is mostly for metal. You know...I've been thinking of you lately. There aren't many DeathEaters in this region of the world. The Clan knows my kind a little better and you appreciate us better than most humans."

"Perhaps because we've seen what dwarves are capable of in large numbers."

"Aye. Aye, I suppose that is true. But most humans would see one of our cities and have a mind to claim it and make it theirs, while The Clan simply see and admire it. I like that about you and your kin."

Skharr nodded. "That is appreciated."

"I had a dream, you know, and a human female entered my dream. She was beautiful, I suppose, if you have a preference for human females. Have you ever been with a dwarf woman?"

"I can't say I have. They don't like a human my size much."

"They wouldn't, come to think of it. But back to my tale. She was beautiful with rich black hair and dressed in flowing silks, she looked rather like a goddess, but not any I have ever heard of or seen."

"From what I've heard, there are numerous gods and goddesses who aren't too well-known."

"Aye, it could be. But the point is, she came into the dream to warn me. She said there is a plot afoot between the local Thieves and Assassins' guilds to kill a barbarian but that the gods were in support of the barbarian in this. So perhaps she was some kind of oracle, although why an oracle would need to peep into my dreams escapes me."

Throk paused, took a few bites from the freshly roasted pork belly that was set out in front of them, and motioned for his guest to join him. It was impolite to allow a dwarf to eat alone when in company, and Skharr cut a slab of the pork for himself.

"I tried to think of who she might have been, and I found one of my kin who prays to the goddess of thieves. She's not too well known and most humans bow their heads to...uh, Neuregh, although I don't think he's a high god in his own right. Still, no matter."

"How long ago did this warning come to you?" he asked. He had a feeling that he already knew which of Throk's kin prayed to a god of thieves, but he didn't want to make any assumptions that could not be withdrawn.

"A few weeks past. I told my kin of my dream, in which the woman asked me to cast protection over the young Brahgen. I did as she asked, and sure enough, there was a slaughter and all those who ruled the undercouncil of Verenvan were killed and a new undercouncil royalty was born."

The barbarian nodded and took a bite of the juicy, well-cooked pork. "I think I know the occasion you speak of."

"Aye. I should have cast a warning your way as well. There aren't many barbarians in these parts she could have been referring to, of course. You were still in the city and I could have acted or found some way to help."

"It's no matter," Skharr answered. "It turned out well enough in the end and I am glad your...nephew?"

Throk nodded.

"I am glad your nephew is safe."

"Your concern is appreciated. And yet...there is a rub. Brahgen has to leave and go to another clan. He can't be seen by the humans here who might know he was not killed and assume he was part of the coup. Too many in this city have a mistrust of us as it is, and I would not see him fall victim to that, especially over something that is not his doing."

The barbarian tugged one of his forelocks thoughtfully before he tucked it behind his ear. "Are there no others you could trust this business to?"

"No." The dwarf shook his head and carefully cleaned some grease that had spilled from the pork belly onto his beard. "You are the only one I trust to accomplish this, especially since you might find that Brahgen himself gives ye the most trouble."

"Is that so?"

"The lad fancies himself as something of a thief." Throk snorted. "Simply because he hasn't the body for smithing, he assumes a thief is what he must be. He's barely reached manhood and he's about to get himself killed. The only wise thing he did was pray to some...demigoddess who gave a rat's ass about his sorry skin."

It seemed as though his companion could have revealed a little more of who or what the dream intruder was. He wasn't sure why the dwarf felt the need for secrecy but he decided not to question it. As long as Throk needed something from him, it was only good manners to at least give the idea some serious thought.

"I have intended to leave the city, in all honesty," he admitted and drew a deep breath. "I was involved in that business you mentioned, and... Well, suffice it to say there are still those who would see a certain barbarian breathing the water in the sewers."

"I see."

"There is a matter we need to discuss, however."

Throk nodded. "Your ax. It isn't quite finished yet but it will be by the morrow. If you wish, I could have the weapon sent to you when you arrive at your destination."

Skharr shook his head. "The weapon was never intended for my hands. I would need it sent to the DeathEater clan."

"Ah...that would be in the opposite direction of where you're going. I know of some who could deliver the weapon safely to your clan at the earliest opportunity. Would you have any... words that you would send with it?"

The warrior nodded, cut a slice from the pork, and added bread to it as he considered what he wanted to say.

"Tell them..." He paused, shook his head, and smirked. "Tell them that Skharr DeathEater has paid The Clan all that is due and more. Should they desire anything more in recompense or deeds, they should look to others among them."

Throk leaned forward, his eyes suddenly focused. "You...you sunder all obligation to The Clan, then?"

"They already sundered it," he answered. "I am merely... rubbing salt in the wound. There is no way for them to ever right the injustice of what they allowed. This ax will ensure that my mother, father, and those siblings who might still be among their number know there is no shame—no greater DeathEater than the one named Skharr. I am my own man and my decisions were correct. The council of the Clans can suck my—"

The dwarf coughed loudly. "I'll...leave that last part of the message out."

After a moment of thought, Skharr nodded and a small smirk touched his lips. "Aye, perhaps that is for the best. There is no need to get your messenger killed."

"I...I doubt it would happen." Throk grinned and cleared his throat. "So that is what the ax was for the whole time. A final declaration?"

"It was always a possibility but not the only one that came to mind when I commissioned the weapon. But as time passed, it proved to be the only purpose it could serve."

They shared a moment of silence, but he tilted his head in query when his companion started to chuckle softly and shook his head.

"I thought I could not possibly rise to new fame, and yet I will be known as the dwarf who forged the ax of the DeathEaters, the...Ax of Infamy. Hmm, the Ax—"

"Of Skharr, Barbarian of Theros," he completed for him. "A name need not be forced. Our chieftain can accept the weapon with humility or I will pay him a visit and leave it buried in his chest, and he can choke his acceptance out through the gaping hole."

"I see your negotiation skills have not improved." Throk sighed. "Barbarian of Theros?"

"The high god and I have come to an agreement," he admitted. "I cannot change who I am and he does not promise me any explicit help."

"That seems like nothing has changed."

He shrugged. "I am who I am."

"We'll be happy to pay you for your efforts to help my nephew," the dwarf said and changed the subject quickly. "You will be tasked with escorting him out of the city through one of the back ways. And with that, I must ask for your oath that you will never speak of the city you've seen to any you might encounter and not even the gods themselves. Not that I do not believe they already know of this place, but if they have no intention to see what occurs under the ground, we have no intention to attract their attention."

Another point of pride for the dwarves was the belief that they never needed the help of the gods—with a few exceptions.

The barbarian smirked. "What city? All I saw were the dank Warrens the dwarves prefer to live in instead of a real city around them."

Throk nodded. "I'll consider that your oath, of course. Brahgen is a fine lad and brilliant in his way, but he's wound himself into the intrigue that fills this city to the brim. Verenvan is no longer safe for him so he needs to go far from the city's walls to where we would know he is in some semblance of safety. Back to his mother's clan's home, I think—in the mountains. I know he'll find himself in trouble there as well but he will be considered an equal instead of an outsider among his kin."

"How long do you think he'll last before they send him away?"

"I'll give them two years, I think," Throk admitted with a subtle grin. "We are a longsuffering folk but there are limits to their reserves of patience. That is about as long as he's lasted here."

"Will they send him back here?"

"I doubt it. There is more than sufficient trouble to engage him between Verenvan and the mountains the dwarves call home. You will become more acquainted with the dangers yourself, given that you will likely travel through them. Across the Sea of Dragon Kites, in particular, seems to be the most danger you will face along the way."

"I have no fear of deep water or sea dragons."

"You're a fool, then."

"Possibly. But sea dragons are far less defensive and violent than their land-living cousins. A few even helped to guide my ship through treacherous waters and asked only for a few pieces of silver in exchange."

"Silver?"

"They preferred how silver shimmered under the water to gold."

"So the sea dragons can speak?"

"Not in words but they are capable of communicating. Not all of them, however."

"You'll have to tell me about how you know so much about sea dragons sometime."

Skharr smirked but looked up when Brahgen approached the table with a couple of guards, neither of whom were those who had escorted him. He had a feeling that the woman had decided to engage in the revelry the other dwarves were enjoying, although it appeared that her charge was not happy to be dragged across the Warrens like some kind of prisoner.

His glare was a little difficult to miss. The barbarian wasn't sure how he hadn't caught it before. Then again, he had worn a hood that covered his face but it was plain to see as he now studied the visitor with all the rage that came with youth. It was odd how similar human and dwarf younglings were.

"You killed them!" the young dwarf shouted suddenly. He jerked forward like he meant to attack him but was stopped barely an inch into his assault. "You killed them all. Some of them were my friends."

Skharr shrugged and pushed from his seat. "Then you had friends who put your life at risk for no reason. My cutting your time with them short saved your life, even if I didn't kill them all myself."

"No?" Throk asked.

"There were dozens of them. I am deadly but even I cannot fight a small army. Those who were with me did, however, kill them all." He returned his attention to Brahgen, who looked like he was still being restrained by the two armed dwarves. "Consider this your first lesson—never find yourself supporting actions intended to harm a DeathEater. Harm generally comes to those who intend it."

The master smith smirked. "I doubt he'll learn that lesson until he sees what a DeathEater is capable of with his own eyes."

"Have you seen such a thing yourself?" Skharr asked.

"Aye. It's not the kind of thing you forget. I watched as a group of your clan, at the request of the AnvilForged, attacked a caravan coming away from the mountains. The group had stolen something precious from us and The Clan overtook them on one of the icy roads. Howls split the air and arrows were loosed from every possible angle before the warriors descended and killed them all without mercy. It isn't the kind of thing a young dwarf would ever forget."

The barbarian smiled and looked at Brahgen, who avoided his gaze and stared at the stone beneath his feet instead.

"We can only hope such a demonstration does not prove necessary."

CHAPTER THREE

He would not be able to find his way through the passages on his own if he had a month in which to attempt it. Dwarves had an instinct for navigating their tunnels, while the barbarian was far more comfortable walking through the open spaces, be it in the fields or the mountains.

Skharr liked to think it had something to do with his size that made him dislike enclosed spaces, but if that were the case, he had no idea why he had spent so much time underground. He would need to think on that another time, however.

"All you need do is knock again and you'll be let through," the dwarf who guided him said. "We'll show you."

With little else to do but agree, he nodded. He was, however, mostly sure they hadn't followed the same route along which he'd arrived. As expected, when he tasted fresh air again, he stepped through into a different alley. The dwarf showed him the knocking code—not only the precise number of knocks but how to perform them, as well as which part of the wall he needed to knock on.

"Stone is not wood," his guide said as the doors began to close again. "You need to have more patience and tenacity when you deal with it."

The door closed before Skharr could answer and left him in the middle of a mostly abandoned alley. The smell of the swamps wasn't too far off as he moved away and he soon regained his bearings enough to return to the Mermaid without difficulty.

By now, the sun was already straddling the horizon and cast long shadows across the entire city and the torches were being lit throughout. A few areas still hadn't been attended to. The slums would not be lit until the morning light appeared, and he thought he could feel gazes following him through the streets.

Whether they were or not, he couldn't tell. A few too many looks lingered but it was possible that folk were simply curious about him. It was one of the disadvantages of being a little too well-known in the city. Perhaps it was merely his mind playing tricks on him.

And yet the barbarian couldn't resist the urge to keep his hand on the hilt of his dagger while he waited for one of those gazes to follow him for a little too long.

None of them did and he soon approached the famed sign of a topless mermaid perched over the docks. He approached the building through the back. Too many people knew he preferred the Mermaid when he stayed in the city and so it was likely that his entrance through the front would place him toe to toe with folks who wished him ill.

The back door had been left open for him, and he continued through the kitchens that bustled with activity. It seemed the whole room was filled with various aromas and with steam as he turned toward the common room.

"DeathEater!"

He paused and looked around until he saw one of the cooks, who stirred a wooden spoon through the contents of a massive cast iron pot and kept her hair out of her face with a thick leather band.

"Aye, Kora," he answered. "It's good to see you working today. The food will be better than usual—no offense to the rest of the staff."

"They can be as offended as much as they like. It's true," Kora responded with a grin. "I have a platter ready with your usual fare. Ansen says not to but it's best to have it ready for you."

He made a mental note of the innkeeper's name. It continually escaped him and he felt the man would be offended if he told him he had forgotten it.

She paused, selected a slab of cooked meat from one of the nearby fires, and checked it with her fingers before she placed it on the platter for him.

"As with a good stud, good meat must needs be checked, so they say," she said by way of explanation and handed him the food.

"A stud's meat needs to be checked as well, although I suppose that is where its similarities to cooked meat end."

"That depends entirely on the kind of stud." Kora winked at him and held the door into the main room open as the innkeeper was about to push through.

"Where's the food for... Skharr." Ansen grunted when he saw him standing in front of him. A quick look confirmed that he already had his food and he nodded. "I would shoo anyone else out of my kitchens but as it stands, Dame Sera is here for you. She's waited nigh on an hour."

Skharr nodded and held the platter with one hand while he tried one of the small chunks of sausage that had been added to it before the roast. His eyes bulged immediately and it felt as though his mouth was on fire. This was nothing like the spices he was generally used to. It was more of a dry heat, made more interesting by the fact that it was unexpected.

"Good spices, yes?" Ansen asked and gestured for him to follow him into the main room. "They arrived this morning. Our patrons have talked about them all day. I thought DeathEaters were used to spices in their food."

He narrowed his eyes at the man. "You said it is how DeathEaters like their food, yes?"

The proprietor nodded. "I might have implied as much."

"For the future, there is more flavor to match the heat. You'll find more success if you add lemon, lime, or orange to blend the spices and mellow the heat."

Ansen grinned at him. "I might consider having you in our kitchens instead."

"You couldn't afford me." Skharr grinned and turned to where Sera sipped a tall mug of something cool and frothy.

Before he could approach, a young man sat on the chair opposite her and the barbarian paused and narrowed his eyes.

"Should I remove him?" the innkeeper asked.

"Soon, perhaps. I have a feeling you might want to watch this."

The man smirked. "Is she as bad as you are?"

"Honestly? I suspect she might be a good deal worse." The warrior placed his platter on the countertop and took another bite of the spiced sausages while he watched and listened for what would come next.

"And how might I help you?" the blademaster asked after a few moments of silence resulted without the new arrival to her table saying a word.

"You might remain precisely where you are and let me watch you," the man replied with a drunken laugh. "I had hoped to find a beautiful woman with whom I could spend the evening, and damned if you didn't arrive early."

Sera tilted her head and sipped her drink. "Truly?"

"Aye."

"And what do you suppose I'm early for?"

"Heavens know, but the gods sent you to me for a reason and I would see their will done for as long as possible. I say we retire to my room so you can inspect my sword."

"Sword, you say?" she asked and tilted her head as she pushed from her seat.

"Yes!" The man almost couldn't believe what she had said. He stood quickly and needed to lean on his chair to stop himself from falling over.

"But I think you might have to inspect my sword first."

"Wha—"

Before the word could emerge fully from his mouth, Sera already had her weapon in hand. She swung the pommel across his jaw and he stumbled and fell heavily. He held the side of his face as she settled into her seat again, adjusted her clothes, and shifted the blade slightly to make herself more comfortable.

"She is a little more...direct than you tend to be," Ansen conceded. "Straight to the point. I doubt any of the other would-be suitors will attempt to approach her now."

"Those who have their wits about them haven't approached her because of the medallion hanging from her neck," Skharr told him. The innkeeper leaned a little closer and nodded.

"Men are somewhat intimidated by a woman like that." The man did not look proud to admit that fact. "A blademaster might have most thinking twice, I suppose."

"I think I should see to it that she doesn't murder any of those who have been in their cups for too long," He moved to where the hapless suitor regained his feet slowly.

"You'll...you'll regret that, bitch! I'll rip your—"

The barbarian caught him by the collar and drew his attention away from Sera. The drunk squinted at the broad expanse of his chest for a moment before he realized that a man stood in front of him. He looked up and tried to jump away when he realized the size of the warrior who still held his collar in an iron hand.

"All she'll regret is having to clean your blood from her sword if you persist, little one," Skharr answered and walked the man to the door. He made sure to bump him into any tables they passed before he pulled the door open and flung him out.

The drunken fool couldn't be blamed for approaching a beautiful woman while drunk. He had done the same in his time, and more than once too. The only problem arose when Sera decided he had gone past the line of impropriety and he had gone even beyond that when he threatened to rip something out of her.

That had taken it a step too far and a blademaster was more than within her rights to defend herself from that level of abuse.

"It's good of you to intercede," she noted as he approached her table again. "But I'm sure you know that I needed no help."

Skharr nodded. "My reasons were entirely selfish. I had been given my meal and I had no intention to have it interrupted by a fight breaking out in the common room."

She laughed. "Since when are you averse to starting a fight?"

"Never. Well, except when I'm hungry and there is a feast to be had. If there was pandemonium and someone spilled my food, I would not be responsible for my actions."

"Are you ever?"

"Have I ever avoided responsibility for my actions?"

Sera considered him while she took a long sip of her drink. "I...don't know. I've never paid attention to that kind of thing, which I suppose means you have never avoided responsibility for your actions. I would possibly have noticed otherwise."

The barbarian grinned as the innkeeper brought the platter to the table, as well as a mug of hard apple cider, likely to help with the heat of the food that was served.

"And here I thought you would need to leave me a gold coin to pay for any damages incurred," Ansen noted with a smirk.

"Not this time," Skharr answered. "More is the pity. I was hoping for a little exercise."

"And I'm sure all the diners would take pleasure in watching your fists beat unwilling flesh," the proprietor responded briskly.

"If you need anything else, milady, tell me." He bowed his head respectfully before he backed away.

The barbarian grinned before he turned his attention to Sera.

"There's no need to look so smug about it." She shook her head and the amusement faded from her features as she cast a worried look across the room.

"Something is wrong." His tone was sharp as he stated the obvious and leaned forward so none of the other patrons could hear him.

"Not here," she whispered.

They both stood and moved out to the front of the Mermaid, which was considerably less crowded than the common room. He had a feeling there were still ears to listen to what they were saying but she would be able to see them a little better when there were fewer folks about.

"Something is gnawing at you, that much is obvious," he muttered and folded his arms. "I was under the impression that the situation with the undercouncil had been resolved."

"It was, but it presents a few...new difficulties," Sera whispered and leaned against a nearby wall. "A few of those who control Verenvan feel as though a power vacuum has formed, and while they deal with it, they would prefer that things be as peaceful as possible."

"Peaceful?"

"They were too...ah, polite to say it outright, but the point is that many folk would see killing you as a stepping stone to taking the power left by those you killed."

"Polite?"

"I did mention they were folk of power in the city, yes? Did you think they would be street urchins like the undercouncil?"

"Did you call your sister a street urchin?"

The guard captain grinned. "I thought you might miss that and yes, I did."

"So, what did the overcouncil think I could do about those

who want me dead for political reasons? Did they want to join the hunt?"

"No. In fact, they want you out of the city as soon as possible so they can resolve the situation."

There was an undertone to her voice that Skharr couldn't quite place for a moment. When the thought crystallized, a smile touched his face and he ran his fingers lightly through his beard. She was worried, and not only for the safety of her city. Sera was worried about him.

He leaned forward and placed a light, tender kiss on the top of her head. "I'll be gone by first light tomorrow."

The fact that she hadn't hit him or stabbed him already was probably a good sign. It might even be an indication that she wouldn't in the immediate future.

"Well," she retorted. "That was an unimpressive kiss."

He lowered his head. "So you've been kissed many times on the head, have you? Enough that you are able to decide which are acceptable and which are not?"

"I merely assumed you had horrible aim," she answered with a smirk and a wink before she turned away and stepped into the street. He could only hope she had left enough coin to pay for her drink in the common room, although he found his attention drawn to the figure that receded quickly into the blackness of the evening.

"I'll need a cold bath," Skharr whispered, shook his head, and entered the inn. The common room seemed the same as it had been when he left and his food and drink remained untouched on the table where he could still catch hints of her scent lingering in the air. He closed his eyes and leaned closer to his food, where at least the heady scent of spices covered almost anything else.

The food was good—better than what was served on most other days—and he wondered why Ansen didn't have Kora cooking every day. Perhaps the woman had work elsewhere or a family that needed tending to. It was unfortunate that he knew so little about these people.

He finished quickly and the warmth of the food filled him as he mounted the stairs to his room. A cool bath would certainly help him to forget the scent that seemed to trail him through the building.

As he reached for the latch to his door, he paused, narrowed his eyes, and tried to determine what precisely was wrong.

The latch was all the warning he needed, of course. It had been pulled to the other side of the wood and not returned, which meant the door was open. He hadn't opened it so someone else was in the room waiting for him.

Skharr took a deep breath and paused at the threshold. No lamps or candles burned inside and he needed to allow his vision to adjust for the darkness he would likely encounter when he entered.

By now, they would surely know he was outside. The stairs needed attention and creaked faintly with every step and the sound was multiplied when it came to a man of his size.

Without giving them too much warning, he barreled into the door with his shoulder. The hinges snapped and gave way as he rushed through it.

The heavy wood catapulted into a figure hidden behind it. Unable to stop himself in time, the warrior tripped over him and the man groaned in pain when the full weight of both barbarian and wood landed heavily on him.

Skharr reacted to the faint suggestion of movement to his side and rolled away. A glint of steel reflected some of the moonlight that filtered in through the windows. He rolled again, this time into the hallway that was thankfully bathed in the soft light of a handful of candles.

The two assassins followed him out. Both were dressed in light armor, and while the one who had been pinned under the door did look a little the worse for wear, he chose not to give the intruder the opportunity to recover.

"A little gentle exercise it is, then. Have at it, you mangy toad-fucking goblin spawn." He laughed and rolled his shoulders as both men advanced on him. Their daggers flicked forward, one aimed at his unarmored chest and the other at his gut.

He took a step back and swayed out of the sweep of their strikes. The one who stood to his left checked his motion, maintained his balance, and withdrew while his comrade stumbled forward. He'd put a little too much power into the thrust and couldn't stop until his victim hammered his fist into his jaw.

The blow was delivered with sufficient force to make him stagger into a nearby wall. It shuddered on impact, and the barbarian grasped the man by the shoulder and twisted him sharply. He drove his opponent's head into one of the nearby doors before he dragged him to the railing that allowed the folk upstairs to look down into the common room. Not many had noticed the sounds of fighting from above thanks to a group that had broken out in song on the ground floor.

A second later, the second man lunged forward to try to help his comrade—or perhaps to take advantage of Skharr's distraction. The attempt was futile. The barbarian jerked around and powered his elbow behind the man's ear with enough strength to launch him over the railing. The assassin plummeted to land on one of the tables that was being cleaned by the staff below.

Plates and mugs inevitably shattered, followed by shouts from the patrons who realized what had happened. He ignored them all and slid his arm around the other man's neck. He started to resist but the warrior simply squeezed tighter as he pulled him around.

Ansen approached the table and tilted his head to look at his large guest, who stood over what was undoubtedly his newest victim.

"Is there a problem, Skharr?" the innkeeper asked as he continued to struggle with one of the assassins.

"Uninvited godsbedammed troll-ass vermin in my room," he answered and thumped the second assassin's head on the railing.

"Well, send the other one down. We'll dispose of the both of them."

"Are you sure it won't be any trouble?"

"As long as you pay for the table, no."

He nodded, lifted the man, and hurled him over the railing to where, thankfully, his comrade was there to break his fall.

Once both men were down, he picked through his coin purse and after a moment's thought, tossed two silver coins down.

"For the dishes," he explained and shook his head as he moved into his room. From what he could hear, a few of the patrons were taking care of his assailants.

Although he had already decided not to remain in the city for too long, it seemed as though someone wasn't willing to let him leave. Or perhaps they didn't know he planned to leave and wanted to make sure he wouldn't be a problem.

Either way, Skharr would have to leave the city as unobtrusively as possible before more of them had the same idea.

With a sigh, he lit a few of the lamps in his room and proceeded to gather the rest of his belongings.

He'd promised to be gone before first light in the morning and intended to keep his word.

CHAPTER FOUR

"We'll leave the city soon."

Horse snorted and the sound echoed through the mostly empty streets.

"Well, if you didn't want to tolerate my untenable hours, perhaps you should have remained in retirement. I asked constantly but you said no, and here you are, complaining."

The beast whinnied softly and tossed his mane.

"You can't say my schedule is worse than the mares'." Skharr stopped and turned to face his long-time friend. "We're going to help some folk who helped us in the past. Well, they helped me, but that means you by association. And they will pay for the help as well, so if you stop complaining, we can get on with it. You'll cease your protests anyway once we're out in the open country. You're the odd kind of horse who likes to walk long distances."

When the stallion made no answer to that, the barbarian began to advance into the alley in search of the telltale signs of one of the entrances he'd been looking for.

His gaze flicked around his surroundings to ensure there were no people in the area before he tapped on the wall in the rhythm and sequence he'd committed to memory. After a moment, he shook his head, moved to another section of the wall, and repeated the process.

"I have no mind for stone," Skharr muttered when he heard Horse mocking him.

This time, the rock echoed the sound of his knock and he could hear movement on the other side. After a few moments, the wall began to move aside to reveal a handful of armed and armored dwarves waiting for him. They were a little surprised to see him but motioned for him to follow them.

"The beast must needs go through another path," one of the guards said.

"We go together."

"No, you don't understand. The tunnels you will travel through are not large enough for him. He'll be escorted to where you'll leave from."

Skharr turned to where Horse stood with his head tilted. "Will that be a problem?"

The stallion snorted and tossed his mane.

"He'll go with you," he translated. "If you have any apples to spare, he would appreciate it."

"Are you...are you speaking to the horse?" one of the dwarves asked.

"No, I am a madman who speaks to himself. Of course I'm speaking to Horse. He says he'll go with you and would appreciate any apples you might have to spare. And he'll be a little grumpier than usual due to having to begin his day this early, so I would suggest you find some apples, or perhaps carrots, to appease his mood."

The dwarves nodded, tried to not look skeptical, and failed desperately. Still, they led him away down another path that appeared to have been designed specifically for horses. The barbarian wasn't sure why, unless the dwarves needed a few to carry their burdens. Perhaps they needed larger horses too, which explained the size of the other path Horse was taking.

None of the dwarves seemed overly talkative, and Skharr could understand their lack of trust in a large outsider. He'd dealt with their kind for most of his life and they tended to be wary of outsiders, even those they were supposedly on good terms with. The DeathEaters had been on good terms with the dwarves in the mountains, but only a few were ever invited to spend time among the clans under the mountains.

It seemed like the same rules applied here. He was a trusted client and a business partner but not close enough that any of them would feel comfortable with him in the subterranean city without having their hands close their weapons. It was understandable, of course. DeathEaters were generally far more hostile than he was.

They reached what looked like a small gate to the underground city, and he could see that he wasn't the only one leaving the area. Throk appeared at the head of a small train of donkeys and a group of his kin, while Brahgen stood near them in front of a donkey that was most likely his.

"Skharr, you've arrived!" the master smith roared and his voice echoed through the chamber. "I thought we would have to leave and have someone else explain the situation for you."

The warrior nodded and noticed that Horse now approached. It begged the question of why they hadn't simply used the same route the horse had, given that it took the same amount of time to reach their destination. More to the point, it explained why they hadn't been able to get Horse an apple or two yet, which meant he would have to dig into his supplies to feed the beast's addiction with.

"What situation?" Skharr asked and patted the stallion on the neck.

"Ah, well, we had already planned to send a caravan to our kin in the mountains and would thus send your gift to The Clan with them. Given the value of the weapon, however, I would trust none other to deliver it than my own hands."

The barbarian raised an eyebrow. "That is certainly appreciated."

The dwarf waved dismissively. "You spent a king's ransom to forge the weapon and I've been due a visit to my homeland after decades abroad, so it worked out rather well, to my mind. With that said, I thought you should have a little something to offset some of the expense you've gone through."

The dwarf looked around at one of the others, who attempted to secure what looked like an ax on Horse's saddle.

The beast almost bucked and kicked him for his efforts and Skharr approached immediately to stand between Horse and him.

"There is no need to be offended," he rumbled and took the package.

"I wasn't."

"I wasn't talking to you." The barbarian hefted the wrapped weapon. "What is this?"

"An ax. While not quite of the quality of the one you commissioned, it's a decent weapon. I thought it would be a good idea to avoid any knowledge that we travel with something quite so valuable into the mountains. As such, your weapon is kept safe with me, while those who might have thievery in their hearts think you carry it."

"And leave the murderous bastards for us to deal with, yes?"

Throk chuckled. "You two will travel faster and will therefore be more difficult to find than a caravan. Even so, you will discover that you are more equipped to handle a sustained attack than we."

Skharr hooked the ax into his saddlebags and glanced to where Brahgen had mounted his donkey. The youth looked uncomfortable and exceedingly unhappy as the other dwarves began to gather and take their positions in the caravan that would soon leave Verenvan.

He approached the younger dwarf, who was braiding his beard nervously although he stopped as he approached.

"Are you ready to head out then?" Brahgen asked as the barbarian clicked his tongue to call Horse to him.

"We will head out west with the caravan for a short distance before we take our own path," he answered and patted the donkey on the neck. "What is her name?"

"Her?"

He raised an eyebrow. "You didn't know much about her when you climbed on? That's a good way to get your knees kicked in."

"Well… I…it—"

"She."

"She's a donkey."

He nodded and scratched the beast's forehead. "Her name is Jenny and she would appreciate it if you avoid kicking her."

"What?"

"Don't kick her. She'll tolerate you riding her if you don't heel her flanks."

Brahgen's eyebrows raised as the warrior patted Jenny on the backside and clicked his tongue for Horse to follow him through the gates along with the caravan.

It was interesting and even impressive that the dwarves had managed to keep a gate in and out of the city secret. The presence of a hidden portal that could lead into Verenvan could break a siege if there ever was one.

He doubted they would be involved in a war, but if this were ever discovered, the chances were good that the officials in Verenvan would start a war with the dwarves under their city to gain control of the gate, if nothing else.

For the moment, however, Skharr doubted they would encounter much trouble. The group was already on their way and used the nearby woods to cover their tracks as they worked steadily toward the roads.

"I've always loathed the western roads," he muttered. "The empire always hated this little section they took control of and never bothered to put any real thought into maintaining it."

"Have you traveled these parts a great deal?" Brahgen asked.

"While they were still fighting for it, yes. I never understood why."

The roads certainly hadn't improved and he thanked his lucky stars that they didn't need to pull a wagon like the caravan did. Moving away from most of the civilization in the region had its disadvantages as they were bounded on all sides by the Green Wilderness, with hundreds of miles of little other than trees as far as the eye could see.

Not that the eye could see much, as the road led them directly into the forest, where massive roots had begun to dig through the cobbles and made them difficult to traverse. Traveling to Verenvan from his farmstead had brought him along the same path, and it never failed to annoy him to realize how difficult it was to move through the region.

That would change the moment a few armies needed to pass through, however. In that case, the roads would be repaired all too quickly.

As the sun began to set on their third day on the road, the barbarian pointed out a small group of smoke pillars in the distance.

"Grenland ought to have a few straw beds for us to sleep in," he told his companion. Not that he expected much of a response from the dwarf, whose silence was marginally more tolerable than his complaints as they began the winding journey into the lake region. The area offered little to draw much attention from the empire that putatively ruled it, but there was enough in the way of fishing and farming to attract a few settlers. These founded a small group of villages that were too far from the empire for it to care that it ruled over them.

They approached the settlement at a steady pace. The dwarf had yet to respond to Skharr's comment and he shifted continually on his saddle and looked away, although he showed a keen interest in not sleeping with roots digging into his back for at least one night.

The village was no hub of commerce but a level of activity in the streets showed that the locals enjoyed something of an economic boom that allowed them to sell to and buy from the nearby towns. The advantage of this was that so many strangers wandered the streets that two more didn't draw so much as a second glance despite their disparate sizes.

As no word had yet issued from the sullen dwarf, the warrior found a tavern that had rooms available. Once Horse and Jenny were situated in the stables, they sat in the common room and were served a pint each of locally brewed ale with promises from the innkeeper that food would soon be forthcoming.

The establishment was not quite filled to capacity yet, but as the sun began to set, more folk wandered in. He had a feeling it would be full before day gave way fully to night.

Brahgen sipped his ale, sighed deeply, and shook his head.

"Do you truly speak to horses?"

Skharr looked curiously at him. It was the longest string of words the dwarf had spoken to him since their journey started. He should have known that all it would take was a little ale to get the youth's words flowing.

"Aye." The barbarian nodded slowly. "They're sharper than folk give them credit for. Donkeys are even cleverer, so you'll have your hands full with Jenny if you don't pay attention."

"Most donkeys aren't so difficult."

"They've been browbeaten into submission to the point where they have been taught that showing any sign of their personality results in punishment. It breaks my heart every time I see it."

His companion narrowed his eyes, leaned back in his seat, and took another sip of his drink. "Throk encourages the use of whips on the beasts. And I don't only mean the donkeys. He might be a mighty blacksmith, but he's a godsbedammed shit-hearted uncle, I tell you. Then again, not many of the other dwarves mind him so much."

"You don't like being put to work, do you?"

"I don't mind working for my keep, but it's become more and more obvious that I don't have the blood of a blacksmith in me—and not the muscles of a fighter either. It narrows what a dwarf can do since my kin aren't given to farming."

"There are many dwarves who farm. How do you think the mighty cities under the mountains feed themselves?"

"I didn't mean dwarves, I meant the AnvilForged. Mining, fighting, and smithing are all that is considered an honorable endeavor for the family. Let the lesser families deal with such drudgery as farming."

"Which explains why you treat your donkeys so poorly."

Brahgen nodded.

"It doesn't take much muscle to be a fighter," Skharr told him after he'd sipped his drink.

"So says a man who is a mountain of it."

"I do not jest. I know my fair share of slim humans who can wield a sword better than I might ever dream of. Dwarves like their long spears and shield walls, granted, but with a little training, you would find some form of fighting ability."

"Perhaps you're right, but it's not only that. I cannot say I like much about dwarves as a whole. I don't like living underground and I hate the…closeness of the clans. I don't even like good dwarven women. Not even my mother."

"And…that is why you worship Ahverna?"

"Yes. She and I have quite a bond, given that she never answered me. It's the best kind of worship. Or at least…I think she didn't."

"All folk can hope for is to avoid the attention of the gods. At best, you find yourself burdened with gifts that allow you to serve them better. At worst, they grow angry with your lack of service and become a pain in your ass for the rest of your life."

Brahgen laughed. "I can't disagree with that."

Skharr took a long, draught from the pint mug and emptied it in a long, slow gulp before he pushed up from his seat and belched loudly.

"I need to bleed the lizard."

The dwarf raised an eyebrow.

"Take a piss. I'll be back."

The inn had no designated cesspits, but a handful of trenches had water running through them and likely led to the communal pits, far away from where folk lived and downwind as well. He undid his breeches and as he relieved himself, he sighed and shook his head.

Most other quests he'd been sent on tended to lead to him to battle a primal evil of some kind by this point, which made him believe that perhaps this would merely be another job, a simple favor he did for a friend.

Two friends, technically. It was certainly true that he wanted to help but leaving Verenvan for a while was also the best thing for him and, of course, for Sera.

Skharr looked around when he heard shouts from inside the tavern. He fastened his trousers quickly and hurried inside after washing his hand under nearby flowing water.

His fears were realized as it looked like Brahgen was well on his way to antagonizing a group of woodsmen.

"Your mother didn't complain about my size last night," the dwarf snapped with a grin. "Then again, I suppose that says more about your da's size than mine."

"Get the fuck up, little one, and let your betters have a table you don't need."

"Do you think you're better than me because you fit in a larger size britches, ya fat pile of shite? I'll show you that better is as better does, not determined by larger size."

Before the warrior could intervene, Brahgen grasped the back of the man's head and thunked his face on the table. The dwarf didn't wait for him to recover or any of the other woodsmen to react, but caught the man by the beard with one hand and brought the other up in a fist to deliver a punch to his nose.

It wasn't the most powerful of blows but was more than enough to stun the man, who stumbled back and tried to stem the blood that flowed from his broken nose.

The young dwarf even managed to throw in a couple more strikes at his opponent's comrades before their size blocked his attempts and they began to restrain him.

"Is that what you need, big man?" Brahgen roared while he continued his attempts to fight them off. "So many big men to fight one small dwarf, is that it?"

Skharr had to respect the youth's spirit, even if he didn't put up much of a fight. He stepped closer, took one of the men by the shoulder, and twisted him to face him.

"If you want a shot at the little pest, you'll have to—"

The woodsman's words cut off when he looked at Skharr and he took a step back.

"There's no need to wait," he retorted. "I have tree-fucking vermin aplenty to deal with."

His fist met the man's jaw with enough power to spin him in place before he toppled and fell. Their comrade's predicament immediately caught the attention of the other fighters. All turned to face the barbarian with their eyes narrowed and fists raised, ready for a fight.

"How about fighting someone your own size, you halfwit forest scum?" Brahgen laughed and adjusted his coat.

"It still would not be an even fight," Skharr responded.

"Closer than five of them against only one dwarf."

The youth made a fair point but it was still far from being a fair fight.

The three woodsmen still standing attacked immediately and surged forward while they yelled some kind of battle cry. They grappled him around the waist and forced him back step by step. He managed to rain a handful of blows on them before their combined momentum made it difficult to keep his balance. Their attacks were focused on his abdomen and a handful were aimed at his jaw.

Skharr couldn't help a laugh and not only because he could see Brahgen undaunted and shouting insults in the common and dwarf tongues. It was an interesting and hilarious sight, of course, but there was something more to the laughter. Three days of monotonous travel had been a weight on his mind, even if he hadn't quite noticed it, but there was now drinking and fighting, and with camaraderie to be enjoyed besides.

He twisted, caught hold of two of the men who attempted a combined assault when they thought he was distracted, and yanked them into each other's paths. Their heads hammered together and he pushed them away, leaving only one woodsman standing against him.

"Well, then, you godsbedammed moss-brained squirrel-fucker. What will it be?"

None could say they lacked in courage, even if it had started with five of them trying to push a single dwarf from his seat. The last woodsman lunged forward as he bellowed their battle cry that still meant nothing to the barbarian, who waited until the last moment. He sidestepped him and he continued his headlong rush into a nearby wall. Before he could recover, the warrior spun swiftly and drove his elbow behind his adversary's ear.

The man collapsed with a loud thud and his eyes rolled to the back of his head as Skharr looked at the other woodsmen. They all displayed some degree of consciousness or another, but it was clear that the fight had leeched out of them for the moment.

"You need to help your friend," he rumbled as two of them finally regained their feet. "A little water will wake him right the fuck up. Your choice was foolish but you can redeem it by showing a little wisdom and common sense. Leave this place for the night."

They didn't answer but they did do as he had told them and helped one another to exit the tavern. A few groans accompanied their pained retreat, although they paused to dart resentful glares to a group of their fellows they were leaving behind.

"Will you make up for what those five would have paid for their stay?" the innkeeper asked as he approached them. He tried to not show the anger that had built inside him but wasn't entirely successful.

"Where were you when they were harassing another of your patrons?" Skharr asked and raised an eyebrow.

"Five spend more than one."

"You haven't met this one," he snapped, took three gold pieces from his purse, and handed them to the man. "Now make yourself useful and find us the kind of food you give to your better-paying patrons. *Now!*"

The proprietor's eyes bulged at the sight of the gold and his grin spread wide although he jumped when the barbarian raised his voice.

"Of course! I will return with your victuals."

Skharr shook his head and winced as he touched a handful of tender places that were likely to become bruises that wouldn't go away for a week.

"You are quite handy in a fight, big-un," the dwarf commented as a group of serving girls exited the kitchens with platters of steaming food.

"You made a good showing for yourself as well," he responded. "You have the speed and dexterity that make a good fighter, but you need more power in your punches."

"I haven't the muscles—"

"Shit from a bull. Power comes from the legs and flows through the body. With a little training, I might make a fighter of you yet. But if you have a moment in the fight when they are distracted, you might want to think about slipping a few items from them when they have their minds on other matters."

"Oh?" Brahgen grinned, took two silvers from his belt, and smacked them onto the table. "You mean like these?"

He nodded. "Aye. Or something like this." He retrieved a heavy coin purse, a ring, and a knife from under his coat and dropped them beside the coins.

The dwarf narrowed his eyes and tried to decide when Skharr had managed to take the items from the men who had attacked him. After a moment, he simply shook his head and laughed. "Barbarians."

They tapped their glasses together before they started enthusiastically on the food brought for them.

"Do you think we will be lucky enough for another fight to find us?" Brahgen asked.

"One can only hope," the warrior answered over the lip of his mug. "With that in mind, we might want to set up a few watches for the evening."

"Agreed."

***

Spymaster. The word almost made him smile.

Only someone with a massive ego would ever give themselves that title. Or someone with an equally pretentious perception of their importance would give that title to those who were supposed to serve them. Tryam had discovered that it was hard to avoid developing an over-inflated ego when so many who gave themselves lofty titles bowed and scraped when they had an audience with him.

The only thing that kept his feet firmly on the ground was

that he knew precisely what they were saying and doing when they thought he couldn't hear them.

Elric stood in the corner, his eyes narrowed and his brows furrowed as he studied the smaller man in front of the emperor. Despite the visitor's appearance, he had no illusions and knew exactly what the self-styled spymaster was capable of. Skin as thin as parchment paper, a hooked nose, and a bald head distracted the eye from his body which was lean as a whip, and the man had a skill for assassination unlike any other.

The young emperor could understand his guard captain's trepidation at allowing someone like Hassim so close to him, but even in a world of shadows, trust was needed. Sometimes, it was even required.

"Unlike what some legends might state, I don't have all the time in the world," he said and motioned for the man to sit. "Tell me what you know."

"Knowledge is my business, and I know many things."

"Of course. Which means you should know what knowledge I am interested in hearing, whether I know it or not."

"Well...I know you have an interest in the redheaded barbarian known as Skharr and I have heard a great many whispers of him regarding his time in Verenvan."

The emperor leaned back in his seat with a frown. He did have an interest in the warrior, and not only because he owed him his current position on the throne.

"Go on."

"Whispers told me of certain criminal elements of great power that the barbarian angered. Their word spoke of a great deal of coin to be paid to any who could kill him."

Tryam scowled deeply. "They need to die."

"That would be difficult to accomplish, Your Grace," Hassim pointed out. "Even for you."

"Why?"

"Because they are already dead. At his hand."

"Huh." The young emperor tilted his head in speculation. "I've seen the man fight and I know what he's capable of. Even that would be beyond it."

"He was not alone. From the reports of the few who survived, he was suddenly aided by a mighty host of skilled warriors who killed all those in their path. They appeared mysteriously, as though they rose through the mist, and vanished in a similar fashion. It was…most curious."

"Curious," Elric growled. "And likely a fabrication told by men embarrassed by their defeat."

"Possibly, but that would raise more questions than it answers. Whichever the case, it is, as you say, curious."

Tryam nodded. "I would like to know more. Both of what is happening in Verenvan and what the barbarian is doing. Leave out no details this time. No mysteries and no old wives' tales. Facts."

Hassim rose from his seat and bowed gracefully. "It is my honor to serve. It shall be done."

CHAPTER FIVE

"Why are we going this way?" Brahgen asked. "It's the least used route."

"It's more direct," Skharr responded calmly.

"Aye and heads directly toward the Druums Woodland. You would have to be an utter madman to travel through those gods-bedammed woods."

"You...have met me, yes?" he asked and raised an eyebrow.

The dwarf scowled and adjusted his seat on the damnable donkey. Jenny had lived up to her word, but a comfortable ride she was not. Then again, perhaps all beasts of burden were uncomfortable rides, which was why his companion had chosen to walk instead of mounting his warhorse.

"Why are we coming this way?" the youth asked. "You wouldn't choose this path unless you were looking for something specific. Death might be what you find if you choose to enter the woods."

"Not death, no," he answered. "I have some business in this region. I once thought I would find peace here so I built a small farmstead."

"You? Peace?"

"A farmer's life does have a certain…appeal to it. But it was not to be. I merely wish to see what became of the farm since I left it. This is not a common route for any journey and I likely will not travel this way again."

Brahgen tilted his head and shifted again on the saddle. Perhaps a pony would have been a better choice for their current journey, although he failed to see how having his rear end jounced continually, no matter what he rode, could be called enjoyable. He sighed and grasped the reins a little tighter as they continued and finally veered onto a fresh path once the actual road had ended. It was newly cut into the thick, lush grass that sprouted all around them.

Finally, a small farmstead appeared in the distance and he could distinguish two people standing out in the open. They had seen the two new arrivals as soon as they had appeared over the distant rise and now waited anxiously and probably not without a great deal of suspicion. Skharr was right in one thing, at least— few travelers used this route. The dwarf had a feeling that if anyone did arrive, they would immediately assume they were hostile.

The distant figures resolved into a man and a woman. Commoners both, by the looks of them, but the man carried a wood-felling ax while the woman held a hatchet, and both appeared to have prepared themselves for a fight.

Skharr raised his hands and approached them from the road. "We come in peace. There is no need to be alarmed."

The two didn't look convinced but the husband took a step forward.

"We welcome travelers with all the hospitality granted by the Lord High God Theros. Please, come."

The barbarian nodded and gestured for his companion to join him. He seemed to know what that was supposed to mean, although Brahgen didn't understand it. The dwarf reassured himself with the reminder that if Skharr knew this place as well as he said he did, there would be history there that he couldn't expect to understand.

"You are his barbarian, yes?" the woman asked and took a step forward, although she still grasped her hatchet in a way that suggested she knew how to wield it.

"I suppose he would say that. I am called Skharr DeathEater."

"Then you are most welcome in our home, barbarian. Will you stay long?"

Skharr looked at Brahgen, who shrugged. He didn't want to show it, but his ass was sore from the saddle and time off it would be more than welcome. They'd stopped for a short while in the town but only to resupply before they had returned to the road that very day.

If his travel companion wanted to spend his time in a small farmstead, his ass would certainly thank him for the respite, however long it might be.

The warrior approached and shook the man's hand while the wife turned away and in a few moments, the sounds of children could be heard from the other side of the house.

"I wouldn't want to stay here without finding some work to do," he stated. "If you have any work that needs doing in the fields, I think there might be a way for us to pay for our keep."

The couple exchanged a look and laughed.

"Now that you mention it, there is a little work we have yet to attend to—the kind that needs a strong, steady hand to accomplish."

Skharr had volunteered his efforts and while it was clear that the dwarf he was escorting was under no such obligations, Brahgen didn't feel it was right for him to stand around doing nothing. Of course, the massive barbarian was better suited to certain kinds of work, while he was undoubtedly better suited to others.

"And if you have a need for tools to be fixed about the place, I suppose I might be of some help," he said finally and tried to hide his reluctance.

"Are you sure?" She brushed some of her long, curly brown hair from her face as the children ran around her. "You look to have been on a dusty road and likely need some rest."

"And he doesn't?" the dwarf asked.

"He offered. And my husband might be a little too quick to take advantage of the help."

"Well…what else would I have to do? Sit around and fondle meself?"

Brahgen's eyebrows raised in mute apology when he remembered there were children around them and he cleared his throat and looked away quickly.

"Well, we have a few items that might require fixing if you find yourself up to the challenge."

Seated on a chair while he worked with his hands was certainly better than the alternative of riding on a donkey and feeling like his ass was being pummeled. A handful of tools needed repair and in the pleasant shade of the house, it was not an unpleasant way to spend the day, especially since Skharr was out working in the sun.

"What is your name?" he asked and wiped his fingers with a piece of cloth before he refocused his attention on the wheelbarrow he was affixing a proper wheel to.

"I am Hanna. My husband is Faron. This is Sateen." She indicated the girl who played around her feet. "And my oldest is Taso."

The dwarf nodded. "I am called Brahgen AnvilForged—a dwarf but not much of one, of course."

"What makes you say that?"

He shrugged offhandedly, finished with the wheel, and cleaned the grease from his hand. "There is not much dwarf in me. It's why I travel with a barbarian now."

"There are places in the world for all," she noted. "Even barbarians."

"How did you do that?"

Brahgen looked at the young Sateen who stared at him as he flicked the planer between his fingers from side to side.

"I…what?"

"How do you do that? With your fingers?"

He twirled it in a few more complex patterns. "Oh? That? It is nothing. Wait until you see this."

After a few more flourishes, he tossed it up in the air and made to catch it with the other hand but let it slip deftly into his coat sleeve before he showed both hands to the young girl.

She squealed, clapped, and looked around. "Where is it?"

"I should ask you since you hid it."

"I didn't!"

"Indeed you did—look!" Brahgen extended his hand past her head and withdrew the planer from his sleeve in a smooth motion that made it appear as though he pulled it out from behind her ear.

She laughed and picked it up like she didn't quite believe it was real. A sound of laughter came from the fields and drew his attention there for a moment. Skharr swung Taso onto his shoulders with one hand while the other lifted the plow that had caught in some stones. The field had not been plowed very well and needed considerably more work. Surprisingly, the warrior appeared to be good at it.

"We all have our gifts, Master Brahgen," Hanna stated firmly with a small smile as she picked Sateen up so she could sit on her lap. "Perhaps he has impressive strength, but you should know that we will eat far easier this winter now that the wheelbarrow has a proper wheel."

"You merely need to clean the dirt and grime from the axle regularly and you shouldn't have any more problems."

"Even so. It's not the kind of thing a barbarian would know about, wouldn't you think?"

He smiled. "Well, if you say so. But rarely does a woman look at a man and say, 'what a fine set of fingers he has.'"

She smirked and shrugged nonchalantly. "You might find yourself surprised on that score."

"I still cannot believe it."

Skharr looked up from the little campfire they had lit for themselves. The farmhouse was small and cramped, even without two extra occupants, and the barn was already a little too full. Sleeping under the stars was not so terrible either as the weather was clear and the open landscape around them seemed surprisingly peaceful.

He looked at the dwarf who whittled a piece of wood.

"Cannot believe what?" he asked after a moment's pause.

"That you lived in this godsbedammed place. No offense to the family, of course. It is a peaceful existence, but I cannot think that Skharr fucking DeathEater would find comfort as a farmer."

"There is an odd peace that comes from simply working with your hands, tilling the land, and other such ventures. A real but somewhat irregular danger from the forest kept me from going soft but even so, it was an interesting change of pace."

He handed the wineskin to the dwarf, who took a long swig from it.

"But you did not purchase the farm from him, did you?" Brahgen asked and handed the skin to Faron.

The man took it with a grateful smile before he shook his head. "No. I think we purchased it from the man who bought it from Skharr. He showed us there was power in the land and a peace to it, despite the forest on our borders."

"Only this particular piece of land," the barbarian noted.

"Yes." Faron laughed, gulped the wine, and passed it to the warrior. "I think the power of the land inside the forest would have resisted us in some fashion if we'd tried to venture in there. It is best to enjoy the peace and let the power protect us through its proximity."

Only a suggestion of a throb lingered in his head as they rose with the sun and prepared to press forward on their journey. Skharr knew that heading through the forest was the fastest route to their destination, but he couldn't help a feeling of trepidation at the idea of entering it.

Perhaps that was why he had decided to spend the rest of the day and the night among those who had purchased his former farmstead rather than proceed the day before. He preferred to brave the dangers once he was rested and ready, not with a half-day's travel under their belts.

Still, they would have to get through it eventually, and this seemed like the kind of day on which to do so. The weather was still fine with only a handful of clouds scattered across the bright orange sky as they turned away from the farmhouse and walked steadily toward the forest.

"Did you always mean to travel through the woods?" Brahgen asked and nudged Jenny forward to walk alongside Horse.

"Aye. It's the shorter way. There is also less chance of us being encountered by folk who mean to rob us."

"Instead, you'd like to find out what is inside the fucking place that means to eat us?"

"I've battled the beasts in these woods before and they are not quite as terrifying as one might think. When it comes to robbers, we might find them in larger numbers and with more sophisticated weapons. It is best to deal with a known kind of creature."

Still, even as he said that, he could feel the weight of the trees as they loomed over them when they began their advance into the forest. There was undoubtedly a power present. Too many stories had rippled from it for him to know fact from fiction but there was some truth mixed in as well.

That truth was enough to send a chill up his spine every time he heard something move in the branches above them.

He could tell that Brahgen felt the same way when he rested his hand on the dagger he carried in his belt.

The only solace he could take was that if anyone thought to relieve him of the so-called Ax of Skharr DeathEater they might think he carried, they would have to venture through this gods-bedammed fucking forest as well.

It wasn't long before something cracked branches a little farther ahead. He loosened the ax that had been forged to take the place of the more expensive weapon that had been sent with the dwarf caravan.

"Trouble?" Brahgen asked.

"Nothing makes a noise here unless it means to do some killing," he answered and unwound the wrapping from the ax. It appeared to be a fine weapon in its own right, even though he knew it didn't come anywhere close to the quality of the one he'd sent to The Clan.

They proceeded cautiously toward the intermittent sounds of cracked branches and dried leaves. Dark-green scales glinted in the sparse sunlight that filtered through the tree cover. He hefted his as yet unfamiliar weapon and found a comfortable and tight grasp on the shaft that brought balance to it. It soon became apparent that more than one of the creatures approached.

A small pack of them—half a dozen in total—moved toward the travelers. They were the size of large dogs, with heavy, plodding legs tipped with long, curved claws. Their jaws were long and gaped to show line after line of razor-sharp fangs that dripped with what he could only assume was some kind of venom.

Of course, it could merely be drool, but it reeked all the same. It seemed reasonable to assume that a bite from one of them would be enough to trigger gangrene within minutes, even if there was no venom.

Long, thin tongues flicked from their mouths and their long tails slid nimbly from side to side. Skharr had a feeling he would have to watch for the tails or he would find himself wounded by one of them before too long.

"What the hell are those? Dragons?"

"You've never seen a dragon, have you?"

"Well…"

"No, they aren't dragons," he snapped and gestured with his ax. "But they'll kill and eat us all the same. It would be best to get off the donkey and help me to kill them."

"Why?"

"Because they are more interested in eating Horse and Jenny than you or I, which gives us an advantage, but only if we can draw them away from the beasts. Now move, boy!"

Brahgen jumped from the saddle, his dagger in hand, but looked uncertain as to what he should do.

Skharr wondered if perhaps he would have a better chance against the sentient thieves they might encounter. The dwarf had evidenced more experience in that quarter but when it came to monsters in the wild, he had no idea how to attack.

Unfortunately, he didn't have the time to teach him how to fight these feral adversaries as he had quickly become the center of attention for the two larger creatures. They flicked their tongues out at him before they opened their jaws and uttered a long, spine-tingling hiss.

"Come on, then, you scaly, muck-brained vermin of Janus' hairy armpit." Skharr growled and twirled his weapon to hold their attention. "Have you a taste of DeathEater."

Whether the monsters understood his taunt or not didn't matter as they rushed at him at the same time.

One stopped short and flicked its tail to catch him by the leg. He jumped to the right, lunged at the beast closest to him, and chopped the ax into the creature's skull. The blow split it open easily and he turned quickly to face two more of them that now advanced on him.

"You were taught by dwarf fighters who thought you would grow into their kind of strength," the warrior shouted to his companion as he leapt aside to avoid the monsters that attempted to encircle him. "Now is the time to learn how to use what you have."

Skharr dove to the right, landed on his knees, and severed the head from another of his adversaries. The dwarf, for some reason, darted to his saddle and withdrew a few lengths of rope.

He only had a few moments to wonder what Brahgen intended when the youth tied the rope quickly into a loop and tossed it out onto the soil in front of the one creature who wasn't attacking. It stepped into the loop and he yanked the rope back before he dragged it toward the other beasts.

The distraction was more than a little effective. The attention of the creatures was pulled away from their intended prey and toward the monster that was being hauled into their midst. They began to snap their jaws at one another in an attempt to push the others away from them and for a single, crucial second, they forgot the two travelers.

The barbarian rushed into the group and his ax cleaved into the necks and skulls of the beasts around him. Two more were felled but the last one stood its ground, snapped its jaw at him in warning, and flicked its tail in a wide arc. In that moment, Brahgen lunged forward with a shout and drove his dagger into the back of its skull.

It jerked hard enough to throw the dwarf from his perch atop it, but the beast was dead. No one could doubt that.

Skharr chuckled and broke into a full laugh as he moved

closer to drag the dwarf's weapon out from where it was embedded in the massive lizard's head.

"That is more what I hoped to see from you!" he said cheerfully as he extended his hand to help his young companion.

"And it was enjoyable, wasn't it?" Brahgen agreed although he sounded surprised. He took the proffered hand and jumped nimbly to his feet.

"You have a sharp mind that should serve you well in shit like this," he said and placed the dagger in the dwarf's hand. "Stop listening to the voices in your head that insist you should attack these godsbedammed poison-toothed fuckers the way I do and find your own way. Come the morning, if we have time, I'll teach you a few more useful tricks to add to your arsenal."

"Why not now?"

Skharr looked around. "The smell of the bodies will bring more of the godsbedammed stink-breath bastards upon us. It would be better to put as much distance between them and us as we can."

Brahgen nodded and cleaned the blood carefully from his weapon while the barbarian did the same. Satisfied with his effort, he stowed it and mounted Jenny.

"You'll have to tell me one of these days why you never ride Horse," the youth said.

"I'm sure I already told you—or I've said it so often that it should be common knowledge. I won't force a brother to bear my weight. I wouldn't carry him so why should he carry me?"

"Because he's a horse. That's what they are for."

Horse snorted softly and derisively, and Jenny answered with a loud, mocking bray as she jumped and almost knocked Brahgen from his perch.

"They think all you're good for is to provide them with food," he told him and patted the stallion on the neck. "There is more to friendship than usefulness."

"You want me to be friends with a donkey?"

"She has carried your lazy ass without complaint. The least you can do is be friendly about it."

Brahgen looked at Jenny, who brayed again loudly before she began to plod forward.

"All right," the dwarf muttered. "I think I understand. But how do I speak to her like you do?"

"You listen. And you pay attention. Horses, donkeys, and beasts of all kinds speak not only with the noises that they make but with every inch of their bodies. Listen to that, and eventually, you'll understand what they want to tell you."

"Truly, it sounds like a load of what Jenny dropped this morning."

Horse nickered.

"Don't be mean," Skharr responded. "What you dropped was not any more appealing."

CHAPTER SIX

"She did not say that."

"Why would I lie?"

"I don't know. Why would a barbarian lie about being able to speak to animals?"

Skharr looked at him where he was perched on the saddle. "If you think I lie about understanding them, why would you concern yourself with what is or isn't being said?"

He made a sound point. Brahgen wasn't quite sure if he believed him when he said he could understand what his horse was saying. It seemed both impossible and ridiculous. Still, the two went about their day with an uncanny silent understanding that made it difficult to deny there was something there.

It felt impossible, and yet a niggling suspicion had settled in the back of his head and wouldn't let him simply discard it as the mad ramblings of an idiot barbarian.

"She cannot mean that I am the heaviest load she's ever had to carry," Brahgen stated finally and realized he had begun to braid his thick black beard again. It was a habit he reverted to when thinking hard and he'd tried to cast it aside but had not been quite as successful as he had hoped.

"Why not?"

"Because she worked for my uncle and I know for a fact that he loaded the poor donkeys with as much as they could carry. And even then, the rest of the dwarves of my clan were heavier than I am."

Skharr leaned closer and Jenny snorted and brayed softly as she tossed her head.

"Ah. Not the heaviest but the most uncomfortable. You lean back in the saddle and your weight shifts with every step. It's uncomfortable for you and makes you feel like every step is jarring into you, and it's uncomfortable for her as well. You merely need to straighten your back a little and you should be fine."

Brahgen narrowed his eyes skeptically. Horse whinnied softly as Skharr approached the warhorse and gave the beast an apple to settle him. Both had been nervous from the moment they had entered the damn forest. It hadn't improved but if the map told him anything, the dwarf could tell that they were most of the way through.

When his companion wasn't looking, he straightened his back and tried to settle his rear end a little more comfortably.

"How's that, then, Jenny?" he asked and kept his voice low. "I don't mean to make this uncomfortable for both of us. I haven't ridden much, and it's…well, this much time spent on the saddle is not a pleasant experience for either of us."

Jenny showed none of the personality she had responded with when Skharr spoke to her, but her tail swished from side to side and she lowered her head to nibble a few stray tufts of grass. If there was any sign that she was at least somewhat happy, that probably qualified.

"There, see what I mean?" the barbarian asked. "And she'll grow more comfortable with you the more you speak to her."

"What?"

"They like it when you speak to them. They won't always

60

understand but they grow more comfortable because they sense that you are making the attempt."

"How do they understand you?"

"The way they speak is through more than only words. It's in the way your body moves, the inflection of your voice, and the smallest of details. The more you speak to them, the more you'll be able to speak in a language they understand."

That almost made sense. It was odd how the more he spoke about it, the less insane it sounded. Perhaps all Brahgen needed was to spend some time with folk who didn't talk to animals for sanity to prevail. For the moment, though, it teetered on the verge of making sense.

Skharr stopped suddenly, tilted his head to listen, and raised his hand to bring their small convoy to a halt. He looked around in silence and finally focused his attention on the path in front of them.

"What's the matter?" the dwarf asked. "More monsters?"

"Aye. This time, the kind that wanders about on two legs."

It took him a few seconds to understand what the barbarian meant. Humans were not common in the area but they still wandered the route, which was what the road was for, after all.

Still, he had hoped they wouldn't have to worry about humans as they proceeded through the forest. There was enough else to worry about, after all.

"What are you— Hey, what are you doing?"

Brahgen looked around to where his companion moved to Horse's saddle and began to retrieve his bow.

"We don't know how many of the godsbedammed shit-faced sneak-thieves will be waiting for us, so we should have a plan ready for how to fight them."

"How to fight—what do you plan to do?"

Skharr shrugged and began to string his bow. "You move in and draw their attention. Once they are focused on you, I'll pick them off from a distance. That should make sure none of us is in too much danger."

"Right, right." Brahgen scowled. "And what do I do?"

"Anything you like, but don't do anything stupid. We work as a team. And do not leave the road."

"Ha. A team. Right." The dwarf shook his head and tugged one of his beard's braids. "So why don't you be the bait?'

"I would have suggested it but you would have to draw my bow."

The youth considered this for a moment, unable to understand where the problem with this might lie. He shrugged, slid from the saddle, and strode to the bow that was taller than he was. It wasn't too much of an issue since most of those dwarves used were taller than they were, especially the larger war bows.

He nodded when Skharr gestured for him to take the weapon, lifted it carefully, adjusted the grip, and tried to draw the string back.

After a goodly number of groans and a few more adjustments later, Brahgen realized the draw weight was considerably more than he thought it would be. He tried to turn it on its side and pull it that way, but with no more success. He could only draw it a few inches before his back shouted in protest.

Finally, he was forced to admit defeat and handed the weapon to the barbarian. The initial disappointment at his failure was soon swallowed by a slew of possible solutions and he scratched his head in thought. "I might be able to add a few gears to this and reduce the draw weight while still giving it the same power. After that, we could let it rest and—"

Both paused and Skharr was the first to shake his head.

"This is not the time," the barbarian muttered. "But we'll have to discuss it soon."

His companion was right, of course. It would take days to work through the gears that might work and longer still to test each one. In the present circumstances, they barely had time for him to conceive the idea before the warrior slipped quietly into the tree cover.

The warning to stay on the road still rang in the dwarf's ears, even though his companion had disregarded that warning. He shrugged and reminded himself that Skharr knew more about the area than he did. There were dangers in the forest that were not accounted for in the natural world, and he was more than willing to leave the risk to others.

Brahgen pulled a few layers of padded armor on over his clothes and clicked his tongue as he motioned for both Jenny and Horse to follow him.

Either they understood or were willing to follow regardless, but they did as instructed. The beasts plodded behind him as he began to lead them down the winding path through the forest.

After what seemed only moments later, he heard the tell-tale sounds of humans in the vicinity. Skharr's ears were undeniably sharper than his to have heard them before he did. They ventured cautiously around another bend and he stopped when he saw a group of three humans waiting for him in the center of the road.

Standing against them on his own made his mouth go dry and his knees responded with a feeling of weakness sufficient that he had to concentrate to not reveal it. The barbarian had promised to help him, but for all Brahgen knew, something horrifying might have already swallowed him whole and left him to deal with the brigands alone.

He swallowed the lump in his throat and advanced with a steady step.

"Damn my friend for leaving me in the middle of this godsbe-dammed forest," he muttered under his breath. "We might have found a nice, longer path around but no, I'm fucking stuck in this shit-mire on my own without so much as a sign that the barbarian is even alive."

"You'll want to leave the beasts and walk away, little-un," one of the brigands shouted. "Don't make a fuss and we'll let you walk out with your life and maybe even the clothes on your back."

"Do you think you can talk them into staying with you?" Brahgen asked and looked pointedly at Horse and Jenny.

"Eh?"

"They talk, you know. The horses and the donkeys. They'll perhaps stay as long as you give them as many apples as they can eat. But I don't see any on you, so I doubt you'll be able to sweet-talk your way into keeping them."

"What the fuck is he on about?" one of the thieves asked.

"Talk...talking horses?"

"Never ye mind what the shit-head dwarf is saying. Take whatever he don't want to part with and be done with it."

"You might as well be horses yourselves given the amount you're talking," Brahgen retorted. "Do ye plan to talk me to death or do you have other plans to part me from my valuables?"

"For fuck—take them from him and be done with."

The thieves were disconcerted by the fact that the dwarf replied to their threats without any sign of being cowed, but it seemed as though they had enough talking. One of them held a boar spear in hand and began to advance toward him, Horse, and Jenny.

Before he'd taken three steps, something struck him in the chest and Brahgen gaped reflexively. He'd missed what exactly had hit the man but in one moment, he stood on the road and in the next, he was knocked off his feet and rolled some five feet away and off the path into the bushes beyond.

"Oy!" One of the thieves took a step forward. "What the fuck is you up to? Where did he go?"

At least they hadn't seen what happened either. Their missing man was still alive, however, judging by his screams of pain inside the undergrowth.

"Follow the sound of my voice, ya daft bastard!" one of them shouted and looked around. "Because I'd rather lick my own balls than come in after you."

The other shook his head. "He's already dead, most like, or soon will be. There's no point in weeping over him now. We can still kill the fucking dwarf and use him as a snack."

They both turned to Brahgen, who was already inching away from them. One drew a hatchet from his belt and the other carried what looked like a war hammer.

It might have been a blacksmith's hammer in another life, his dwarven brain pointed out, but one side had been honed to a fine point.

He nodded, drew a deep breath, and held his dagger a little tighter. The one with the hatchet advanced on him and shouted a battle cry and the dwarf sidestepped neatly and immediately put a little distance between himself and the two.

It wasn't something he would be able to do forever, of course. He would need to fight back.

"There's some courage in you," Brahgen whispered. "You'd better fucking find that some or you're a dead godsbedammed dwarf."

He stood his ground when the man with the hammer attacked, recalled what he had seen Skharr do, and remained in place until the last possible moment before he bounded to the side. The hammer sailed past a few inches from his head. The dwarf bellowed—more to bolster his courage than to try to intimidate his adversaries—lunged toward his opponent, and thrust his dagger forward with as much power as he could manage.

It cut easily through the man's clothes. He wasn't wearing any armor so the blade went in deep and sliced his stomach open in a neat, long gash.

The youth stepped back, feeling almost as surprised as the man looked as he tried to make out precisely how he'd been wounded.

"You...motherfucker!"

The wounded brigand tried to attack again but he slipped on the blood and guts that poured from the wound. The other man was probably already attacking, but Brahgen forced himself to focus on the one in front of him. He kicked the hammer away from his hands, drove his dagger through the robber's throat, and yanked it out when warm blood spilled onto his hands.

The life began to fade from the bandit's eyes before the dwarf turned to face the third man.

He stared for a moment when he realized that the man with the hatchet was no longer there. A howl of pain drew the dwarf's gaze to the side of the road where the thief sprawled, most likely punched off his feet by the power of a strike. An arrow jutted from his chest, almost as long as a javelin.

His back arched from the ground and he cried out in pain again as he tried repeatedly to pull the arrow from his chest.

It was a futile endeavor. Even if it wasn't barbed, it would take a feat of immense strength to draw it out.

And if he did succeed, he would face a quick death from blood loss.

Before either could occur, however, Brahgen took a step back when he noticed movement in the bushes. The first thought that came to mind was that the third brigand had finally recovered and now returned to help, but as the movement continued, he realized it wasn't something moving in the bushes.

The plants themselves were strangely in motion.

A vine slithered forward, wound around the dying bandit's neck, and dragged him slowly deeper into the underbrush.

Something else moved in them as well, and it seemed as though jaws snapped into the man to cut the screams off as the body disappeared into the brambles and the earth below.

The barbarian had been right about the bodies drawing more monsters. He merely hadn't expected them to be in the trees themselves.

"Skharr?" Brahgen called and peered into the darkening forest. He tried to make out something—anything—that might have been his giant companion.

But nothing moved and he heard no sound beyond a low rumbling from the bushes, complemented sickeningly by the snapping of bones.

"Fuck me," he whispered and looked furtively around. "We'd best keep moving, yes?"

Jenny walked forward obediently but Horse stood his ground and tossed his mane rebelliously.

The dwarf knew he could pull and tug at the reins as much as he wanted, but the beast would not take another step forward until he was assured that Skharr would join them.

"Come on, you stubborn shit. We need to keep moving," Brahgen insisted and hated that he now tried to reason with a horse. "You know we cannot stay here. It will be the death of us."

The stallion still showed no sign that he was interested in moving and nickered softly.

"Skharr said it himself. Bodies will attract more of the monsters. Now, if you're interested to find out what other monsters might crawl out, or what those fucking plants will want to eat when they have finished gnawing on the dead bandits, stay where you are. See if I care."

He did care, of course. Not only because he'd come to feel some affection toward the damn beast through their time traveling together, but also because he knew the warrior would never forgive him for leaving Horse behind in the damn woods.

Whether the barbarian was alive or not didn't matter. He knew well enough that the dead could be as terrifying as the living—sometimes even more terrifying.

Finally, the stallion lowered his head, neighed softly, and pawed the dirt before he took a tentative step forward to follow Jenny.

The donkey had enough of waiting as well and looked as close to panic as he'd ever seen her. She brayed loudly at Horse, whose head lifted sharply. He stamped his hooves in surprise with his ears flattened against his skull.

But she had the last word and she turned away and walked toward Brahgen. A few moments later, the stallion proceeded to follow with no further argument.

The dwarf couldn't understand what their exchange had been but he had a feeling that Jenny had snapped at him to recollect whatever balls he had and start walking.

The warhorse seemed to listen to her far better than he listened to Brahgen, but the end result was the same and the youth felt an odd rush of success as both beasts plodded after him down the road.

Perhaps Skharr wasn't quite as mad as he seemed. The two beasts were intelligent enough to reach the same conclusion as he had, after all.

The fact that Horse was willing to stand his ground and risk death while waiting for the barbarian was admirable as well. He could only wish that he might develop a similar bond one day—perhaps with Jenny or some other beast.

It might even be the two-legged kind, but that was a thought for another time. All he needed to think about now was that he had to get them out alive. He looked at his hands, still covered in blood, and slowly wiped them clean with a kerchief he carried in his coat pocket. The steady clops of the horses behind him were oddly comforting.

All he could hope for now was that Skharr was still alive and would meet them somewhere along the road. He had possibly run into trouble but his words had been clear in directing him to stay on the road.

Hope seemed like an odd thing to consider in the gloom of the forest around them, but it seemed strangely clear in the moment. He'd stood his ground against the fucking bandits and won. With help, of course, but he hadn't dreamed that he would be capable of that before. Perhaps Skharr was right.

But that was a matter for another time as well. Brahgen shivered when he heard another crackle from the forest around them and he increased his pace. The two beasts followed suit without need for him to urge them to move faster.

CHAPTER SEVEN

Many rules could be learned about the world. Skharr had discovered that most of those could only be learned after experience had taught them as lessons. Of course, this could have been because he was a fool who could not learn from the mistakes of others.

One rule he thought he did not need an object lesson on, however, was to stay away from godsbedammed fucking bears.

The beasts could be found almost anywhere in the world, even in the Druums Woodlands, although there was always a sinister twist to any creature in these woods. A massive bear stood its ground against him as he took another arrow from his quiver and put it to the string. Without so much as a whisper of warning, the mountainous bundle of fur and angry muscle rushed toward him.

The arrow flew and he could see it pierce the beast's shoulder a few inches behind the skull, which was what he had aimed for.

He had a feeling the wound would merely anger it and he flung himself aside and narrowly avoided a swipe from a massive paw. The claws grazed his shoulder but not hard enough to cut through the padding of his clothes. In seconds, he was on his feet again, two arrows in his hand, and he nocked one as the beast whirled to attack him again.

There was no time for careful aim and he loosed the first of the arrows into the bear's hindquarters while the other sailed a little high and barely grazed the creature's skull before it thunked into a nearby tree.

The war bow was not the finest weapon for the situation. It took him too long to draw and his aim was compromised when the creature surged into another attack.

Skharr tossed the weapon aside and circled behind a heavy pine tree as the bear charged blindly toward him. All the arrows had done was enrage it further, and he took a step back as its impact with the tree felled a handful of branches above him. He drew his ax and darted around the trunk as the beast swiped at him again. With a roar, he pushed forward and buried the ax head into a massive paw.

It was the bear's turn to roar and it jerked back and inched away while it inspected its wounded paw. The barbarian tried to keep the tree between himself and it before it rushed into motion again. The beast was about the size of a small troll and it took all the willpower he had in him to stand his ground as it closed on him again, wounded and angrier than before.

He dove under a swipe and his shoulder caught a root and twisted awkwardly. A jolt of pain streaked through his body before he found his feet and attacked his adversary before it had the time to turn and attempt another assault. He swung the ax down on the creature's neck as hard as he could as a paw swiped his legs out from under him. The weapon bit deep and he twisted it and felt the crack of bone breaking under his falling weight.

It could only be the spine from the way the whole beast suddenly stopped and fell like all the life had fled from it. The head continued to move and the massive jaws snapped at him as it tried to swing to catch him.

The rest of its body did not cooperate, however, and Skharr

dragged himself slowly to his feet. He scowled at an ache in his legs where the claws had caught him.

"My apologies, big-un," he said quietly. "It was a choice between you or me."

The bear didn't appear to understand what he was saying but he felt the apology was necessary regardless. He had intruded on its territory, after all, and it had reacted to defend itself, even if he hadn't meant it any harm.

But in the end, he wouldn't lay down and die for that, nor would he regret fighting for his life.

He did feel like there was a painful lack of purpose in their fight, however. The barbarian shook his head and swung his ax to finish the beast before he plucked his arrows from its body.

"Now," he muttered, "where the fuck was that road?"

He didn't want to wait to find out what scavengers were probably waiting in the shadows.

He wouldn't leave Skharr behind. The barbarian had gone off to do things his way, and Brahgen had no doubt that he was capable of looking after himself.

Dozens of stories, tales, and ballads had begun to circle that described the wide variety of reasons why doubting his abilities was a bad idea. Still, as he trudged on in silence, he did have a few moments where he wondered how much of what he'd heard was fact and how much was good storytelling. He hadn't walked very far, however, before he heard more footsteps ahead of them, breaking branches, and the crunch of dry leaves.

Skharr had said that the only creatures that moved about and made that much noise were those that didn't worry about what else was out there.

There weren't many humans who would feel that way in these woods, and Brahgen wasn't entirely surprised when he saw the barbarian standing on the other side of a bend in the road.

He was covered in blood and sucked in deep breaths as he looked around the forest like he was annoyed over the necessity to work a little harder than he intended to. Claw marks were visible across his shoulder, back, and legs, although it was difficult to tell which of the blood was his and which was that of whatever owned the claws that had left those injuries.

Although he also favored his right leg a little, it wasn't enough to suggest that the wound was deep.

"So you had a fight of your own, did you?" the dwarf asked as he approached the barbarian. Despite his relief at seeing his travel companion, he made sure to sweep his gaze continually over the forest around them in case something still lurked, determined to attack the man.

Skharr shrugged and scowled into the forest as he walked to where Horse had come to a halt and showed no sign whatsoever of having missed him.

"It was a little bloody," he explained as he took some cloth from his pack, doused it with water, and began to clean himself. "If you are bored, it is certainly a good way to get the blood flowing."

"There are ways to accomplish it that don't involve charging into a cursed forest without so much as a second thought."

"I did have second thoughts," the warrior admitted. "And third thoughts, if the truth be told. It was about the time that the fourth thoughts started that I regretted having gone into the forest."

"You think a lot, don't you?"

"I do. It is a pity that it usually comes after I've put myself in a position where thinking might have avoided it."

"The kind of thought where you realized we could have dealt with three attackers without you braving the forest?"

Skharr grinned and nodded. "Even so, you acquitted yourself

quite admirably against them. You might not need me to keep you safe for very long."

Brahgen chuckled and shook his head as they began to move again while Skharr continued to clean himself. "So, will we stay on the path from this point forward?"

"All things considered, I think that would be best, yes."

That admission seemed a little unlike him, but the dwarf chose to not argue with him over it as long as they stayed on the move. The sooner they were out of this godsbedammed forest, the better.

"So," he said once the warrior had changed his shirt for one that was not ripped or covered in blood, "what did you think about the fight? I thought I did rather well, all things considered. But what the hell were those...plants that ate the men once they were dead?"

Skharr shrugged. "Fucked if I can tell. There are far too many dark and horrifying monsters in this place to keep track of. We might be the first humans to have seen them at work and survived."

"Ah." He wasn't sure why, but the knowledge didn't appeal to him as much as it might have. Knowing there were plants out there that were as dangerous as the monsters was a terrifying thought given that they were surrounded by the damn things as far as the eye could see. "What do you think we'll do the next time we are ranged against a group of humans?"

"You mean aside from heading out into the forest?"

"Naturally."

The barbarian tilted his head. "Next time, I think we should simply kill them from afar."

"And if they are civil? Not hostile?"

"We shouldn't have to guess once they state their purpose. They'll have to walk into the range of my arrows and we can discuss whether or not they have a mind to kill us and take everything we own. I feel that would bring out the most honest part of their natures."

The youth laughed at that and Jenny nudged him gently in the back. "And if they were to be a problem? And were too many for you to handle alone?"

"It's a good thing I don't travel alone, then."

"Do you honestly think I would be any help to you if we were engaged in a skirmish?"

"I'd say that I have a better chance of surviving with you than without. You have a weapon and the willingness to use it. All you need is training and tactical direction and you'll soon be in a position where you would be able to bring your strongest talents to bear."

"How do you mean?"

"A large barbarian can be the center of the attention and take the brunt of the attacks. Of course, I won't be there to do so for you in the future, but if you are in a situation where you need to fight, you must know what your strengths are and apply them effectively. You won't be the burly warrior type. You could adapt your combat skills to that particular day but for the moment, for survival, fight as you are, not like what you wish you were."

"And what am I?"

"Quick, for one thing. A sharp eye and a quick hand allied to a keen mind are difficult to beat."

"Would I be able to beat you?"

Skharr grinned and shrugged. "Perhaps one day. Although I would say your keen mind might tell you to back away if you were ever to find me as your opponent without any support."

Brahgen nodded, drew his dagger, and flipped it smoothly over his fingers. "What kind of weapons would you recommend for one my size?"

The barbarian thought about it for a moment. "Well, I would say you could handle a spear rather well. With fast, deft strokes, you could use it as a staff as well, which would allow you to take advantage of your dexterous hands and sharp eyes as well help with what you lack in…well, range."

"Are you calling me short, barbarian?"

After a second, Skharr realized that the dwarf was joking and shook his head. "If you're looking for something a little closer and tighter than a spear, I would suggest possibly a falchion of some kind—a well-balanced one that could be whipped around with all the speed you could muster."

"I like that idea. I could be the first pirate dwarf to sail the seas."

"Is that something you've considered?" Skharr asked and narrowed his eyes.

Brahgen shrugged. "Why the fuck not? The whole world is before me."

"Right. But for the moment, you'll need to find out how to keep yourself alive on dry land."

The dwarf grinned, flipped his dagger from his left hand to his right, and tried to thrust it toward his companion.

His eyebrows raised sharply when his companion's hand snapped down to catch his hand before it had traveled more than an inch.

"You're not the only quick one among us," Skharr said and chuckled. "Another strength of mine is that many who see me underestimate how fast my hands and mind are. It's something to keep in mind. Folk generally have thoughts about what dwarves are like. Some are true and some are not. You can always find some way to put yourself in an advantageous position by using that kind of thinking."

Brahgen nodded, flicked his blade to his left hand again, and thrust it toward the barbarian. The blade scored his sleeve faintly before he withdrew the weapon.

"For instance, if you thought I was right-handed."

The warrior laughed and nodded. "Aye, something like that."

The forest felt like it went on forever, and the idea of

spending a night in its confines was not a pleasant thought. He had a feeling that Skharr felt the same as they continued along the winding road at a good pace. It wasn't long before the young dwarf had to mount Jenny again to keep up with the man's long paces.

As the sun was about to set, however, a hint of hope appeared as well. The tree cover started to thin slightly above them and before too long, he could see the sun setting out in front of them, away from the trees and out in the open.

"I'll admit that I did not look forward to spending the night in that godsbedammed place," he stated and looked over his shoulder at the trees as they cleared the woodland.

"Sleeping inside the Druums' Woodland is a good way to find yourself dead in the morning," Skharr agreed. "If we had still been inside the tree cover when night fell, we would not have stopped. The beasts prowling through there during the day may be terrifying, but those that come out at night are true nightmares."

The barbarian left the description at that and Brahgen could thank him for it. There was no point in fearing what they would hopefully not have to deal with ever again.

"It looks like we might not need to sleep out on the ground again tonight." The warrior looked up and raised his hand toward where the sun was setting. "I thought I had chosen the path that led us through a narrower section of the woods, but I don't remember that village being there when I last traveled these parts."

Brahgen followed his pointed finger and his gaze settled on a village a few miles away nestled gently alongside a small lake. Fishing vessels had already begun to pull in for the night.

"I wouldn't mind having a real bed to sleep in tonight and food not cooked over an open fire," he muttered.

"Does that mean you don't like my cooking?"

"It's good enough, I suppose, but in the end, there is something appealing about fresh food instead of the dried rations travelers are forced to use over longer distances."

Skharr clearly had no argument against that. The man was a skilled cook, of course, but Brahgen knew he was right. And having food possibly freshly caught from the lake would certainly be a pleasant break from the humdrum fare that traveling on the open road necessitated.

CHAPTER EIGHT

The town was small but like Grenland, despite the lack of interference from the larger governments, protection was provided by the fact that none of the bandits and deserter groups were brave enough to traverse the region of the Druums Woodlands.

It was an interesting thought but it wouldn't last, Skharr knew that much. Eventually, war would find the area and the peaceful existence the folk enjoyed would be rudely interrupted. For the moment, however, the peace and considerable natural resources in the region were more than enough to give the locals some sense of prosperity.

All the folk in the village were dressed well, not quite in the silks that were seen in larger cities but not the rags that Skharr had seen in other, similar villages across the continent.

"It seems like a pleasant little place to live," Brahgen commented. "I could see myself settling here in my later years."

"No palisades."

"Hmm?"

"It has no palisades. No wall, moat, and no defenses. They've become lazy. Eventually, the fear of the Druums will not be enough to drive deserters and bandits away and they'll push through and burn this settlement to the ground. If you were to live in this region, the first thing to do would be to build some defenses around the outside, if only to keep the weaker groups away."

The dwarf nodded. "I think I would be able to turn my mind and my skills, such as they are, to that kind of work. But if there were walls, wouldn't that attract larger groups?"

"Possibly."

The barbarian didn't like that his mind went immediately to what could go wrong for the folk in this village. Perhaps he would find himself in a better situation if he was able to better focus on the nicer things in life.

Of course, that wasn't quite in line with his reality. There would be enough time to indulge that later, he decided, possibly in his old age but almost certainly not before.

Signs along the road through the village indicated an inn where they could find rooms for the night closer to the lake. To reach it, they needed to walk across a planked pier to the entrance, which overlooked the water.

It was an interesting choice. Skharr liked the idea but it meant the rooms were likely pushed out to the back with the stables.

"Welcome, welcome." A stout, shorter man greeted them, stood from his seat on a barrel, and coughed a lungful of pipe smoke. "Not many outsiders come to visit us here but we do have a few rooms available if you have a mind to spend the night."

He nodded. "We'll need stables for the beasts and food for us all."

"Right then, of course. Where did you come from if you don't mind me asking? I didn't see you along the main road around the lake."

"We came the other way," Brahgen answered. "Through the woodlands."

"Well. Huh." The man tugged his beard gently and seemed

genuinely flustered by the idea that someone would willingly come through the forest. "What would you do that for?"

"Shorter route," Skharr responded bluntly.

"Aye, if you're willing to die on the road. I didn't know that any folk of character wandered through those roads. Well, except one. A mad barbarian set up a little farm on the other side of the woodlands from here. I cannot tell you what might have touched his mind to see him make his home that close to the Druums but then, barbarians have always been a little off in the head. Speaking of which, you do seem to be...would you happen to know the man?"

The warrior realized that the innkeeper talked more than he meant to and had allowed his tongue to run rampant before he had an idea of what he was saying or the consequences that could result from what was said. He soon realized how his guest might have taken what he had said if the redheaded giant wasn't, in fact, a barbarian.

"The farm was mine," Skharr admitted. "But it has been handed to another family who is in the favor of the gods."

"Ah. I see. Well, your beasts should want for nothing as we bring in the freshest and sweetest hay that can be provided."

"Apples too, if you can spare," he requested. "Does this village have a Guild Hall? For mercenaries?"

"Ah, you are a fighter? Yes, you'll find it closer to the road. Not many travel this way but enough for a small guild to be established."

Skharr nodded. "Right. Dwarf stays for the evening. I return soon."

"What?" Brahgen asked. "If you think I'll be hidden in a corner while you find extra work, you're a madman."

He tilted his head and shrugged. "Do as you please."

It was his job to keep the youth safe but there likely wasn't going to be any trouble for him in a tavern this small. And in an area of the village where there were fighters, he was the most likely to be involved in a dangerous situation anyway.

Once it was clear that Horse and Jenny would have a comfortable place in the stables, Skharr followed the innkeeper's instructions to the outskirts of the town where the guild's sigil was raised above a simple log house. The structure wasn't remotely comparable to the kind of Guild Halls he had seen in the past, but at the same time, the village was the smallest settlement of civilization he'd ever seen have a Guild Hall of its own.

Unsurprisingly, simplicity defined the building. Once they were inside, his focus was immediately drawn to a massive fire burning in the center of the room. Smoke and embers rose through a hole in the ceiling.

The building had a few elevated stories where a few rooms had been set up, but it looked like most of the business went through a single desk on the far side of the room. It was probably a good thing that very little work took place. A handful of mercenaries were clustered around one of the tables near the fire, and while they cast their gazes to see who the new arrivals were, they weren't overly interested.

The barbarian strode immediately to the table of the guildmaster, whose nose was buried in a stack of papers. The man had difficulty reading through them and had to peer through a pincenez and squint to see anything. He had the look of a former warrior himself, although many years in his past. His head was bald and his chin clean-shaven, which left his thick, bushy eyebrows as the only hair on his head as he focused on the new arrival.

"More fighters coming along this way, eh?" he grunted. "Chano is the name, and they call me guildmaster around these parts. If you look for work, find it on the board above. If anything interests you, come to me for the contract."

He recited the words in a practiced manner and delivered them quickly despite his heavy accent while he returned his attention to his papers. It took a moment before the reality of what he'd seen finally penetrated and his gaze shifted to stare at the massive warrior framed against the firelight. The guildmaster's eyes almost bulged and his pince-nez dropped from its perch.

"I say...are...are you... You would not happen to be Skharr DeathEater, would you?"

The barbarian smirked as he approached the board where the contracts were posted. "I suppose many barbarians look like me. But yes, that is the name that I am known by, among others."

"The other name known is the fucking Barbarian of Theros." The guildmaster stood. He wasn't a tall man but he possessed a stocky build that made him look like there might have been a trace of dwarf in his blood as well.

Brahgen leaned against the table. "He is well-known, then? I thought his legends didn't go much farther than the civilized world."

"Maybe not among the common folk, but much has been said about your travel companion among the fighters for hire on the continent."

"What kind of stories? I've heard the one about how he killed a dragon to bring the emperor to his throne."

"I didn't kill the dragon," Skharr corrected them, his focus fixed on the board. "I ran away from it, to be honest. Survived a dragon, I suppose you could say."

"That is as may be, but we all know ballads have a tendency toward exaggeration," the guildmaster replied. "Not much in the godsbedammed world can kill a dragon aside from magic. And even then, I've seen powerful spells strike the scales and simply bounce off. But, no. The stories I heard were a little more interesting, although perhaps not the kind to sing about. How he would take coin from ladies of the city of Verenvan to abuse their less desirable suitors. Of course, as the tales go, he is known to take a little more than coin."

"What do you...oh. I see." Brahgen narrowed his eyes and looked at his companion. "Is that true? I didn't think ladies had a taste for that kind of...well your kind of... Never mind."

"I couldn't tell you if I wanted to," the barbarian answered cryptically. "And I wouldn't want tales of how I take payment for my services to have any credibility."

"That means yes," the guildmaster whispered. "Still, the genuinely interesting tale was when one of those suitors decided he wanted to marry the woman regardless. She had other plans, of course. Skharr had beaten the man before, but the tale being woven was that his feat was not quite as impressive as all that. I forget what excuses the lordling supposedly wove, but come time for the marriage, the bride invited Skharr to the ceremony and after it was completed, he dueled her new spouse again, killed him, and left the lady in possession of her late husband's estate. It reputedly angered most of the underworld of the city enough that they put all their resources out to kill him. I think we know how that worked out for the sodden fools, wouldn't you say?"

The guildmaster chuckled and returned to his papers before he saw the conflicted expression slide across the dwarf's face. Skharr wondered if that meant the boy had never heard the full story of what happened and only been given scant details from the perspective of those who were likely to not see it in a positive light.

"How did he think he would get away with spreading that kind of rumor?" Brahgen asked.

"Well, I suppose the man has a certain nature about him. It makes folk underestimate him."

"Have you seen him?"

"He's physically imposing, yes, but there is something about him that leads one to think he is a little slow on an intellectual level."

"An idea I have consistently taken advantage of," Skharr interjected. It was a little annoying to be spoken of as if he weren't in the room, but it was something folk had started to do a little more often lately. He would have to put a stop to that.

"Right." Chano cleared his throat and shook his head. "Did you find anything you think you'd like to take on?"

"Aye," the barbarian answered. "There is mention of a dungeon on the Island of the Groll Oak Orcs. It seems like the kind of battle that would fill our time to our advantage."

"Aye. You'll need supplies for the journey as well. Not to mention transportation to the island itself. It is a little too far to swim. Perhaps much too far to swim."

He nodded. "Would we be able to buy the supplies here?"

"Most of them, provided you have your weapons and armor. You won't find any of quality for sale around these parts."

"We have our weapons and armor, for the most part. What kind of orcs live in the region?"

"A handful of fishing tribes and few others. The isle is said to have been home to a coven of emerald hags and the orcs generally stay away from the center of the island where the dungeon is found. The tunnels are said to be too small for the full-sized creatures, so only their youths venture in and then only in shallow delves."

"Hags are nasty, fiercely intelligent, and with an uncanny grasp of the magical elements." Skharr shook his head. "I tangled with one who was abandoned by her coven in a swamp a few years ago. I've never thought I might have to face a full coven."

"And if you're lucky, you won't have to." The guildmaster chuckled. "All we know is that there are rumors of their presence and nothing else. Of course, rumors come from somewhere, so you might encounter them, if not worse. And the guild would need to know what is present on that fucking island."

The barbarian nodded and looked at his companion. "How is your orcish?"

The dwarf looked around before he realized he was the one being spoken to. "Oh, me?"

"Who the fuck else?"

"My orcish?"

"Aye."

Brahgen shrugged. "I've…uh, I've never had the opportunity to learn."

Skharr scowled deeply. "Neither have I. Well then, we'll have to hope they know a language other than stick the pointy end in the dwarf and human."

"So do you want the contract?" Chano asked and looked from one to the other.

"Aye, we want it." He took the scroll from the man, performed the short rite to bind the contract to him, and turned to his companion. "Now, it's time to have food and rest, then we can procure the necessary supplies we will need to take with us."

The dwarf grinned and turned away from the table. A small group of mercenaries began to gather at the door. They spoke quickly and looked agitated and seemed to grow more so by the second.

As the two approached, they stood their ground and would not allow either of them to pass through the door. Behind them, a handful of irate locals had converged on the Guild Hall and their vociferous complaints incensed the mercenaries even more.

"You two!" one of the fishermen shouted. "You thieves have stolen precious items of great value from the inn. They are the thieves. They have to be!"

Skharr narrowed his eyes and turned to where Brahgen stared at him, aghast.

"How many times have I told you to not take the shiny baubles, you massive idiot?" the dwarf roared and drew himself as tall as he could.

The boy was playing at something, and as much as he wanted to demand to know what he was doing, they had little time to resolve this before the whole village was in sufficient an uproar to hang them. For now, he'd play the part he thought was expected of him and hope the plan worked to their advantage.

He grunted softly and rolled his massive shoulders. "Take?"

"Yes, you always take what doesn't belong to you."

"Not take!" the barbarian roared and picked the dwarf up with one hand. "Always say give it back. If had, would give."

With that, he hurled the surprised Brahgen into the group of mercenaries and villagers alike. Some fell while others stumbled over one another in their effort to catch him, surprised that the two newcomers were arguing between them instead of contesting the claims outright.

Skharr shook his head and marched to where the group now attempted to struggle to disentangle themselves from their fellows and stand. Those who hadn't fallen began to draw back slowly at his approach and he lifted Brahgen and set him unceremoniously on his feet.

"My apologies," the youth shouted to the group. "He has something of a temper but has redeeming qualities. Now, did you take the baubles, big-un?"

The warrior shook his head. "Did not take."

"Well then, we'll have to find out where the godsbedammed things went before they decide to…uh, do whatever it is that they do to thieves around here."

The group members looked around, seemingly unsure of what the penalty for thievery was. Before they could reach any consensus, however, one of the mercenaries on the ground shouted, jumped up, and gaped at a collection of pendants and ornaments scattered around him, including a garish broach with a pin that had poked him.

"There's my wife's broach!" one of the villagers shouted and immediately, the townsfolk scrambled feverishly to claim the lost items.

"See now. I knew that there was a peaceful solution to all this." The dwarf smiled and bowed politely.

No one appeared to fully believe his act and they glowered at them, but they had what they'd lost with no proof that the two companions had committed any thievery. When faced with the fact that they had whipped a mob up over items they might have had on their persons all along, they chose to simply hurry away.

Skharr and Brahgen continued through the door and set out on the road to the inn.

"Now, why did you steal their shit?" the warrior asked once they were out of the group's earshot.

"You said I should do so if I was smart."

"That is only if someone has picked a fight with you. Collecting a few spoils of war while you defend yourself will draw no blame. You cannot steal simply for stealing's sake."

"Isn't that the definition of a thief?"

"Not an intelligent one."

"Why the hell not?"

"Do you need to face the angry mob again?" He sighed, exasperated. "Besides, you're merely someone who steals. A true thief is above that kind of nonsense. You have to earn the right to be one. A quality thief is someone others want alongside them when things turn sour like they would, for example, in a dungeon. Not a...rabid animal who takes whatever his hands happen to touch whenever it pleases them."

Brahgen shook his head. "You might have been speaking orcish there because what you said made no fucking sense to my mind."

"Well, think on it."

"Maybe I'm the barbarian here," the dwarf muttered as they approached the inn.

CHAPTER NINE

"What else do we need?"

Skharr assessed the supplies they collected. They had enough food for the two of them for the journey based on the map he'd purchased from one of the locals. He hadn't expected to find a mage in the village so wasn't surprised when he didn't, but he still carried a handful of amulets he had collected for previous excursions that would have to suffice.

Still, they would face a handful of unknowns. He had never dealt with the fishing orc tribes and he'd heard they were more hostile than their desert-dwelling brethren—who were excessively aggressive so this was a matter of some concern. The possibility that there might be hags on the isle as well was a worrying development, but the magic dampening amulets would hopefully keep the creatures away from them. They would feel the effects and move away before the travelers even approached.

Which left one last issue.

"We'll need a fucking boat."

"A…a boat?"

"Aye. How else do you think we'll get there? There is no chance that we'll be able to swim across the lake, down the river, and through to the island. We must have a boat. What? Did you think that I would swim and you would ride on my back?"

Brahgen coughed in what sounded suspiciously like laughter but he wisely chose not to pursue it and they left it entirely unexplored. Skharr led him to the small village docks where most of the boats—small craft, as a rule—were already out at sea in search of the day's catch.

A handful of vessels were still docked, and one of the barges, in particular, seemed likely to ply the smaller waterways.

"It'll be a silver apiece to take the two of you down the river," the captain stated before either of them could say a word. "You'll have to bring your food and we won't bring your horses."

Skharr looked around to make sure the man was speaking to them.

"You already knew we were coming?"

"Word came that you were headed to Groll Oak Island. We happen to be the only vessel that travels down the river, but we will only go as far as the delta. From there, you'll have to find other means to travel."

The barbarian inclined his head and looked at the smaller boats strapped to the barge's side. "Could you spare one of those?"

The captain grinned to reveal a number of missing teeth behind his beard. "I'd part with it for a gold piece if you can spare it. If not, I'm afraid you'll have to find other means of travel. There are a few fishing and whaling inlets you could bargain with."

He knew the man demanded far too much but shrugged and took out two silvers and a gold coin. "We'll take the one on the left. It is in considerably better shape than the other."

"A bargain well-struck."

Skharr knew that they were being robbed blind, of course. The dinghy was barely worth the price of two silvers, much less a full gold coin, but he wouldn't bargain, both because they had little time to waste and because it would not have much success. The man was, after all, their only means of transportation out of the village.

"When do we sail?"

"In an hour. You'll bring your supplies on board."

They hurried to the inn and took a moment to make sure Horse and Jenny would be stabled and fed in their absence before they returned to the barge as it was about to set off. Two men at the front began to push the vessel away from the dock before the wind filled the sails.

"What you said about thieves before..." Brahgen said tentatively. "You seem to have given the whole concept considerable thought."

Skharr scowled. The vessel was slow-moving, the kind that would take them a while to reach their destination. Still, they would follow the river directly through the mountain ranges that spanned the western frontier of the continent. Without it, they would have had to spend weeks looking for a pass that would take them out, whereas the river delta led them directly to the island.

Or at least as directly as anything could given the alternative.

His eyes narrowed. The dwarf was talking to him and had made a statement that needed an answer. He shook his head to clear it and tried to remember what it was.

"I merely thought that you are the type who would prefer to find a better situation than the one that compelled you to flee Verenvan," he replied. "You have a mind and a hand for thievery but engaging in it thoughtlessly is the action of a starving child on the street. You are neither a child nor on the street. And not starving either, I should add."

"So...there are different levels of thievery?"

"Aye. What do you think the fourth level is named?"

"What?"

"A businessman," Skharr grumbled.

Brahgen smirked but looked intrigued. "And...shall we say, the seventh level?"

"Lawyer." The barbarian nodded emphatically. "And the highest level of thief is the tax collector. Of course, they have all the power of a country to give them a legal writ to steal. And they all work for the nobility so in those cases, when you find yourself elevated to such status, you'll discover that the best way to be a thief is to do it for others with the blessing of whatever law you happen to need."

"I doubt any of them think of themselves as thieves."

"Who cares what they think? Their actions speak a great deal louder than any of their loud and offended denials."

"So you think that I should become a tax man. Or a lawyer."

"Or a businessman. You already have the skill and the mindset for it. All you need is the proper title for it."

"And do you suggest we steal from the orcs who will no doubt be waiting for us when we make landfall on the island?"

That was a question Skharr had hoped wouldn't come up. He still had no idea what they would do when they arrived. Orc tribes were unique in how they treated outsiders, which made it difficult to predict what the attitude to strangers of one or the other would be.

"We might need to sneak around the tribes," he said cautiously. "Escape if we are discovered or move directly to negotiate with the smelly bastards for safe passage."

"Why don't you simply treat them the way you usually handle problems?" Brahgen asked. "Shoot your bow first, swing your ax second, and once all are dead, negotiate with the bodies?"

"Orcs are notoriously difficult to kill. Negotiating first will be far easier."

"Negotiations might be a little difficult if neither one of us speaks orcish."

"Which should tell you how difficult killing an orc is."

Brahgen nodded and chuckled. "True. No one lives to teach

others the language. Well, I imagine we'll find out when we get there."

The barge increased speed as the wind finally pushed them free of the lake and into the river, which allowed the current to pull them gently downstream toward the sea.

It was an impressive sight to watch the mountains rise on either side. Trickling streams flowed from the snow-capped peaks that chilled the water to near ice before they plunged into the river to feed the current. Their progress rapidly reached a point where the two men with oars at the front had to use them to keep the barge away from rocks and the shore as it surged forward, driven by the swift flow of the water.

Sheer rock rose on their left as if the water had worn through the mountains themselves over thousands of years, perhaps even longer.

If nothing else, it was a pleasant distraction before they curled away from the mountains and the delta came into view.

Beyond it lay their destination. It looked much larger on the horizon than it had on the map. Skharr's mind went immediately to the question of whether they had brought enough supplies to traverse the godsbedammed island—and how inaccurate their map might prove to be—but they were beyond such worries now. If they needed something, they would simply have to improvise.

If the need arose, he was more than capable of keeping himself and his dwarf companion alive against the harsh elements and the problems that arose from hunger.

A few nights of slow travel on the water passed before the barge changed course to the edge of the river, where a handful of whaling and fishing villages were visible. These were much smaller than those they had left behind and edged up against the coast to take advantage of small harbors to protect themselves from the elements.

The barge likely bought provisions needed by these villages and took their catch back, from the rich, fatty blubber of the whales to the larger numbers of fish that could be caught in the open sea.

It was morning, but the sun had barely peeked over the horizon before the captain approached them again.

"This is where we part ways, barbarian," he said bluntly. "The dinghy has been readied for you and is ready to sail. It should serve to take you safely to the island and provide you with a way to return, should your luck hold."

"You don't think we'll return with your dinghy?" Skharr asked.

"There is a reason why the barge stays away from those waters. Orc ships are sneaky and fast, and we would be boarded and attacked before we could raise much of an alarm. And they are frankly the least of the dangers you will face. No, I do not believe you will return my dinghy to me."

The barbarian grinned and patted the man heavily on the shoulder. "All we can do is prove you wrong, then. Thank you for bringing us this far."

The dinghy was lowered from the side of the barge and the two companions climbed aboard.

It was apparent almost immediately that the dwarf was uncomfortable being aboard a smaller craft. He clutched the sides and looked almost too terrified to help with preparing to cast off or even bring their supplies on board.

"It is a joke among humans that dwarves don't like to travel on the open sea," Skharr noted cheerfully. "And it's interesting to see that a few rumors of your people still hold true in you."

"Fuck off."

He grinned and raised the sail. The dinghy moved faster than the barge and they sailed rapidly out of the delta toward the island, where the waves began to increase in size.

Skharr had been at sea in smaller craft before, but Brahgen didn't seem to react well to the way the dinghy was buffeted by the waves.

"Dwarves...were never meant...to be on water," the dwarf

muttered and shook his head. His face had taken on an uncomfortable shade of green.

The barbarian could understand and so quelled the instinct to mock him for the moment, at least until they were on dry land.

The waters calmed somewhat as they approached the island, and as the sun continued to rise in the sky, it became more difficult to see it due to a thick mist that seeped slowly over the area. The wind calmed to the point where the sail no longer propelled them any farther, and with Brahgen still trying to keep his stomach contents down, it fell to Skharr to row them through the mist-covered waters.

Eventually, his companion recovered somewhat and his gaze flicked around to inspect their surroundings.

"I didn't see this mist when we were coming in," the dwarf commented after a while.

"Me neither. It might have been a reaction to our arrival."

"Magic?"

"Possibly. Or it could simply be that the island is plagued by mists coming in over the sea."

It wasn't a pleasant situation to be all but blind, but he still had a rough idea of where they were going, if only from the movement of the sea around them. They now approached dry land, and when he peered into the water, he could see the bottom rising gently with each stroke of the oars.

The dinghy stopped suddenly and he whipped around. It felt like they had struck a rock, and while the jagged edges they had hit might have seemed as hard as stone, it was suddenly clear that it was wood reinforced with steel.

He snapped his hands to his weapons, but he could see movement on the ship they had collided with and bows strung with arrows already pointed at them. The fact that they hadn't been fired at yet was an interesting development and it meant they needed to be incredibly careful how they acted over the next few minutes if they wanted to survive.

"Raise your hands and make no sudden movements," he told Brahgen quietly.

Contrary to his instruction, the dwarf leaned over the side of the boat and heaved loudly.

Skharr closed his eyes and waited for the twang of bowstrings that would indicate their imminent demise, but none came. Instead, a loud clanking was heard as hooks caught on the side of the dinghy and began to pull them around.

Once they were dragged to the port side of the ship, a rope was dropped for them.

"I don't think I can climb that," the youth declared weakly.

"I'll lift you," he answered and after a few attempts, he managed to heave the dwarf up the side without tipping the dinghy. The fact that he still couldn't hear any sounds of violence coming from those on the vessel meant they hadn't encountered a tribe that intended to kill them out of hand.

He climbed up the rope, pulled himself carefully over the side, and immediately raised his hands to show no sign of aggression. There were at least a dozen crossbows pointed at both him and his companion, as well as numerous spears. The orcs on board looked larger than their kin from the deserts and wore garments in dark-green shades that almost helped them to disappear in the mist.

The ship itself was larger than Skharr had thought at first—at least twenty paces from bow to stern with oars positioned on the sides and a mast that was currently lowered along the deck. How they had managed to move so silently along the water was a mystery he had no time to ponder.

One of the orcs stepped forward. She was taller than her sailors and wore intricately designed mail armor. A sturdy steel helm also set her aside from the others, who mostly wore padded armor if they wore any at all.

She carried a heavy scimitar on her hip but it wasn't drawn

when she approached and she tapped her tusks gently before she made a few quick gestures with her hands.

He narrowed his eyes as she repeated the series of motions.

"Are...are they speaking to us?" Brahgen asked.

"Yes. I think so. How did you know?"

"They look like the hand signals that imitate a spoken language." The dwarf grunted.

"Do you understand it?"

"More or...yes. She's asking us...I think why we are not...in fleet waters?"

Skharr tilted his head in some confusion before it became clear. Orcs didn't like to speak any of the common tongues since the words felt uncomfortable in their oddly shaped mouths. It appeared, however, that they understood what they were saying from the nods he could see from a handful of those who held the crossbows.

Not all, however.

"I think they have an agreement of some kind with the fishing villages," Skharr answered. "Fleet waters suggests the fishing fleets, which means these waters belong to them, yes?"

Another smattering of nods followed and the orcs grunted between themselves in their guttural language, likely translating what he had said to those who didn't understand the common tongue.

The chieftain made the gestures again and grunted firmly to demand an answer.

"We are not with the fishing fleet," the barbarian explained.

Her eyes narrowed and another series of gestures ensued.

"What is she saying?" He turned to Brahgen.

"She asks...if we were banished because of...the sick one? Do they think you're sick?"

The chieftain shook her head, pointed at the dwarf, and indicated in a way that even Skharr could understand to refer to his small stature and the fact that he threw up.

"No, he's not sick," he stated quickly when he realized that they were afraid of having a sickness spread among their tribe. "Being on a boat over the water unsettles his stomach."

That brought a ripple of what he could only describe as laughter among the tribe members. As the translation spread, more laughter followed.

"Well, let's see how they handle being under the ground for years at a time, then we can laugh," Brahgen muttered and rolled his eyes.

Once the laughter died down, the chieftain made another series of gestures.

"She asks why we are here."

"We are…" Skharr paused and looked at the group before he continued. "We are not with the fishing fleets. We are here to raid the dungeon on the island. There has been word of monsters spreading from it and we are here to kill them."

Her eyes narrowed as she focused on him specifically. She appeared to assess him critically, unsure if he was capable of doing what he said he would do. It was an unsettling moment but he steeled himself, very much aware of the crossbows and spears all around them like they were prickling into his skin.

After a few moments, she shrugged and uttered what sounded like a chuckle before she gestured for the tribe to lower their weapons, which they did without question. Skharr's eyes narrowed as she began to speak in the sign language again.

"She…she says that they'll take the boat in exchange for safe passage through their lands to the dungeon," Brahgen translated. "There…are monsters on the path, and we might need help on the way in."

"How are we supposed to get off the island when we return?" the barbarian asked.

Another round of laughter rippled through the orc ranks as the chieftain spoke again.

"She doesn't expect us to survive," the youth muttered.

"I've survived more than my fair share of dungeons," he answered firmly. "Which is not to say I won't die, but I always make plans based on my survival."

The orc looked like she understood and nodded.

"We can buy the dinghy from them if we make it out," the dwarf translated again. "But we'll need our supplies. You can have the boat but we need what's inside."

It took Skharr longer than he would have admitted before he realized that his companion had directed the last two statements at the chieftain, who nodded and motioned for them to bring the dinghy up.

"Well...that went smoother than expected," he said as they began to unload the supplies from the small craft. "How do you think they learned sign language?"

"I assume the fisher villages might have taught it to them as a way of communicating," Brahgen surmised although he didn't sound convinced that this was the right explanation.

Even so, the barbarian had a feeling the orcs were only willing to grant them safe passage because there was something on the island they needed killed as well.

There wasn't much in the world that scared an orc into compliance. Dragons were all he knew that they feared openly. A few tribes even worshipped the creatures.

Which meant there was likely something even worse waiting for them in their adventure.

Once the dinghy was secured on the side of the orc ship, the large vessel began to turn toward the land that became more visible as the orcs rowed toward it.

"So there was no need to steal from the orc tribes, then?" Brahgen asked. "What level of thief is a negotiator?"

"Among the highest, although that skill is necessary for any who wish to stay alive long enough to be among the most accomplished in the profession."

It was soon apparent that their destination wasn't one of the villages and instead, they simply steered toward one of the nearest beaches, which was covered in what looked like black sand. The rowers pushed harder and the ship was thrust onto the beach, and a handful of the orcs leapt out and dragged it onto the sand and fully out of the water.

No more weapons pointed at them, not even when Skharr collected their weapons again and climbed out.

If he were to guess, he would have thought they had more dangerous things to worry about. This was annoying in its own right, as he much preferred to be the most dangerous thing in any region he happened to be in.

A number of them gathered their crossbows and spoke quickly in the guttural language he was starting to get used to hearing. None of them made any of the gestures that Brahgen would be able to translate, unfortunately. Still, their demeanor and the way they held themselves in readiness were fairly universal—something was out there and they anticipated that it would attack them directly on the beach.

None of the orcs stopped him as he hefted his bow, strung it quickly, and selected three arrows from his quiver.

Brahgen looked around. "What's happening?"

One of the orcs signed something to him deftly. This one was better at it than the chieftain, and the dwarf took a step back.

"What did he say?" Skharr asked.

"He said that they follow the ships and attack them when they land," the youth answered. "He didn't mention who they were."

"I think we are about to find out," he responded and nocked an arrow to the bowstring when he discerned movement deep in the mists.

There was no mistaking the clattering in the street. A group of horses had ridden up outside the Guild Hall and raised a clamor that couldn't be ignored. Chano grunted and pushed out of his seat when he realized that the mercenaries all hurried to find out what the disturbance was about.

There were few real rules in this corner of the world, and if he didn't take steps to resolve the situation before it escalated, he had a feeling they would have a fight on their hands.

The guildmaster moved quickly out the door to where a group of ten or so horsemen had gathered outside. A few of them looked like they had sustained wounds and weren't likely to continue riding, but the others appeared uninjured and like they were ready for a fight.

One dismounted quickly and marched to where Chano calmly struck flint over steel to light his pipe.

"Are you the guildmaster in this backwater hole?" the man asked as he removed his helm.

"Aye, and I advise you to not call it a backwater hole again. I'd like to see what happens to you if you do."

The stranger smirked and ran his fingers through his long, golden locks to loosen them where the helm had flattened them against his head.

"A giant barbarian and a small dwarf came this way not too long ago. Do you remember them?"

"Aren't all dwarves small?" one of the local mercenaries asked.

"Aye, but this one would be smaller than usual."

"I've not seen enough dwarves to know which are too large or too small," Chano admitted. "But a barbarian of some size passed through here with a dwarf as his companion. Do you have business with the man?"

"You could say that." The golden-haired fighter looked at the rest of his troop. "He has a weapon of great value in his possession that belongs to us. Tell us where the man hid himself and there will be no more trouble."

"It is odd that a man who obtained a weapon of great value

would choose to put himself on the path to suicide," one of the mercenaries muttered.

"Suicide?"

Chano shrugged. "They went to find a dungeon on Groll Oak Orc Island. It's covered in orcs and heavens knows what else might be prowling there. Frankly, it does not seem like the action of a man with a treasure of a weapon in his possession."

"And yet he has done it," the mercenary snapped before he turned to his men. "Gather supplies, regroup, and we'll leave as soon as we are physically able to do so. Go!"

The men hastened to obey the command of their leader and mounted up immediately to find a trader where they could buy supplies.

"Well, it seems we have more than a few who are willing to throw their lives away," the guildmaster muttered and shook his head. At least the group hadn't attempted to start any fights, although some of his mercenaries certainly looked like they were ready to retaliate at the slightest provocation. The villagers would never forgive him if that happened.

CHAPTER TEN

The monsters that moved through the mist seemed almost reluctant to attack once they realized the group was waiting for them, but it wasn't long before a loud, sustained roar echoed through the fog and they began to edge closer.

Skharr still couldn't see enough of them to enable any kind of accuracy, but he drew his bow and felt the weight of it on his back as he held his aim. With as much patience as he could muster, he waited for one of the creatures to finally show itself.

When it did, there wasn't much thought involved in the process of selecting his target at almost fifty yards over the black sand beach before he loosed the arrow.

It streaked toward the creature with enough power to cut it down before it could take another step. He'd made a decent shot, especially in the circumstances. At first glance, it looked like it was vaguely humanoid, but when it toppled, he could see a thick, sinuous tail that whipped violently in its death throes.

As more of the monsters approached, it was clear that these were the mythical lizardfolk. They stood on two legs like humans but their three-fingered hands were tipped with long, razor-sharp claws. A long, dangerous tail, powerful jaws that were said to break bone, and long fangs that could rend flesh made them foes to be reckoned with. A few myths even mentioned the tails being tipped with poison.

Skharr wondered if he would discover the veracity of that. He had heard a few myths about the lizardfolk that lived in swamps, far from where humans were capable of living or even visiting safely, but he had never seen one himself, and he'd never met any person who had.

That changed now, he realized, but it wasn't a particularly appealing thought.

Dozens of the creatures emerged from the mist. They still looked like they weren't too keen to attack, and a handful darted forward to pull the one he had killed back.

He drew another arrow and chose another target as they began to brandish their spears. Another monster was punched off its three-toed feet as the orcs fired a volley from their crossbows to cut them down in a heavy barrage.

Before Skharr or the orcs could prepare for another volley, the monsters scuttled in, gathered their dead, and vanished into the comparative safety of the heavy mist.

The barbarian scowled and raised an eyebrow as he waited for them to attack again, but the orcs began to take their formations in preparation to continue moving. A few turned to return to their village and a group readied themselves for more fighting.

"Where did the creatures go?" he asked. He decided not to complain about them taking his arrows but it was certainly something he wasn't happy about. There were only a limited number of them available, after all, and he'd already lost enough of them in the forest.

One of the orcs heard him and made the now-familiar gestures.

"What's he saying?" he asked and nudged Brahgen's shoulder.

The dwarf started as if he'd been lost in thought and now paid attention as the orc repeated what he'd said.

"The beasts are cowards," the youth translated. "They will not attack landing craft if they take losses. But...they become more... hungry when they attack farther ahead?"

The orc shook his head and repeated a few of the movements.

"Aggressive." The dwarf nodded and the orc grinned. "The farther into the island we go, they'll grow a few more balls."

That elicited a few of the grunted chuckles from the orc who motioned for them to join the group that would proceed to the dungeon. Skharr adjusted his grip on his bow, slung his sword over his shoulder, and hooked the ax to his belt before he collected the supplies they would carry with them.

Brahgen carried what he owned as well, although the dwarf didn't have much in the way of armor or weapons to weigh him down as they started out. The barbarian would have asked if the orcs had any weapons the boy could borrow, but there was no telling what kind they would have to spare and how much they would cost.

With things as they were, he didn't trust them to not suddenly decide they were expendable if he showed them the coin he carried on him. The purse was considerably lighter than it had been when they left, but there was still enough to tempt the greed of any creature.

The chieftain motioned for them to follow and they proceeded deeper into the island. There was no sign of the lizardfolk attacking as they followed the winding paths to where he assumed the dungeon was situated. He didn't know of any powerful wizards who might have spent time in the area, but he was learning the long, hard lesson that he didn't know everything there was to know under the sun.

As the day progressed, the mist showed no sign of lifting and the fact that none of the orcs seemed surprised by this was a little worrying. Still, he didn't want to ask them if it would remain. The fact that they couldn't see anything farther than fifty feet around them was certainly a new and concerning experience.

"The mist unsettles you too, doesn't it?"

Skharr turned as Brahgen pulled his cloak a little tighter around his shoulders.

"Why do you ask?"

"Because it unsettles the fuck out of me. How in seven hells does a mist this heavy linger for so long?"

One of the orcs made a gesture, circled her head, and patted her chest twice.

"Magic," the barbarian muttered.

"You're catching on, then?"

"Perhaps. But that was fairly obvious, in all honesty. The hags who are said to inhabit this island doubtlessly keep the fog in place for the protection of the lizardfolk. It makes life a little more tolerable for them while making it difficult to see them when they have a mind to attack something."

The dwarf nodded and tightened his hold on his dagger as they continued along the winding paths that interestingly began a slow descent after a brief climb.

It wasn't long before Skharr could smell the rotten odor of a bog nearby. He should have known that the lizardfolk preferred to live in swamps based on the legends, but he had truly hoped it wasn't the case.

Fighting in a bog was a particular kind of nightmare he'd hoped he would never have to endure again.

Unfortunately, he was doomed to disappointment. His feet soon sank a little deeper into the mire with every step. Horse would have hated the swamps as well. Most horses hated them. Hooves sinking into the ground was not a pleasant experience for the beasts and worst of all, there was always the chance that they would get caught in a sinkhole with little chance of being dragged to safety without considerable effort.

He looked up as the orcs began to grunt and growl something

in their tongue. None of them took the time to signal to the two newcomers what was amiss. Still, Skharr could determine what they were saying at least from context and from the way the formerly still water had begun to move around them.

"Stay away from the water," he warned his companion.

Brahgen did as he was told and remained close to where the orc warriors were for the moment. The barbarian drew a handful of arrows from his quiver and looked around for any sign that the creatures were approaching them.

This time, the orcs were the first to loose a volley of crossbow bolts into the swamp when they saw something move. They knew the swamp better, of course, but he wondered how they'd seen the movement in the water before him.

When one of the creatures reared its head to lunge at the group with its spear in hand and claws and fangs bared, Skharr loosed his first arrow and caught the beast in the side of the neck.

It punched straight through and pierced the chest of one of the monsters behind it.

The shot was impressive, he had to admit, even if he didn't fully intend it to be so. He hastily brought another arrow to nock, drew without pause, and loosed it as almost a dozen of the creatures emerged from the swamp water to attack the orcs.

Another was felled quickly, followed by a handful of others as the crossbows twanged loudly to drive the heavy bolts through the lizardfolks' thick skin almost effortlessly.

In moments, however, the enemy had pushed their assault. One of their tails whipped around to catch him on the leg and he landed hard on his back as one of the beasts rushed from the water, a little too anxious to kill him.

"You godsbedammed hell-spawned scaly slime-sucker!" He raised his bow to push it back a step before he thrust one of his loose arrows into its eye.

It fell away but was quickly replaced by another. He'd yanked the arrow free and now nocked it to the bow and loosed it as rapidly as he could. It burrowed into the monster's chest and drew blood but the wound wasn't deep enough to kill as it hadn't been pulled back far enough to bring the full power of the bow to bear.

Still, it was injured, and he snatched his ax from his belt and swung it with all the power he could manage while still half-prone.

The impact cut deep, broke the creature's jaw, and spun it into the water.

"By Janus' lice-infested, snot-filled scrotum, you fuckers chose the wrong barbarian to fight."

Another dove forward to catch him while he was still on the ground, but it stopped short when Brahgen rushed in, drove his dagger hard into its side, and elicited one of the hiss-edged roars that issued from all around them. The beast wasn't dead but it certainly was wounded. The dwarf screamed at it, pulled his dagger free, and stabbed it repeatedly to make sure it was dead.

Skharr's face broke into a grin at the sight. He pushed to his feet as another two monsters surged out of the water and swung their tails to try to upend him again.

He would be damned before something like that worked a second time and jumped back before they could strike at him, then rushed in before they could recover.

A spear scored across his shoulder, barely enough to break the skin, and a scream bubbled from deep inside his chest as he sank his ax into the creature's skull.

He realized he had been a little too enthusiastic as it was now buried too deeply, and when the beast twisted away, the weapon was yanked from his hands.

Another tail arced viciously and he leapt to the side, unslung his sword from his shoulder, and drew it in a single, smooth motion. The blade gleamed even in the dark of the mist, and he immediately felt like he should have had the weapon in hand a little sooner as he swung it at the creature that was still standing.

It raised its spear to block the strike but it wasn't effective. The blade cut cleanly through the weapon, into its shoulder, and all the way to its ribs. He felt like he was sliding a hot knife through fresh butter.

With his adversary dead, he removed his weapon in a clean pull and turned his attention to three of the creatures that looked like they had a mind to attack Brahgen. None of them had realized that they were now the focus of his attention.

A smooth swipe was all it took to behead one of the beasts, and as another lashed its tail, he brought his blade down to cut into that as well and left the appendage to writhe on the ground with no creature attached to it.

The other turned and screeched loudly as he deftly parried the strike from its club and slashed his blade across the lizard-folk's stomach to disembowel it smoothly before he turned to the one that had lost its tail.

It looked like the monster had difficulty keeping itself on its feet as it struggled to swing its spear to strike him.

He smirked, leaned out of the way of a lunge that came a little too close, and buried his blade in the beast's chest.

"Are you all right?" he asked when he noticed the dwarf was covered in blood.

"Aye…it's not my blood." Brahgen nodded before he touched a small gash on his cheek. "Well, not all mine."

"That sensation you're feeling—half a sense of elation and the other half invincibility?"

"Yes." The youth narrowed his eyes. "How did you know?"

"I've felt it enough times myself. Learn to enjoy the first without indulging the second. It is the reason why many young fighters throw their lives away in battle."

Brahgen nodded and carefully wiped off some of the blood that had collected on his beard.

The orcs appeared to have dealt with the rest of the lizardfolk. Either they were sick of fighting and had withdrawn or their numbers were depleted. Skharr had a feeling there were many more of them spread throughout the godsbedammed swamp, but it would take time before the other fuckers reached the area where they were standing.

The orcs had lost a couple of their number and tended to the bodies carefully to prepare them to be carried to their tribes for a proper burial instead of leaving the bodies for the monsters to eat.

They seemed in good spirits, oddly enough, and a few of them gestured at Skharr, made a motion like they were swinging a sword, and laughed. They made the signs for his benefit, of course, as they had no issues communicating between themselves.

"They are calling you the Killer," Brahgen told him.

"Do they not have archers of their own?" he asked.

One of the orcs laughed, shook his head, and repeated the gesture, this time slower so they could see him signing what looked like a square before he swung an imaginary sword.

"I don't understand." The dwarf shook his head. "That's...kill, yes? But I don't understand the other one."

An orc coughed and rolled his eyes before he leaned forward and spoke in a thick, gravelly voice.

"Reaper."

It was good to know they could speak at least some of the common tongue, even if they chose not to. Whether the name had any alternative significance for them, the barbarian couldn't tell but it seemed to amuse them greatly.

"Why?" Skharr asked.

The orc made another series of quick gestures, one where he drew his arm back like he was shooting a bow.

"They are impressed that you shot an arrow that killed two of the lizards," Brahgen explained. "And your skill with the sword is another item of note. I think they approve of your fighting skills."

A quick nod was the answer to that.

"I've been called worse," he replied. "I suppose that is somewhat similar to DeathEater too, so I think I'll take it."

The orc grinned and nodded before he turned to join the others.

Still, it didn't look like he'd been in a position to help them. They were solid fighters with all the skill in the world but there would always be casualties in this kind of fight.

Yet he could see the orcs didn't look like they were preparing to continue. In fact, it appeared that they had every intention to return the way they had come.

The chieftain checked her people to make sure they had suffered no injuries before she turned her attention to Skharr and Brahgen. She began to talk in the signals that had begun to frustrate the barbarian because he couldn't understand them.

"Dwarf?"

"They...they're saying this is where they stop," the youth answered. "The lizardfolk have been scared away and the dungeon is a short distance ahead. Stay...stay on the path, and do not trust the water."

That seemed fairly direct and in truth, this was more than what he'd expected in the way of help. Still, now that they had an idea of what they were facing, he didn't want to think about the possibilities. The lizardfolk were no doubt working under the influence of something, and he had a feeling he knew exactly what.

Skharr nodded and raised a hand in farewell as the orcs lifted their dead and set off the way they'd come. They hadn't so much as paused to try to collect anything from the creatures they'd killed.

"Without so much as a goodbye," the dwarf muttered.

"I don't think anyone could blame most orcs for not abiding by human concepts of politeness." He took a moment to collect his ax and arrows from where they were still buried in the dead lizardfolk, careful to clean them and his sword of blood before he stowed them. "Come along, dwarf. We don't want to be caught out here at night."

"You'd prefer to be caught inside a dungeon at night instead?"

"No, but it's the better of two poor options. Although we wouldn't be sleeping either way."

It was impossible to tell what time it was as the mist was even thicker over the swamp than over the rest of the isle. Skharr hefted his bow again before he focused his attention on the path they would have to follow.

At least it was straight as if even the people who had built it were afraid of getting lost in the bog. He held his bow a little tighter and retained an arrow in hand and ready to draw at the slightest provocation.

Even so, it didn't seem as though they would need it. The lizardfolk had committed whatever forces they had to the first attack, and if the others had only now begun to converge on their location, it gave the two of them the chance to continue toward their destination.

A short while later, Skharr noticed something rising ahead of them through the mist. It resembled a large mound like the kind the folk in the north used as a burial ground for their dead kings.

The closer they got, the larger it seemed to get. The ground rose as well and moved them out of the bog and directly to the entrance in the side of the mound, which was about the size of a hill at this point.

"I've never been to a dungeon," Brahgen commented as they approached the darkened doorway. "And yet, oddly enough, that is exactly what I pictured one would look like."

"There was one that looked like a castle built directly into the side of the mountain," Skharr told him, raised his bow, and aimed an arrow at the door, expecting something to come through it out of the darkness.

When nothing did, he scowled deeply. It felt almost like it had been a little too easy.

"Is that what they usually look like?" the dwarf insisted.

"No. One was a tower that appeared out of thin air. Another was buried in the ground, hidden by tunnels and protected by a dragon. I've seen a temple as well. There was even one that was merely a trapdoor into the earth, although it had already been cleared for the most part when we reached it."

Still, the boy's assumption was understandable. It was more or less what one might expect a dungeon to look like if all he'd heard about them were stories and legends.

"Well, there's no point in simply standing here while we wait for something to happen," Skharr muttered. "We might as well find out what awaits us inside."

It was clear that nothing would emerge from the dungeon to attack them and as they had taken the contract, they would need to act. It occurred to him that he had accepted it without discussing the matter with the dwarf. Brahgen had essentially joined him by default, although he likely needed the coin as well. Starting a new life was not a cheap endeavor.

He moved into the darkened door, took a torch from his pack, and handed it to his companion. The youth was keen enough to know it was his job to light it to illuminate their progress through the darkened tunnel that led them unmistakably downward.

How the original creators had managed to make the dungeon without having it flooded by the swamp all around them was a question he felt needed asking. At the same time, he was reminded of how powerful the hags were to use their magic to keep the fog in place and the water from seeping in through the tunnels and this, in turn, begged the question of exactly what they were capable of when pushed.

Skharr was certain that they knew they were there and could harass them at any moment. Why they hadn't mounted a greater resistance to their arrival nagged at the back of his mind, but they wouldn't learn anything if they lingered in the swamp, where more of the lizards would inevitably find them.

They pushed in deeper and the tunnels began to resemble what Skharr had seen in other dungeons. Instead of merely a passage dug into the ground, the stone around them displayed signs of skilled craftsmanship. Most of the figurines and other carved details on the walls were gone, corroded or worn away, but the evidence of the craftsmanship was still there.

Before too long, he raised his hand, drew a deep breath, and pointed at the torch. Brahgen shook his head.

"Put the light out," the barbarian whispered. "I can smell more of the creatures ahead."

It was interesting that the dwarf hastened to do as he was told and didn't even question how he could smell the lizardfolk. Under normal circumstances, he wouldn't have, but the deeper they walked into the subterranean stronghold, the less he'd smelled of the bog they'd left behind.

A waft of swamp stench had caught him when he least expected it and intimated beyond a doubt that the monsters lurked somewhere ahead of them. The tunnel was plunged into absolute darkness, and Skharr could hear Brahgen inching forward using the wall to guide himself. He had good instincts but so did most dwarves when they were underground.

It wasn't long, however, until fumbling through the darkness was no longer necessary. Lights flickered in the distance, which told him that fires had been lit. The dwarf saw them too and they both proceeded down the narrow tunnel at a slower pace, careful to not make a sound.

Soft screeches and growls issued from inside a chamber that opened out from the tunnel they had traversed. As expected, numerous campfires burned inside and small rivulets of murky water ran through the area.

At least a dozen of the creatures were gathered in circles around the fires while they cooked food and chattered amongst themselves. It didn't look like they lived in the area or at least hadn't for long. If Skharr had to guess, he would have said that this was a guard camp with soldiers stationed there to protect something.

He had a feeling he knew what they were guarding and adjusted his bow to ready it for use. The beasts didn't look like they expected any kind of attack and if he intended to do so, now was the time.

"All right," the barbarian whispered and hunkered close to his companion to make sure he could hear him. "You hide under those rocks and stay low and out of sight. I can eliminate a few of them with my bow and when the rest rush, wait for them to focus on me and attack them from behind, understood?"

Brahgen's eyes were wide but he nodded and carefully and skillfully maneuvered himself to a small group of rocks. There was always the possibility that the monsters would be able to attack him there, of course, and it would be up to the large warrior to defend him and give him time to retreat.

Risks were being taken by both of them at this point.

Skharr nodded and tried to convince himself that his plan was a good one. Tactical decisions would always be second-guessed and not least by those who made the decisions, but in the end, there wasn't much even a brilliant tactician could do with an army of two.

His first task was to lower his pack without making any noise and he followed this by placing his sheathed sword carefully on the floor in front of him with the quiver next to it. He then took five arrows from the quiver and placed them carefully within reach at his feet. With three more held in his free hand, he drew a deep breath and selected his targets. There would be no time for him to choose when the fighting started.

He took a few seconds to estimate where the monsters would move to after his first shot before he placed one of the arrows to the string, drew it slowly and carefully, and watched the creatures intently for any sign that they'd heard him.

There was none, fortunately, and he focused on a target farther away and closer to the fires. It appeared to be tasting what must surely be a massive swamp rat being cooked over the open flames.

It stood about twenty paces away. While it wasn't the longest shot he would ever take, Skharr knew that speed would have to complement accuracy in this.

The bowstring sang and the arrow streaked away. A moment later, the creature jerked to the side as the arrow hammered into its arm and pushed through into its chest. It was dead and falling and he gave it no further thought. He already had another arrow fitted to the string and dropped to one knee as he drew, his attention on one of the creatures that had seen its comrade fall and stood to investigate.

His arrow struck and the beast toppled, and more of the lizardfolk stirred with the awareness that they were under attack. They snatched their weapons up and their tails flicked from side to side as they tried to determine the source of the assault. He realized that their hearing wasn't keen enough to tell where the arrows had come from.

They could see the direction, though, when he loosed the third arrow and caught one of the creatures in the jaw, and it stumbled into one of the little streams.

Nine were left, he tallied mentally as he scooped two more arrows from the floor beside him, drew, and fired one without so much as a thought.

Another of the creatures fell back into some of its comrades with an arrow buried deep in its chest. The other arrow launched without pause, but Skharr scowled as it sailed a little higher than he intended. It struck one of the creatures that pushed forward from behind in the shoulder and seemed to simply bounce off its scaly skin.

They had recovered quickly from their surprise and now scrambled over the pile of rocks Brahgen was hiding behind. With a single-minded focus on the barbarian, they showed no sign that they had detected his companion's presence as they surged into a combined attack.

One more fell from the last arrow he felt comfortable launching before he discarded the bow at his feet, retrieved his sword, and unsheathed it smoothly as they tried to overwhelm him in a swarm.

A spear was thrust at him but the warrior knocked it aside easily, turned, and swung at his attacker's throat to inflict a long wound that immediately gushed dark blood. Skharr retreated quickly to the tunnel to force them to cease their combined assault, which wouldn't work in the narrow space.

He grunted when one of the tails whipped around his legs. It was barely a glancing blow but it stung a little and warned him that one of the monsters tried to flank him. He swung his sword and missed his strike but forced the creature back a step, determined to not leave himself open as an easy target for more than one to attack at a time.

Six of them remained now—much better odds than twelve, of course, but still not optimal. He leapt back to avoid two tails that lashed out to catch his neck and his leg.

"You'll have to move faster to kill a DeathEater, you stinking slime-brained troll turds."

They were more cautious now and attempted to knock him from his feet before they attacked. When the next one tried, the barbarian swung his sword low and severed the tail halfway up before he countercharged with a brutal slash of his blade that beheaded one of them. He continued his swing to impale another with the tip of his blade.

Skharr moved one hand from the sword to take his ax from his belt. He used this to deflect a club that arced toward his head and sliced easily into the creature that wielded it.

With his ax in one hand and sword in the other, the warrior turned to the three remaining lizardfolk. They showed no expressions on their hardened faces, but the way they inched away from him said they had second thoughts about attacking him directly.

It was time to press that advantage.

"Come on, you fucking scaly swamp-vermin." He bellowed a challenge and the sound echoed off the walls around him and amplified it as he rushed forward and cornered them before they could escape. One fell to his ax and he slit the throat of another with his sword.

The last one seemed to suddenly recall that it had a weapon, a crude-looking ax made from flint and wood. It hissed, swung it at him, and caught the side of his shoulder as he twisted in an attempt to avoid it.

He kept the creature that clutched its neck wound between him and its surviving companion and waited for the right moment to drive his sword into its chest. It cut through effortlessly and impaled the monster behind, and both sagged as they succumbed to their wounds. He drew his blade out and inspected the glancing blow he'd taken on his shoulder.

"No, dwarf, never mind me," Skharr muttered. "I fought them on my own this time. I suppose I can count on you to stay out of it next time as well, eh?"

When he turned to where Brahgen had been hiding, he realized the dwarf was no longer there. The godsbedammed short-assed bastard had run off.

"I'll remember that come time to divide the reward," he snapped and turned his attention to where his arrows had gone.

He froze and stared at the chamber that was no longer empty. Three figures huddled close to one of the fires. They were dressed in rags that covered their entire bodies aside from their hands which hung low, almost to the floor. Their backs were bent and they moved like old women. That kind of disguise might have worked on an unwary traveler but the barbarian could see the talons that curved from their fingers.

"Barbarian meat, yesssss," one of the crones hissed. "It has been a long time since we've tasted human and longer still since we tasted barbarian."

"He is a killer of many. His blood will be sweet."

"His muscles will be tough but it won't matter in the stew."

Skharr kept his weapons in hand and advanced slowly on the creatures. Their faces were covered but it was obvious that they watched him intently.

"I won't surrender willingly to your pot," he told them and twirled his ax and sword in his hands.

"Your compliance was never a factor," one of the hags muttered, lifted what looked like a waterskin, and blew into it.

Out of the skin flowed the same kind of mist that seemed to fill the whole island, but when it touched him, the power leeched from his muscles. He scowled in concentration but try as he might to hold fast to his weapons, they slipped from his fingers and fell with a loud clatter.

"It'll make him taste wrong," one of the crones complained.

"Don't worry," the other replied. "We'll steep it out of him first."

CHAPTER ELEVEN

The fucking mist would not go away.

Their ship sailed through the still waters and had encountered no real difficulty. He'd been through the region before and knew which areas to avoid. The orc settlements were nestled away from the shoals since they happened to ground their ships often enough as well.

They had the lamp raised to the bow of the ship to alert the orcs of their arrival and moved slower than they needed to. This was simply a precaution to make sure none of the tribes were tempted to attack.

He was there to do business with them, after all, and the best way to do that was to avoid making them nervous.

As expected, one of their ships moved beside his but showed no sign of aggression. They were escorted through the bay and into the region where a collection of simple-looking buildings were surrounded by palisades and watchtowers.

Samor had heard that they were dealing with monsters in the region, which explained the improved defenses since his last visit.

When they reached the dock, he was the first one to vault off the ship and strode along the jetty as the rest of his men tied the vessel to secure it and began to unload their supplies.

There was no sign of the chieftain, but he could safely assume she had gone to deal with some attack or another. Hell, from what he'd heard of her, she could as easily have gone out on a fishing trip. She wasn't the type to sit on whatever passed for a throne and let others do the work for her.

One of the orcs approached him, tapped his chest with his fist by way of greeting, and gestured to ask what he was doing among them again.

He shifted, pulled a few strands of blond hair from his face, and made sure his men were unloading the supplies before he replied to the question. "We've come looking for a dwarf who was said to have come to your island."

The orc narrowed his eyes, shook his head, and asked what that was.

"A...have you never seen a dwarf before?"

A shake of the head provided a simple answer.

"They look like humans but are shorter, uglier, and smell of smoke and bad cheese," Samor explained. "This one would be smaller than most, and he traveled with a human who is larger than most."

After a moment of thought, the orc nodded and spoke again in their silent sign language. The tribe had seen the large and the small human. They were brought ashore by the chieftain and headed off to kill the lizard creatures.

These beasts had plagued the area for a while, but if the chieftain had elected to escort a human and a dwarf, the chances were that enough would be killed to leave the roads clear for a few days at least. Not that he would trust that reasoning but he would work with it in mind.

"And you're sure that the dwa—the small human was with them?"

The orc nodded. It seemed the small human had no intention to leave the tall human's side.

"Perfect. We'll need a scout to show us where they were going."

It seemed the orc he spoke to was the one for the job and Samor smiled, walked to where their supplies were being unloaded, and divided them amongst those who would carry them. They knew better than to expect that he would share the burden. They couldn't bring horses to the island, not with the swamps that covered them, and he would carry his weapons and armor, nothing more.

If they didn't like it, they wouldn't be paid. The chances were that they might not leave the island but besides that, they knew better than to question his abilities.

He selected a handful of beaver pelts they had brought for the purpose of payment and handed them to their waiting scout. Coins had little value among the orcs, be they copper, silver, or gold, but trading resources like pelts was a sure way to make them more compliant. Beavers were a favorite as they were warm and resisted the water that was a part of the lives of the orcs who lived and made their living there.

Their guide took the skins gleefully and motioned for them to follow him. The team had already assembled their supplies and despite the glares at their leader, none of them voiced any complaints about their workload. He repeated the motion to follow and before long, they had moved beyond the palisades to the black sand beach and up the road from there.

"It sounds like the DeathEater is as crazy as the stories make him out to be," Samor muttered.

The orc looked at him, raised an eyebrow, and signed to ask if he knew the man.

"No, but I've heard tell of him. As I said, he is crazy."

Before long, the group that had escorted Skharr approached from the other direction on the same route. A few quick grunts and growls in their orcish tongue were exchanged, and a few of the returning orcs gestured to Samor as they passed.

"Good luck with the...Reaper?" he asked.

The orcs had named the barbarian already. The moniker seemed fairly fitting, given what he knew of the man. He accepted that it would take work and effort for him to kill the fucker, and he was only glad the orcs didn't seem to show any sign of remorse over the matter. Perhaps they didn't care what humans did to each other.

They pushed forward into the marshlands and as he'd predicted, none of the lizardfolk attacked. At any other time, he would have expected the scaly swamp bastards to make an appearance in large numbers. If an attack had already taken place in the swamp, they would be a little more reluctant to face another.

Why the different clans didn't simply clear the area of the beasts in a coordinated effort was a question he had yet to find a reasonable answer for. Perhaps the dumb shits weren't civilized enough to combine their efforts to their mutual advantage. Of course, he wouldn't have charged into the swamp but orcs were used to that kind of dirty work.

Their scout paused, motioned them forward, and indicated that the dungeon was a short distance ahead.

"All right, you maggot-brained shits," Samor snapped. "Set the traps up. We want to kill the fucking barbarian but the filthy dwarf comes out alive. We'll be paid if the half-pint is dead but we'll be paid more if he's alive."

They nodded. He had already told them what he expected from them, and a series of traps were set up around the entrance of the cavern. A few of the braver souls even managed to position a few of the dart-casters inside. Tipped with a substance that would put anything from a barbarian to a godsbedammed bear to sleep in seconds, it would be enough to catch their dwarf.

And catch him alive, which was the preferred outcome.

"It simply doesn't make sense," Samor muttered.

The orc signaled that he needed an explanation.

"Barbarians are barbaric but at least they are human. But no, we need to take the fucking dwarf back alive. I can't find the logic in it. Why wouldn't they want the DeathEater alive?"

Their guide shrugged. All humans looked alike to him.

"Of course they do." Samor was a little too intelligent to mention the fact that all orcs, even the female ones, looked the same to him as well.

"Oh shit, oh shit, oh shit."

Brahgen hadn't intended to leave Skharr alone to deal with the lizards. He'd been poised and ready and fully determined to help when he saw the hags come out of a secret passage in the wall. There was no way to warn his companion without alerting them to his presence as well. And of course, the barbarian didn't bother to look for him either but had gone directly to deal with the new arrivals.

It hadn't worked out so well for him.

He was still alive, however, and tried to fight the crones off as they attempted to drag him closer to the fires. Two of them struggled with him while the third hauled a massive cast iron pot to the fire.

The warrior put up more of a fight than the pot, which spoke to the man's strength.

"Give him another dose," one of the hags snapped.

"That will ruin the meat. Put your backs into it."

The dwarf scrutinized the floor near the tunnel. He'd managed to snatch the packs and most of Skharr's items and drag them with him, and he wouldn't rush in like his companion had. It hadn't worked for the barbarian, which meant he would have to find a better way that would hopefully be more effective.

A quick look through the barbarian's belongings revealed something that could help. Skharr had tipped a handful of his arrows with blasting powder, the kind that a few of his kin liked to use to light their furnaces and to dig deeper into rock that was particularly resistant to their efforts.

It was possible that it would create a thick, acrid smoke that would allow him to hasten in undetected, kill the bitches, and get the warrior out. But how could he launch it?

If he'd had the damn crossbows the orcs were using, that would have solved his dilemma, but in this instance, all he had was a bow.

"Think, you useless pint-sized shit," Brahgen muttered and picked the bow up. It was still strung and seemed to mock him. If he were only a few feet taller, he would be able to at least draw the godsbedammed weapon.

He scowled as he inspected it carefully. Talk about fitting it with a few gears would not help him draw it and he certainly didn't have time for that in this situation even if he was able to do anything. He settled his feet firmly and pulled the string.

Before his frustration could swamp him, he had a moment of clarity. He wouldn't need to draw the bow the way Skharr did. As long as he could aim the weapon and launch the arrow, the positioning of the bow wouldn't be a problem.

Encouraged, the dwarf sat quickly and rested the bow over his feet. After a few attempts, he managed to pull the bowstring back. It wouldn't go the full length but it would have to be enough.

He collected the arrows and inched closer. Courage hadn't been something he would have ever claimed for himself but for some reason, showing the barbarian that he wasn't simply a rotten little thief mattered. He would never be the mighty warrior his companion was, but he would find a way to make it work.

There was a perch directly above the flames and he crept

toward it and settled himself securely. Thankfully, the hag who had put the cast iron cauldron over the flames now added water to it and made considerable noise, while the other two continued their struggle to drag their victim to where they wanted him.

"Keep fighting, you big lummox," Brahgen muttered and shook his head as he shifted slightly to stabilize himself in his improvised firing position, nocked the arrow, and tried to aim at the fire. If he could hit it squarely, it would give him the opening he needed to attack.

"Give him another godsbedammed fucking dose!"

"Do you want his meat to be bitter? His strength must surely run out soon. He can't fucking breathe."

Brahgen drew the bowstring back slowly, strained against the power coiled in the limbs, and pulled again with all the strength he could summon before he finally released it.

He watched in horror as the arrow sailed too high and into the far corner of the cave. The clattering was lost in the sound of one of the hags clanging a large wooden spoon against the inside of the cauldron.

"I'm hungry now. And he killed all our food too."

The dwarf snatched another of the arrows tipped with the powder and this time, used his feet carefully to guide his aim as he pointed it into the fire and drew back as hard as he could. He doubted that he had the strength to draw the string a third time. His fingers ached and his short legs trembled under the strain as he pulled it back as far as it would go. Then, with a pained gasp, he released the string.

This time, the arrow flew straight and true.

The impact of the arrow striking the fire manifested almost immediately as a bright flash followed by a loud crack that echoed through the chamber. He rolled away from his position and unsheathed his dagger as he climbed down from the perch and rushed to where the hags had been standing. They shrieked in pain and anger but they still didn't have their attention focused on him.

He approached the one closest to the fire, who had fallen and tried to drag herself to where her spoon had landed while she wailed miserably. He might have had a little compassion for them had they not been talking about killing, cooking, and eating Skharr only moments before.

The smoke filled the entire chamber and made it difficult to breathe, but it wasn't much worse than the usual conditions in his uncle's forges. Relatively unperturbed, Brahgen attacked the creature, drove his dagger hard into her back, neck, and then her head until the screeching stopped and the body fell limp.

He pushed up again and covered his mouth and nose with his cloak as he hurried to where he remembered the hags had been dragging his companion.

Sheer luck made him run almost directly into one of them. He jerked his dagger out immediately to catch her in the side and buried it deep and true. She shrieked and he yanked it free to thrust again. Warm blood flowed and spattered as he hacked and stabbed and his yells echoed his sudden battle lust through the cavern.

"Not so fast, you little rat!"

Brahgen's bellow turned to a squawk of surprise when a hand caught him by the wrist and dragged him away from the hag he was killing. He turned his attention to the creature. Her hand was like a vice clamped around his flesh as she hauled him from his feet.

"You'll join the big one in the stew pot," she snapped and cackled.

"Isn't that too much for a hag to eat alone?" he shouted.

"What?"

"Your bitch friends are dead."

The rags covering her face showed no expression, but from the way her grasp tightened on his wrist, he could tell that perhaps goading her when she had full control of his weapon hand wasn't the best idea. Still, he couldn't help himself. She screeched and raised her other hand, her talons drawn and ready to slice him to ribbons.

The dwarf readied himself for the inevitable but she didn't strike. He paused, a little disconcerted to discover he was still alive, and looked up. Skharr had caught her hand and now held it immobile. He looked like it took every ounce of power he could muster to do so, but it was an effective distraction and it was all the dwarf needed.

Brahgen dropped the dagger from his right hand, swept it up smoothly with his left, and thrust the blade to the hilt in the monster's chest. That done, he repeated it in a violent rhythm until the hag gurgled blood instead of screeching and the vice-like grip on his hand weakened to the point where he could pull free.

Panting with exertion and an odd sense of satisfaction, he dragged himself clear and almost stumbled from the effort before he approached again to spit on the corpse.

"Rot in the labyrinth, you shit-faced slime-begotten hell-spawn," he yelled and kicked her for good measure before he turned his attention to the warrior.

Skharr had sagged onto the floor and now sucked in air like he hadn't breathed for weeks. A draught through the tunnels cleared the smoke quickly to provide fresh and clean lungfuls to recover with as he sprawled on the rock and closed his eyes.

"Are you all right?"

The barbarian glared at him.

"Do…I look…like I'm…fucking all right?"

"Honestly? You look better than you did a moment ago when you struggled to overpower a couple of old ladies," Brahgen told him cheerfully.

"Godsbedammed…cheeky tunneler. Come here and…I'll close…your fucking mouth…for you."

Still, there was a smile on the barbarian's lips as he finally seemed to gather enough strength to regain his feet.

"Now," he muttered, still wheezing like he was out of breath. "We should find the passage the damn hags came through, yes? There might be treasure hidden away for us to…uh, pilfer. Take. Steal."

The dwarf nodded and pointed to the far side wall. "They used a passage that opened out of the wall. I think it shouldn't be difficult to find."

Skharr nodded and half-stumbled to where he had pointed.

Once his companion was out of earshot, the dwarf looked at the ceiling and tilted his head. "I know I might not be the smartest dwarf to ever wield a hammer, but…I appreciate the help, nonetheless. Keeping us alive might count as a miracle and I thank you for it, Ahverna."

As usual, the goddess had no answer for him. He wasn't entirely sure if she could hear him this far out or even if she had anything to do with keeping them alive, but it was best to give thanks in case.

"Stop mumbling and help me find the fucking passage," Skharr snapped. He sounded more like himself with every passing moment.

CHAPTER TWELVE

"You cannot be too disappointed."

Skharr shrugged, looked around the small living area, and hefted a small, iron-capped chest with a selection of baubles, coins, and a few jewels. Hardly a king's ransom, he conceded irritably.

"You have to consider that there isn't much in the way of precious metals and the like in this area," the dwarf continued as they retraced their steps through the passage to the chamber they'd entered from. "Those fucking hags had more interest in fresh meat than whatever that meat happened to carry."

The dwarf was right, of course, but he couldn't help the feeling that he had somehow been cheated. It was better than nothing but the amount likely wouldn't match what they would receive for completing the contract.

"Another job well done," he muttered as they reached the chamber. The corpses were where they had left them, which he chose to take as a good sign. The moment bodies started to disappear from where he'd left them was the moment that they very possibly were no longer bodies.

"How did you accomplish what you did?" the barbarian asked

as they reached the room that still smelled of the blasting powder. "I thought you weren't able to shoot the bow. Did you throw the arrows?"

"No." Brahgen grinned, ran to where he'd left the bow, and picked it up. "I used my feet to draw it."

When his companion frowned in what might have been confusion, he sat quickly and used one foot to push the bow and the other to keep it in place while he dragged the string back with both hands. He didn't pull it very far but it would suffice as a demonstration.

"I would have fitted a few gears to it, settled in, and let them do most of the work, but there was something of a time constraint—along with a dearth of suitable materials, of course."

Skharr nodded. "What with the hags trying to manhandle me into their cauldron."

"I was only able to discover that you had the blasting powder on your arrows and how to fire the bow because you continued to fight them." Brahgen stood and handed him his bow.

"Even so, you showed a great deal of resourcefulness and cunning, both of which are some of the mightiest weapons in the arsenal of a master thief," Skharr pointed out. "You not only saved my life but you saved me from a particularly gruesome and painful end as well. Thank you for that."

"I did save your life, didn't I?" The youth tugged his thick beard gently. "And you thought I'd left you to fend for yourself with the lizardfolk too. But who came to your rescue when you charged in dick-first to deal with hags notorious for using magic to defend themselves?"

The barbarian nodded. "I suppose you did."

"There is nothing to suppose about it. Not that I do not realize that you've saved my life while we've traveled together, but to know that the tables have turned and I returned the favor... Well, it is a gratifying feeling."

"I hope you don't twist your arm trying to pat yourself too hard on the back."

"I don't need to. I have you to pat me on the back instead."

"Well, I would say that it was an equal effort on both our parts," Skharr told him. "And as such, the reward—as well as the treasure—should be divided equally between us."

"Did you ever intend to do things differently?"

"It crossed my mind," he admitted. "But you may consider that thought gone."

"Because I saved your life?"

"Because you saved my life. And because you are and have been an equal partner in this venture."

Brahgen grinned and showed a little more life in his step as the barbarian collected the arrows that were still intact, as well as the rest of his weapons. It had been a terrifying experience to feel like his body wasn't his own. The hags weren't strong enough to drag him easily or quickly, which had been the reason why the dwarf was able to come to his aid.

Still, for the longest of moments, Skharr had thought he was alone. He had felt like he was drowning on dry land while all the power drained from his body.

Few things in his life could ever prepare him for that feeling. He was used to being able to rely on his strength, if nothing else. And with a snap of the fingers from a creature of magic, all his amulets and wards had failed him and he'd been almost powerless.

Then again, maybe the amulets were what allowed him to put up the meager resistance he had. The hags hadn't been pleased that he'd been able to fight against them, no matter how ineffectual his efforts had been.

Or perhaps the magic they used was so unique from what mages offered in the civilized world that his protections had struggled to do their work to keep him alive.

Either way, he would have words with the mage who made it

to ensure that no hag would be able to overwhelm their abilities again. It was not an experience he intended to repeat, of course. At least not until he grew old and his body started to drain of strength the natural way.

"How much coin do you think we'll make from this endeavor?" Brahgen asked once they had gathered their weapons and supplies from around the cavern.

Skharr paused where he examined a few of the lizardfolk to see if they had anything of value to take. "I would say we might find ourselves with…somewhere around twenty-five gold coins each. Perhaps a little more if one of the baubles proves to have magical properties. Mages will always pay dearly for unique items like that. It isn't exactly a haul that would allow a master thief to retire young but it's a good start."

The lizardfolk didn't have much aside from their weapons, and even those appeared to be crude creations. It made him wonder if it was the influence of the hags that forced the creatures to make them as they were more than capable hunters and fighters with their tails, claws, and fangs. In fact, it had seemed like fighting with weapons was foreign to them.

With the hags dead, perhaps that would allow them to retreat into the swamps to hide and stay away as they generally appeared to do. It was likely why they were mostly mythical since finding them had proven all but impossible by even the most astute and persistent of scholars. They were intelligent and had no interest in interacting with the other intelligent species.

And given their interaction with the hags, Skharr honestly could not blame them for it.

The crones didn't carry anything of value either, although he knew a handful of folk who would likely pay a few gold coins for the cast iron cauldron. Still, he wouldn't lug it around for anything less than a real dungeon's worth of treasure.

"Did you find anything?" Brahgen asked.

"Nothing worth taking with us. Unless you feel like hauling that cauldron back for a few gold pieces."

The dwarf made a face. "I think not. We've done enough and I am quite happy with whatever our gain from this little adventure will be—in equal shares. I don't know if you remember, but I did save you from having your limbs chopped up and served in what I am sure would be a delightful and delicious stew."

"I've always heard that humans taste like pork."

The dwarf gaped at him. "What...who would know such a thing?"

"Folk who eat folk, I suppose. I've never tried it myself but in certain desperate situations... Well, the mind does go to the oddest of places when it is desperate to survive."

"The oddest of places should not include eating your friends."

"Perhaps they weren't friends."

"I don't know if that makes it better or worse."

"There are innumerable horrifying things done in the world," Skharr pointed out. "And sometimes for reasons that are far less horrifying than the actions themselves. For the moment, however, you should keep your mind on the task at hand."

"What task? They're all dead in here. The only problem we'll have now is to find a way to buy our boat back from the godsbe-dammed orcs."

"For some, this is the most dangerous part of an attack," the barbarian insisted. "When your spirits are high with victory and thoughts of what you'll do with your newly-acquired coin fill your mind. It makes it the most dangerous moment, as something might assail you when your guard is down."

Brahgen shrugged. "What could attack us here? The lizardfolk are still keeping their distance and between you and me, they likely won't be a problem for the orcs or us anytime soon. Hey, do you think we might be able to leverage that into making them return our boat to us?"

"Dwarf—"

"Hell, for those kinds of heroics, we might be able to talk them into giving us the finest ship of their fleet."

Skharr stopped and peered ahead. They had reached a point in the tunnel where he could see where they had come from and interestingly enough, they didn't need a torch to navigate like they had before. Light streamed in from somewhere—a light that hadn't been there earlier.

"The sun is out!" Brahgen laughed and shook his head. "The mist the hags had created over this island has been blown away and the sun is shining through for the first time in…shall we say years? I think we can say years."

The barbarian narrowed his eyes and scrutinized the tunnel.

"Hells, we might be able to convince the orcs to give us two ships. One for keeping the lizards away for good and another for bringing the sun back to their desolate shores. We might have a few songs written about this little caper yet—if orcs were known for writing music, of course."

Orc music was one thing he had never heard of, but his mind was on the entrance to the tunnel. Something about it unsettled him although he couldn't quite put his finger on it. He continued to study the area as Brahgen advanced toward it without a second thought.

"I might simply write the song myself, you know? That way, I could make sure they get all the details right. Especially the detail about how I saved your life."

Skharr suddenly realized what unsettled him. A gleam was reflected through the tunnel that didn't quite match the stones. It meant only one thing and the dwarf walked directly toward it.

"Look out!"

He rushed forward but something sprang against his boot, followed quickly by a click.

In that moment, three sharp pricks touched his neck. A few more struck his chest and he looked down at two thin darts that had pierced through his shirt and into the skin beneath.

They weren't deep enough to wound but he could already feel something swimming in the back of his head as another three pricks stuck him in the ass.

The effects were stronger than before and he wavered and leaned against the wall of the cavern as he shook his head.

"Look....look..." He struggled to recall what he had wanted to say.

"Shit!" Brahgen jumped away. "I'll get some help—hold on!"

The barbarian wanted to warn him but the words froze on his tongue as he dropped to his knees. Helpless, he could only watch as the dwarf reached the end of the tunnel and a net was cast over him.

All energy left his limbs and he planted face-first onto the ground.

"Not fucking again," he muttered before the world turned black.

CHAPTER THIRTEEN

B rahgen had no idea what he had expected to do. The orcs were already gone and he knew for a fact that he wouldn't be able to help Skharr himself. But something had to be done and he had still been full of his previous success in the cave.

Racing out had seemed like such a good idea before a net closed around him. He hadn't thought about who might have set the trap that caught his companion before he acted. Although perhaps that wouldn't have made much of a difference given that they had traps both within and without the tunnel.

All he knew was that a net had been thrown over his head and he now struggled to reach the dagger at his waist.

There was movement all around him, and he thought for a moment that the lizardfolk were attacking, even though they were no longer under the control of the dead hags.

But the sight of weapons and armor around him told him unequivocally that all was not well, and the primitive reptile creatures had certainly not arranged the traps that caught both him and Skharr.

He began to hack at the mesh around him and even managed to pull it away from where it restricted his movement. Moments later, he felt a rush of elation when he escaped it entirely and crawled out from under it, but he realized he was still surrounded by a group of humans, all with their weapons trained on him.

"Drop the weapon!" one of them shouted. He was the only one not wearing his helm and the dwarf wondered if his long, golden locks were the reason.

"Come and take it!" Brahgen snapped in return as two sword-wielding mercenaries advanced on him.

He lunged forward, ducked under one of the swords, and slashed an attacker's arm. Any thoughts that he was in a position to win the fight were put to rest, however, when pain seared across his leg. He looked down and grimaced when he realized that one of the swords had opened a shallow gash in his thigh, and it was quickly followed by a rapid blow across the jaw with the pommel of the second man's weapon.

Almost before he could blink, Brahgen was on the ground with the dagger forced from his fingers before his hands were yanked roughly behind his back.

What did surprise him was that once his hands were bound, one of the men approached with what was clearly a healing potion and dabbed it lightly over the wound. It stung like he was being attacked by a dozen bees, but as he twisted to see what was happening, the gash began to heal quickly and left only a splotch of bright pink skin.

"What…what are you doing?"

The golden-haired mercenary chuckled and lowered onto his haunches next to the dwarf. "We need to make sure our product arrives alive. There's no point in you developing an infection and dying along the way before we deliver you."

"Deliver me to who?"

The man ignored his question and looked at the rest of the men. "Go on in and make sure the bastard barbarian is dead. Bring me his ax and his head."

"Why his ax?"

That question did catch the man's attention and he focused on the fallen dwarf.

"It is said that he spent a fortune having it made. It would be a waste to leave a weapon like that to rust in an abandoned dungeon in a forgotten corner of the world. While dwarves generally tend to resemble little more than stacked shit, your single redeeming quality is your work with steel."

Brahgen grinned and was unable to stop himself from laughing as the other mercenaries looked at him curiously.

"Oh... You're serious." The dwarf cleared his throat and shifted until he was in a more comfortable position. "You are doomed to disappointment, then. My uncle saw to it that they would transport it far away from here in exchange for his escorting me to my family."

"The last I heard, you abandoned your family when you joined the thieves guild, dwarf," the apparent leader retorted. "You abandoned whatever familial connections you have with the dwarves. I can't blame you for the change, of course, even if I cannot fathom why a human guild would want to have a dwarf among them. You're all merely fatter versions of kobolds with slightly better smithing skills."

Brahgen finally managed to force himself into a seated position and narrowed his eyes. "Why would you pursue me, then? If you came looking for the fucking barbarian and the weapon he was reputed to carry?"

"What? Did you think yer uncle was stupid?" The leader laughed. "We know you told the barbarian about the guild's plans and there are those who want you to pay for that kind of treachery. I don't know why they wouldn't simply let me kill you when I found you, of course. That's what you do when dealing with a rabid dog."

"I didn't betray the guild!"

"Then how did you know to not be present for the fight that got most of them killed?"

"I was warned by Ahverna."

"The goddess?" The human smirked and shook his head. "Now why the hell would a human goddess care to save your pathetic two inches?"

He narrowed his eyes. "You truly hate dwarves, don't you?"

"I would have to care about you to hate you. All I care about is having to share cities with pests like you tiny creatures. You might as well have stayed in your mountains and saved decent folk the trouble of having to deal with you."

Brahgen had heard that kind of rhetoric before and while he wanted to continue taunting the man, there would be trouble given that he was still bound and a sword rested on his captor's hip.

Infuriated by both the mercenary's arrogance and his helplessness, he decided he would find time to mock the man's primitive views on dwarves but at a more appropriate moment. Preferably not when he was still tempted to kill him.

The leader straightened and glowered at his men. "Well then, will none of you bring me the fucking barbarian's head?"

The group exchanged a quick look before one of them stepped forward.

"The man's already been struck with the darts," he pointed out. "And since he doesn't carry the ax you told us about, there isn't much point. It is still a dungeon. We have what we came for. There is no point in risking our lives for no reason."

The leader seemed about to break out in a rage over what had been said but he caught himself immediately and calmed quickly.

"That...is a sound point. But we don't want the godsbedammed shit-for-brains to pursue us should we wake from however much poison is swimming through his veins. Put a few more traps outside and we can start heading northeast."

"Where the hells is that?"

He narrowed his eyes. "We can see the sun now, yes? The fog has lifted, quite literally."

The rest of the group continued to look blankly at him.

"Right. Put your left shoulder to the sun and point a little to the right, you brainless oaf. Have you never traveled without a compass before?"

"What the fuck is a compass?"

"It's what I fuck your mother with!" Brahgen shouted as he scrambled to his feet for mere moments before one of the mercenaries hit him hard enough to topple him again.

The golden-haired leader rolled his eyes as the rest of the men began to prepare the traps in case Skharr managed to get out. It was probably a good idea, even if the dwarf hated them for it. Before he could find his feet again, one of the men hefted him unceremoniously and tossed him over his shoulder like he was a sack of grain as the group began to move out again.

It was all his fault, the dwarf realized as he watched the dungeon recede slowly from view. He had been lost in congratulating himself and hadn't listened to his companion when the barbarian tried to warn him that something was wrong. He'd said it was the most dangerous part of a mission and yet he'd moved forward regardless and been captured, and his foolishness had likely killed the barbarian as well.

Indirectly, of course. The mercenaries were to blame for it but a hint of the blame lay squarely on his shoulders as well.

"I don't know if you're listening," Brahgen whispered. "You never did in the past. But Skharr needs your help."

"Shut it, you!"

It was extremely odd. It wasn't like most things in the world ever lived up to expectations, but when someone talked about a dungeon, this was almost exactly what came to mind.

A barrow with a tunnel leading into untapped depths. It was probably one of the oddest things she'd ever seen.

The landscape did feel like it was changing, however. The lack of a malevolent force on the island was always a good way to start. Even magic that wasn't malevolent had a tendency to leech from the earth that surrounded it. Now it was gone, it would begin to return to normal and correct itself.

She liked the thought that it would heal itself. Perhaps that was the most magical sight of all. Most humans didn't appreciate the concept since it happened so slowly but in the end, it would be here when humans and their mighty cities and empires were nothing but dust.

When she had almost reached the barrow's opening, she crouched and narrowed her eyes to inspect the devices that had been set up around it.

"A trap," she muttered, plucked one of the long, silk strands, and watched a series of light darts bury themselves in the mound. The poison they were tipped with was noxious simply to smell, and she had no intention to see what they were like up close. She moved closer to the entrance and paused a little shy of the shadow cast into the opening by the setting sun.

There was no way to tell who had created the dungeon. Too many had gone power-mad and hog-wild in creating these places and some of them did not appreciate having unauthorized visitors.

Still, she slipped through and waited for something to happen —a crackle of energy or some sign of annoyance—but only silence greeted her. She shrugged, moved in deeper, and approached the soft sounds she could hear issuing from inside.

They sounded like they were coming from something big although she couldn't quite determine what it was precisely.

"Ah, a human," she muttered and approached the fallen figure. "I suppose I should have guessed."

He was a large one too—powerfully muscled with bright red

hair—and was armed to the teeth, although seven of the darts she'd avoided outside protruded from him.

At least he was alive, although from the way his body twitched and the soft sounds he made, he was lost in a deep dream and not the pleasant kind. A bright sheen of sweat covered his skin and his brows furrowed as whatever he faced in his nightmare demanded his full attention.

She knelt beside him and rested a hand on his forehead. There would be no harm in seeing what caused him to worry so. Hopefully, it would allow her to bring him out of the nightmare.

The fight seemed to have gone on forever.

His limbs felt like they were carrying lead instead of meat and bone. Even the weapon he wielded, once light and nimble, now felt as clumsy as a club.

But he refused to stop. He couldn't. The battle wasn't over and the enemy continued to attack in waves. Their armor was brilliant silver and bore the colors of the Red Dragon. They renewed their assault and another wave surged forward.

"Come on, you rabid spawn of steaming godsbedammed lizard dung," Skharr roared and lifted his sword and ax. "You'll have to fight much harder than that if you want to kill me."

Dozens charged his line where they held the breach in the wall. Flames crackled and spread as the siege continued. This was merely one battle among hundreds across dozens of battle lines. A city as large as this one with a wall that went on forever merely meant that much more to defend.

The line was holding behind him but barely. The men were as tired as he was but they expected the massive barbarian to break the enemy charge and sift them through in a weakened condition while arrows were fired from above.

"Come on, you snot-sucking bastard spawn of Janus' poxy

whore!" His weapons still felt heavier than he could carry, but he rushed forward, parried a spear thrust toward his gut, and retaliated with the spike opposite his ax blade. The blow was hard enough to leave a powerful dent in the helm and the wearer stumbled back.

The others raised their shields, ready to continue the fight as the barbarian was forced back. Still, the charge was slowed and the rest of the troop rallied and rushed forward.

Another melee erupted when the opposing forces met. A spear was thrust toward him and Skharr moved to the right to avoid it. He sucked in deep breaths as sweat began to drip down his forehead. It stung his eyes and made it difficult to see through his helm as he deflected the spear to the side and drove his sword into his attacker's neck. Blood gushed from cracks in the armor.

More of the enemy joined the fray. They seemed desperate to take the godsbedammed breach this time. There were fifteen others in the wall but they wanted this one.

"How many of you cowardly ass-fucking lizard pricks do I have to pile up before the wall is repaired again?" Skharr growled his frustration as he cut another of them down and drove his shoulder into the two who followed. The force stopped their momentum and they barreled into the group that approached behind him.

It was getting hard to breathe. All he wanted to do was lay his armor down and rest for a moment until another group began to assault their battle line. He'd spent weeks training the godsbedammed bastards to hold a fucking line and he wouldn't give it all up because a warmongering king heard a prophecy about how he was meant to be the emperor of the whole continent.

The group counter-attacked, which left him with nothing to do but push forward with them. He willed his arms and legs into movement as he hacked into the closest attacker and hurled him out of the way before he drove his sword through the next man. His blade sliced through his mail hauberk and into the padding and flesh and emerged from the other side in a powerful thrust that drove the man hard into the ground.

His men were forced back when a sudden surge of attackers rushed at the walls. They sensed some kind of weakness and intended to exploit it.

A fire seared through Skharr's veins, one that hadn't been in them for a long time. Something deep, hungry, and angry had begun to bare its teeth.

The roar that rumbled from his chest was not something strictly human and for the first time all day, it was more than only the boisterous verbiage meant to keep his men's morale up.

He attacked the group from the flank that they hadn't defended properly, and three were dead almost before they realized he was there. His sword dropped from his fingers and he swept a shield up instead and swung it hard into the closest fighter. He raised his mace and spun his whole body to swing the weapon as hard as he could to crush the skull of another. His target's helm was shattered and blood poured from inside.

"Skharr!"

The barbarian snatched his sword up again and wielded it to bite deeply into another attacker's mail. He could almost feel the blood pumping from the wound as he hacked into it repeatedly. Warm blood spattered across his armor as he dropped his sword, the blade nicked and dented from the treatment it had endured. He retrieved a nearby spear that had fallen as the fighters around him began to inch away, trying to escape the madman.

One fell and was soon followed by another. The spear broke where it was buried in the warrior's chest and Skharr whirled and hammered the broken haft into a nearby head. The blow wasn't hard enough to kill but it forced him back as he swept up the closest weapon to him, a war hammer, which crunched hard into another skull.

He swung it, shifted his grasp, and drove it hard into the belly of another.

"Skharr!"

Someone called his name but it felt like it came from a great distance and through fog with no recognizable tone or voice.

He screamed and buried the spike in the warrior's chest and gut repeatedly until the man sank to his knees and clawed at half a dozen wounds.

"Oh...fuck. You....got the better of me this time, eh, Skharr?"

The voice, even through the pandemonium around them and the man's helm, was a little too familiar. The barbarian approached, dropped to his knees next to him as the battle continued to rage, and pulled the visor of his helm up to reveal a battered and bloody face. Blood seeped from between the man's lips.

"Tristan?" he asked. "What the fuck—how the hell did you get here?"

"The coin was too good to refuse." He coughed and the blood flowed a little faster now. His pale-blue eyes began to lose their focus. "Not...sure I'll be able to spend it, though..."

Ahverna yanked her hand away like it had been stung. Whether this was a dream or a memory, she wasn't quite sure, but the pain in it was only too real. Instinctively, she pulled herself back from it as it began to increase in intensity. She'd never been one to intentionally injure herself simply for the sake of it and nothing else.

After a moment, she shook her head and placed her hand on Skharr's forehead. She could still feel the strife roiling through his body.

"Sometimes, you carry a debt too long," she whispered and closed her eyes. "No longer will this trouble you, Skharr DeathEater."

Pulling it free was like sucking venom from a wound and she

could see the poison seeping out as well. The small darts fell from his body until he was visibly more relaxed. The sweat began to dissipate and the dream faded.

The pain didn't ease much. Nor did the ache or the weight in his limbs, but there was something else that pushed at his consciousness. The battlefield was gone, replaced mostly by blackness as Skharr blinked a few times in an attempt to force his eyes to adjust.

It was odd how they hurt and ached like he had looked directly into the sun for a little too long.

But as he felt his heartbeat thump a steady rhythm through the whole of his body, they adjusted slowly to the darkness of the passage he was in.

Finally, he came to the realization that he wasn't alone.

A slim woman knelt over him. She appeared to wear light armor that was fitted a little too closely to her form. Her hair was black and long and hung almost halfway down her back and he could see her eyes, even in the darkness.

It surprised him that they were what was easiest to see about her. Even with her pale skin and a dip in her armor around her collarbone showing a little too much of it for it to be genuine armor, his gaze was drawn to her bright green eyes instead.

They practically glowed, even in the darkness of the tunnel.

"Ahverna?" Skharr asked and groaned as he propped himself up on his elbows.

"Hello, barbarian," she answered with a pert smirk on her bright red lips. "Of my half-brother, Theros."

"Your half-brother would be ashamed to see me now," he admitted as he pushed into a seated position and inched closer to the wall so he could lean against it and sit with some semblance of dignity. "I thought this would be a simple journey—an escort and perhaps a little coin to be made along the way."

She tilted her head and moved to lean against the wall next to him. "And here I'd heard so much of the vaunted DeathEater stamina."

The barbarian narrowed his eyes. "I hate to tell you but I am in no mood—or condition—to fuck you at the moment."

Ahverna laughed. "Perhaps another time, DeathEater. I am not nearly desperate enough and in all honesty, you reek."

"Reek?"

"You smell of the swamp. You may not know much about women but we are not aroused by the scent of rotting vegetation."

He nodded. "Fair enough, I suppose. If you wouldn't mention that to Theros, I won't have to endure his rebuke again."

Skharr winced as he stretched but managed to retrieve his pack from where it had fallen. His whole body still felt like he had spent three days running without rest and he needed help. After rummaging through it, he found a smaller healing potion he still had from a previous adventure. He couldn't remember which one but the vibrant red color said it was likely still functional. In his current circumstances, he couldn't afford to wonder about its efficacy and instead, he pulled the stopper out and sipped the contents slowly.

"And why would my half-brother rebuke you, barbarian?"

"I…might or might not have had a dalliance with one of his paladins. There was a mutual agreement and consent of all parties involved—if it happened at all, which I do not admit to."

She smirked again and he realized that the sardonic look suited her features quite well, especially with the dark makeup that surrounded her brilliant eyes.

"A Paladin of Theros is not a conquest to scoff at," she noted.

"I wouldn't call it a conquest. Merely a…moment of comfort we both enjoyed."

"How?"

"Vigorously." It was his turn to smirk. He began to feel better as the potion coursed through his veins. "And with more than enough of the famed DeathEater stamina."

They both laughed, although he regretted it as his ribs felt like they still needed a little more time to recover.

"I suppose I can understand what my brother sees in you. And why my other brother does not share the sentiment. Which does still beg the question of why Janus chose to help you with your little skirmish with the underworld of Verenvan."

Skharr shrugged. "A service was performed and Janus felt the need to return the favor."

"He expects loyal service regardless."

"From his people. I serve Theros. As such, I did Janus a favor and he returned it. Not willingly, of course. Theros needed to give him a nudge for it, not least of all because I was in dire straits and needed the help."

Ahverna nodded with a small frown. "I heard a tale of how some of Janus' followers managed to kill a magus lich. I didn't believe the claim, of course, and thought the group looked a little too...incompetent to handle a threat of that magnitude. But now that I think about it, Janus owing you a favor might make up for that level of competence."

"I don't know what you speak of," Skharr responded blandly. "But that does sound like Janus. He's an ass."

"Of course he is." She regarded him quizzically. "Aren't you wondering where your companion has wandered off to?"

"He hasn't wandered, he was captured," he corrected her firmly. "And...I planned to wonder once I was in a condition to follow them."

"How would you do that?"

"Follow their tracks."

"You're in the middle of a swamp. There will be no tracks."

"Then I'll ask the orcs. They know all who come to this island or so I've been led to believe."

"You don't speak their language."

"I'll find a way," Skharr snapped. He realized after a moment that he'd lost his temper with a god and continued in a less confrontational tone. "I...I'll find a way. I'll rescue my friend, no matter what."

"Your friend? Not your charge?"

She was asking many questions, although he wondered if she was playing some kind of game with him now.

"He was my charge in Verenvan but is my friend now. I will kill them all."

"How very...barbarian of you," she quipped.

"There is no denying who or what I am."

"Perhaps I can help," she suggested, pushed to her feet, and offered him her hand.

"How?" Skharr asked. He took it and felt some strength return to his limbs so he let her help him up as well. "I was under the impression that gods weren't allowed to interfere directly in mortal affairs."

"Rules set for the more powerful gods do not apply to me," she answered. "And by way of a for instance, I would be able to direct you since the orcs will likely be of little help. They are headed to Tachan, a port city south of here. And if you are looking for another for instance..."

Her voice trailed off as she leaned closer and pressed her lips lightly to his. The warrior stiffened and surprise prevented him from enjoying the passion she put into the sign of affection.

She pulled away after a few seconds and ran a long, delicate finger over her bottom lip with a small smile. "You should clean up."

"Hmm." The barbarian grunted and tried to make sense of what had happened. A little more vigor had filled his body, the kind that could not be attributed to the healing potion he had taken. "Perhaps after I get my friend to safety. And…thank you."

"Now, rescue my follower," Ahverna answered firmly. "And kill them all."

He chuckled. "How very barbarian of you."

"Every barbarian has some humanity, exactly like every human has a trace of barbarian in them. I merely happen to find myself angry enough to tap into that side of myself."

"Anger is a good place to start," he commented and turned to collect his pack and his weapons.

And in the moment when his attention had been elsewhere, the goddess had vanished and was nowhere to be seen, even in the dark tunnel.

"I'll kill every one of them," he promised no one in particular. "And I'll be sure to make their deaths last."

CHAPTER FOURTEEN

Ahverna had been right, of course. There was no sign of tracks anywhere in the area. The soft ground had quickly shifted to fill in anything that he might have been able to see and the darkness did not help.

It looked like they had left a trap to catch him if he survived whatever had been in the darts fired into him, but it had already been tripped. The darts that had been intended for him were caught in the mound.

After a moment of thought, he collected them and confirmed that they were still tipped with poison. He bound them carefully in cloth and retrieved the abandoned mechanism. It was interesting, to say the least. Thin copper springs were mounted along barrels that were meant to guide the darts on their path. The springs were released when the thin silk strands were tripped.

A keen mind had devised them, although it wasn't likely that they would be able to launch anything but the thin darts and not fast enough to kill a man. That was what the poison was for. He assumed that the only reason why he was still alive was that he was too large for conventional doses and so they had merely drugged him. His light armor had no doubt also helped somewhat, although it had let most of the darts through.

They would not be effective if the victim wore heavy armor or thickly padded leather, but they were an interesting weapon to have in his arsenal if he ever needed to use it.

But that was something to think about later. Night had fallen over the region and while Skharr believed the lizardfolk would not attack, he had no reason to rely on his reasoning. Besides, the swamp had its dangers too. In the darkness, traveling through the bog would be treacherous and if he lost his way, he would either be caught or unable to find a way out. Both those possibilities would almost certainly end in death.

Which meant Brahgen would be left to a painful death.

He made slow progress as he followed the stars for direction. It was odd that he didn't feel the need to rest a few hours later, although Skharr was willing to explain that with whatever the goddess had done to him with her kiss.

His luck was truly bizarre. Most folk didn't gain the attention of the gods once in their lives and there he was with the full attention of three, if not more.

The island was fairly large but it wasn't long before he was out of the swamps. Now, he moved slowly for another reason entirely. The possibility that the orcs had no idea that the lizardfolk would no longer attack them made his imagination immediately leap to the notion that he could be turned into a pincushion by a volley of orc crossbow bolts.

He therefore moved slowly and carefully and walked in the very center of the path. Even in the darkness of a moonless night, there was no way they could mistake him for anything but a barbarian who meant them no harm.

Hopefully.

His instincts—or perhaps simply his imagination—proved correct. As he moved along the path, he began to hear the soft grunts and mutters he recognized as the orc language. Before too long, three of them appeared in front of him, their crossbows at the ready.

They began to make the gestures they used to communicate, and Skharr shook his head.

"I can't understand you," he replied. "The hags are dead, the mist is gone, and the lizardfolk will no longer bother you. And now, my friend was kidnapped and taken away and I don't have the time to play any games."

The orcs paused and two of them took a few steps back and grasped their weapons a little tighter. One paused to talk to those he now realized didn't understand what he was saying. After a moment, they lowered their crossbows and motioned for him to follow them.

They could see a little better in the dark than he did, and he remained close behind as they led him to a palisade guarded by another group of the orcs.

The guards were still awake but it seemed like the rest of the tribe was asleep. One of them began to pull the gates open and another immediately went off in search of the chieftain. The barbarian was prevented from going much farther than a few feet past the gate itself, and while he was in a hurry, he did not intend to antagonize the orcs. If they thought he was a threat, he had no doubt that killing him would not be far behind.

Thankfully, he didn't have long to wait before the chieftain appeared. She looked tired and very much the worse for wear as she approached. He noted that none of them questioned where his smaller companion was, which meant they knew precisely where Brahgen had gone and who he had gone with.

"You've been plagued by the fucking hags, lizardfolk, and mists for how long now?" he asked and tried to keep his tone as level as he could.

The orc realized that he couldn't understand their regular means of communication and signaled with two fingers, then a circular motion.

"Two years?"

She nodded.

"And today, aside from what we dealt with, have you seen any of the lizards? Or noticed that the mists are gone? The hags are fucking dead and the dwarf who killed them was carried off under your noses."

She shrugged and began to go through the familiar and yet unfamiliar hand signals.

"I can't fucking understand you." Despite his good intentions, he growled his frustration.

The chieftain's eyes lit up and she took a step forward. She was almost as tall as he was, although a good deal leaner, but the barbarian did not doubt that she would rank among the toughest fights he'd ever engaged in. Chieftains were not elected among orcs, after all. They had to fight their way to the top and fight to stay there as well.

After a moment during which she stared balefully at him, her expression softened and she shook her head and cleared her throat before she tried to speak. "Humans…kill…humans. Orcs… not…bother."

Skharr narrowed his eyes as he tried to translate what that meant. Eventually, he decided she meant that orcs wouldn't bother with the altercations of humans. They had done what they'd done for their reasons and these had nothing to do with the orcs, who would not interfere as long as the fate of their tribe was not on the line.

"Even so," he answered, "I intend to save him. I know where they are headed. I need to know what they look like and I'll need my boat back. If you feel no sense of…gratitude for what the dwarf did for you, there must be some kind of arrangement we can reach."

The chieftain nodded. "Gra…gratitude…we tell. Boat. You pay."

The information would come thanks to what Brahgen had done for them. Skharr would have to buy the boat.

"Leader...Samor." She indicated his height compared to the barbarian and pointed to her hair. "Gold. Follows..." She tilted her head and finally held ten fingers up.

A golden-haired man named Samor, tall for a human and leading ten men. He could tell she was as annoyed as he was but she did a good job of providing the information.

He nodded. "How much for the boat I came in on?"

"No coin." She shook her head. "Only...trade."

It took him a moment to understand that and when he did, it made sense that they were interested in something more useful than gold or silver. He nodded, unhooked the ax from his belt, and ignored a dozen or so crossbows being drawn around him as he turned it carefully and slowly to offer it to her handle-first in a non-threatening way.

Her eyes narrowed as she took the weapon from his hand. Her grasp was firm and experienced but after a moment, she handed it to one of her lieutenants, who examined it as well. He nodded after a few test swings and returned it to her.

The chieftain focused on Skharr and gestured to show that more was needed. He narrowed his eyes, shrugged, and lowered his pack. The sword he carried and its paired dagger were not anything he would use to redeem a small boat, but something he carried would have to be.

Finally, he paused and drew a deep breath before he withdrew a small, simple wooden box and handed it to the chieftain. She looked curious and opened it carefully to see a handful of corked vials with powders, dried leaves, and other assorted spices.

"DeathEater spices are famous enough that even you must have heard of them," the barbarian said. "They'll stop the food from spoiling and it will taste better once eaten. Perhaps not enough for your whole tribe but they are certainly worth more than the boat we arrived in."

After a moment, her eyebrows raised and a smile appeared on her lips around the thick tusks as she handed him his ax but kept the spices.

He would regret making the trade but he didn't have the time to haggle. It was all he had to offer and he doubted they would take the trap he had found either. Orcs would have little need for it.

"Now?" she asked.

Skharr nodded. "There is no time like the present."

"What...will do?" the chieftain asked and still struggled with the common tongue.

"Do you mean when I find Samor and his merry band of pox-spawned idiots?"

She nodded.

"I will kill them. Every last one. Some will have to die quickly, I suppose, but Samor will likely be at the back of the line, away from the fighting. I'll kill him slowly."

"How?"

That was a good question and one he had considered during his walk through the swamp. "There is a practice in the north among humans called drawing and quartering that might serve. But perhaps I'll squeeze his throat until he has no strength left and gut him with a dagger. I might cut his manhood off as well."

"Manhood?"

"His cock and balls."

She grunted.

"Done right, he'll be alive for the whole process as I pull his guts out and put them on a fire in front of him. It won't take him long to die after that but he'll know what his entrails smell like being cooked over an open flame before he goes to whatever hell he has waiting for him."

The orc laughed and nodded in approval, and as others translated what he said to those who didn't understand the common tongue, a few mutters and laughs followed.

Skharr didn't know if it meant they approved or merely thought it a funny way to kill someone. Either way, it was irrelevant to the matter at hand.

The chieftain continued to chuckle as they approached the beach where all the ships were kept. They had been dragged out of the water to rest on the black sand and he soon located the small dingy he'd come in on. He paused while a handful of the orcs piled in a few extra supplies of dried fish and sea salt for the journey, which he took as a good sign.

The barbarian put his belongings aboard first and, with a little help, pushed the boat to the water. He climbed in smoothly and took hold of the oars.

"Gods…watch you," the chieftain said from the beach as he began to row out into the murky water. Without any mist, it was easy to keep his little vessel from running afoul of the rocks all around the island even at night, and it wasn't long before he reached the open water that was still calm even with the unnatural fog gone.

That probably wouldn't last but this time, at least, he wouldn't have to worry about Brahgen spewing his guts over the side again.

Thinking about the dwarf was not a good idea and his mood darkened as a touch of wind caught his sail and pushed him to the mainland. At least he no longer needed to row.

CHAPTER FIFTEEN

Whatever the goddess had done to him wasn't the kind of thing that faded in a hurry. The sun had begun to come up as Skharr approached the mainland again and continued up the river. Day turned to night and then day again and he still felt like he was relatively well-rested and alert. Even so, it was something he knew would make its demands eventually but for the moment, he could appreciate both the winds from the coast that drove him upstream as well as being able to stay awake for the duration.

Although he was a little sore and tender in places when he steered the dinghy to the docks, he still felt ready to put in a day's worth of travel heading south.

He didn't like the fact that he had to leave behind a boat that he'd had to pay for twice but the situation made it unavoidable. Hopefully, he would be able to return and sell it for a fair price but for the moment, hunting Brahgen and killing his captors took precedence.

Given how long he'd been drugged for, he doubted that he even had time to collect on the reward for the contract, but there was no way to tell how long he had to accomplish his purpose.

Ahverna had described Tacham as a port city to the south but he knew better. It was an alcove that pirates had taken a liking to, the kind of location that was a little too difficult for the empire to reach and control.

It would happen eventually, but for the moment, it was barely worthy of the title of a city. The reality was that the original fishing village had become engorged with folk with ill-gotten gains who came and stayed to spend what they'd stolen until they had none left. It was the kind of cycle that led to folk engaging in crime and returning for the vices available in the town until they died or ran out of coin.

As long as he kept his wits about him, it was the kind of place a barbarian tended to do well in.

Skharr marched immediately to the stables where he'd left Horse and Jenny and paused when he arrived and noticed that the stable was half as full as when he had left them.

The stallion was there, although he showed no sign of being particularly happy to see him. But Jenny was gone. He turned and strode to where the innkeeper was still seated in front of the lake. The man puffed calmly at his pipe until he cast a massive shadow over him.

"Oh. You've returned."

The barbarian chose to believe that the man's surprise was not because he knew he had gone to fight in a damned dungeon. Without pause, he caught him by the shoulders and lifted him roughly off his comfortable seat so they were more or less at the same height, although the innkeeper's feet dangled almost a full foot from the ground.

"The donkey," he stated calmly. "Where did she go?"

"I haven't—"

He clamped his free hand on the man's mouth before another word could be said. "Allow me to interrupt what I'm sure was a very creative story about how the damned donkey disappeared. I will tell you what I think happened and you'll correct me if I'm wrong. A group of eleven men came through, asked for directions for me and a dwarf, and took the donkey. They paid you a great deal to be silent on the matter. You believed I would not survive long enough to come and reclaim the beasts and let her go. How close is my tale to the truth?"

His hand was still over the man's mouth, which meant he could only nod and whimper pitifully.

Godsbedammed fucking blood-leeching thieves were all over the place these days.

"The coin I paid you to care for the animals. Where is it?"

The innkeeper looked reflexively toward his purse and Skharr snatched it before he dropped the man on the wooden boardwalk. It was suspiciously heavier than an innkeeper's should have been, and he took the two silvers he'd paid so both animals would be stabled and fed before he tossed the purse to him.

"If you try anything like this again, I'll be sure the guild knows that you sell what isn't yours to the folk who are killing your patrons. I'm sure they'll be happy to learn of it."

The man's terrified gaze followed him to where Horse had wandered calmly out of the open doors and was browsing a few patches of grass near the stables.

"I suppose I should count my lucky stars that they didn't take you," the barbarian muttered and patted the stallion on the neck before he began to put the saddle on his back, followed quickly by his supplies.

Horse snorted loudly.

"Oh. And you didn't go along with them." Skharr tilted his head. "I am touched although we both know you only did it with self-interest firmly in your mind. You know I'm the only one who pampers you with apples and time spent at a pleasant farm."

The beast showed no sign of denying this.

"I know your only concern is for yourself. My safety did not even enter your mind."

Talking to Horse again certainly helped to calm his nerves.

Heading to Tacham would be an unsettling experience for him. Finding himself face to face with Samor was another situation he would rather have avoided. He'd heard the name a long time before and there were numerous dead bodies associated with it. Many were enemies but too many were those who had signed up to fight alongside him.

That did not change anything, but at least he knew who he would have to fight to free his friend.

Tacham hadn't changed much. The rich smell of alcohol still drenched the town's many inns, most of which doubled as whorehouses for those who were in the mood to indulge in more than one vice at once. It also was home to a few gambling dens and purveyors of substances that could alter the mind, most of which were illegal anywhere else in the world.

It wasn't like the folk cared that it would kill them. Skharr knew from experience that few of those who spent their time in the area expected to see too many winters even without the dangerous habits.

Ahverna's kiss ran out half a day into the trip and he dragged his feet in the last few hours of the day and was barely able to make camp before he was out like a torch caught in a mountain wind blast.

He woke with the sun but the whole of the day's travel had been spent feeling like he was paying for the time when he'd pushed on without rest. His back and shoulders ached like they hadn't since he'd started using his fucking bow, his legs felt like they would buckle at any moment, and his midsection made him groan with every misstep.

The day had involved far too many missteps.

Thankfully, things had improved after a quick sip of a healing potion. Returning to Tacham certainly helped on one level, he conceded.

There was nothing even resembling a wall around it, and Skharr could understand that it had to do with the knowledge that anyone who attacked would be met with reprisals from hundreds of battle-hardened pirates and mercenaries, even if most of them were drunk.

He kept a firm hold on his possessions and made sure that none who approached him came close enough to have a good look at him or to sneak a hand onto his coin purse. It helped that this was the kind of town where folk liked to ignore each other unless there was business to attend to.

And for a place that had more than its share of criminals, there was considerable trust. Folk didn't want to see themselves banned from the inns, brothels, and gambling dens, so they mostly maintained the order.

A few wagons bringing food and supplies to one of the inns had even left their wagon out in the open without so much as a guard as they watched an altercation that took place on the streets outside.

Skharr was not worried about being banned since he doubted that he would return there in the future. With a quick look around, he helped himself to a few packs of food as well as a couple of apples from a barrel for Horse.

The true treasure he discovered was the small glass bottle of a rich auburn liquid that he knew a little too well.

"Of all the things I don't miss about this place," he whispered and tugged Horse around the corner from where he could see the owners of the wagon returning, "you are not among them."

He bit into the cork and yanked it out before he took a long sip. No one would look twice at another brute getting drunk on the streets of Tacham. The rum was powerful enough to make him splutter with the first sip but his confidence returned with the second. The feel of the city began to return to him. Everything about it felt a little more natural as he wandered through the streets and the familiar sights and sounds flooded back to him.

It felt only too natural when he stopped to share his ill-gotten bottle with a younger-looking man who leaned outside of one of the brothels. He looked like he was out for a walk or perhaps looking for work.

"You are a big bastard, aren't you?"

Skharr nodded. "So I've been told. Do you happen to know if any of the local captains are looking for a big bastard on his crew? I am light of coin and eager to earn a little more."

"I...the *Empress Vassan's Redress* was looking for a crew, I think, and they'll leave sometime tonight. Something about a group paying money for an escort through our dastardly waters. I don't know why anyone would serve on a ship named after some tart's dress."

"Redress means revenge."

"Oh." The young man scratched at his bald head. "Well, the group they took has their own fighters, and Captain Thatch wanted to have fighters on his crew if they tried to take over his ship. It's not the kind of thing he said for all to hear, of course—very quiet-like."

The barbarian nodded. "Do you happen to know the group with the fighters? Have you seen them?"

"Aye. Even I know well enough to steer clear of the murderous bastard. I don't know how Samor still finds folk to follow him when they know he kills them all to keep the coin for hisself. They must be desperate is my thinking."

"Did they have any prisoners with them?" he asked.

"Prisoners?" The youth laughed. "It sounds like you know more about the shit here than I! But yes, they had a dwarf with them. He did not look keen to remain with the group, of course, given how he was bound. Perhaps he was a prisoner. He was small for a dwarf, though, so might have been a halfling. I've never seen a halfling before..."

Skharr left the man, who continued to chat to the air while he clutched the bottle in his hands. The barbarian hadn't expected Samor to find passage so quickly, so either he was incredibly lucky or he'd made the arrangements beforehand.

The fact that the captain wanted more fighting men meant it was likely luck on Samor's part. The whole situation reeked of improvisation, which might prove useful if he intended to follow them in.

He clicked his tongue and Horse increased the pace behind him. He could see the *Redress* docked and with movement all around it, far enough away that the men and women looked like insects from a distance.

"This...is probably not a good idea," he said quietly as he patted the stallion's neck. "But aside from starting a brawl in the middle of the city and hoping that the confusion is enough to let us escape, I don't see any other way. So unless you have any better suggestions?"

He looked at Horse, who merely stared at him in return.

"Right. That was indeed a stupid question. But we will find a way through this. You have to trust me."

It was one of the largest ships that Brahgen had ever seen. Not that he'd seen too many in person, but he had read numerous writings on naval battles with sketches that showed massive ships with dozens of men aboard. These were usually depicted in vivid detail as they emptied flaming pots of oil, loosed arrows, boarded other vessels, and tossed their enemies overboard.

Who exactly had made the sketches was never said, but as a young dwarf, he had dreamed of being a pirate of some kind. That was, of course, before he was aware that being on the open water made him sick. The trip from the island to the mainland had been the worst.

The only small comfort was that Jenny was there waiting for him once they arrived but not Horse. Perhaps that meant Skharr was still alive. It wasn't likely but he preferred to cling to any shred of hope that not all was fucked and not all was lost.

It was probably a vain hope but it was all he had while carried along on Jenny's back. Vain or not, it was certainly a hell of a lot better than thinking about what would happen to him once he was among the folks he had once thought were more interested in his well-being than his family was.

Once they arrived in the piss-soaked city, it felt like it was almost impossible to not wonder what would happen to him. Death, of course, but there would surely be a little more to it than that—most likely some more creative form that he would have to endure for days before he finally succumbed. He'd heard stories about mages who could make a painful death last for days by healing the victim's lethal injuries and repeating the process endlessly. He had been told that wasn't quite how healing magic worked but the stories were still there.

"Is something on your mind?"

Brahgen almost jumped and the ropes around his wrists dug painfully into his skin.

It was the leader of the group, a man the others called Samor. The dwarf thought he looked about the most normal and he carried himself like a man of standing or perhaps a nobleman. He wore a medallion with a pair of panthers cast in bronze around his neck and kept his hand close to the sword he carried on his hip.

Interestingly enough, he was very proud of his long, golden hair and he carried a brush and used it to groom his locks on a regular basis. The fact that he was so vain said something about him, but Brahgen couldn't think of what it could possibly be.

How close he was also showed that he wore some kind of perfume, likely to keep the smells of the city away from him.

"My imminent demise and how painful it might be," the youth answered finally once it was clear that Samor didn't intend to move away.

The swordsman tilted his head and smirked. "How odd. I never pegged you for a self-centered little shit, although it does not surprise me. Dwarves have that nature bred into them."

"What is your problem?" he asked. "Did a dwarf fuck your mother? Is that why you have so much resentment toward us? Do you feel a little insecure about such a small character hefting a larger cock than whatever your cuckold of a father blessed you with?"

Samor chuckled and shook his head. "No, I thought about how you might be in a situation where you realize you are at fault for the death of your comrade. While all you see before you might have my actions as their cause, you know in your heart of hearts that your tiny shoulders bear some of it as well."

Brahgen nodded. "So...insecurity over cock size it is, then. We could simply establish this once and for all. You whip yours out and I do the same and we'll know that you have the larger endowment. Unless, of course, you doubt that you would come away from such a contest without the scorn of your men. I imagine shame and scorn is the kind of thing you kill folk over. But I will no doubt die regardless, and if you did it sooner rather than later, I would thank you for it."

The man smirked and ruffled his hair. "You do have a mouth on you, little dwarf. I might simply choose to take your tongue out instead of killing you outright. That might leave you less time to drown your guilt with rabid ramblings. Perhaps it might also give you more time to pray to a human god who won't ever listen to you."

He wandered away and Brahgen spat reflexively at the man's back. It fell a little short but his point was made. He didn't need any help to feel guilt over Skharr's death and he had already told himself repeatedly what the man had to say—and in a more creative fashion than the vain piece of gilded shit could devise.

It didn't help much, of course, but being able to lash out at someone other than himself was certainly a pleasant distraction.

The dwarf froze when he noticed a sudden shift in the people around him. A bell rang on the massive ship and suddenly, all the sailors jumped into action, picked crates up, and began to carry them on board. It was large enough that even horses were loaded, including poor Jenny. About a dozen of them were led carefully along a special plank into the lower deck of the vessel.

He narrowed his eyes and tilted his head, unsure if he was seeing things or if that was truly Horse following the other animals aboard.

It looked like the stallion, at least. He recognized all the same markings on his forehead and back, although he appeared to be missing most of the saddlebags that Skharr generally saddled him with. Perhaps they'd gone back and taken him? No, that didn't seem possible. The beast seemed intelligent and attached enough to the barbarian that he wouldn't simply accept being horse-napped.

"Come on, dwarf. It's time to die," one of the mercenaries stated before he flung the dwarf over his shoulder again and carried him on board like he was another piece of cargo.

But, oddly enough, a hint of hope was buried in the depths of his mind and he had a feeling it wasn't false.

CHAPTER SIXTEEN

Hiding in the hold of the ship had not been a simple affair. He was mostly helped by the fact that nobody expected anyone to be stupid enough to stow away on a pirate ship.

Getting Horse into the pen of creatures that would be transported aboard the *Redress* had been the easiest part of his plan to accomplish. He'd simply walked the beast in with his packs. No one had questioned someone bringing his horse in like they would have questioned him taking a horse away.

Once that was done, he was forced to carry his packs as he slipped into the water a few hundred paces away from the ship. He came in from beneath the vessel and found a window into the hold that allowed the livestock to breathe and have some light. It could be closed from the inside in case there were storms and opened again if their archers wanted a safer place to loose their arrows from in case of a battle on the open water.

Skharr pushed his packs inside while he hung from the side of the boat. He dragged himself carefully aboard, slipped belowdecks without being seen, and stowed away in the hold mere moments before the bell from above announced that they would raise anchor soon.

Boots and bare feet pattered above him and soon, the horses were guided into the hold as well. He remained as motionless as possible in his dark corner while more cargo was packed into the hold to further hide him from prying eyes. None of the crew was interested in searching the area and all were in too much of a hurry to have everything stacked and secured.

All he needed to do was make sure that Horse was loaded along with the other beasts before he settled into his corner and remained hidden.

It was an uncomfortably small haven, and he knew he would battle through aches and pains before too long. The itchy nature of the damp hay that covered the decking was also an issue but he was on the ship. Soon, there were no more tasks belowdecks and it wasn't long before bells rang again. He couldn't make out what was shouted but it was safe to assume they were calls to raise the anchors since the ship began to move soon after.

It was a gentle movement at first, but Skharr could tell when they reached the open water since the ship rolled more.

It was a massive vessel, the kind that wasn't as easily affected by waves in the manner of the smaller craft, but he knew that Brahgen would have issues with how the ship moved as well.

He knew it for a fact too as he could hear the dwarf complaining on the other side of the hold. It wasn't quite as bad as the smaller vessel they'd been on, but he supposed his companion's stomach didn't care. There were none of the tell-tale sounds that said he would be sick, but it was only a matter of time.

It wasn't time for the barbarian to reveal himself yet, however. Timing would be everything, and he realized that he hadn't planned much of anything beyond getting on the ship with the dwarf. That had been solved. What came next would have to wait until he knew where they were going.

For the present, he focused his mind on trying to make out how many men there were. His attempt to tell one from the other from their footsteps above brought no success, and they came regularly to the hold to either inspect their cargo—living and otherwise—or collect personal items. A few even paused beside Brahgen.

"It's time for you to start praying to your god, little one." One of the men laughed. "We know she won't listen to you, but it should provide us with a good measure of amusement before we return to Verenvan."

That explained where they were planning to take the captive at least, although Skharr doubted that a pirate ship would be so bold as to drop anchor in the port. They would likely follow a roundabout route to avoid detection.

He grasped his sheathed sword a little tighter when he heard one of the men kick the dwarf and laugh before he wandered away. Another bell was rung to indicate that it was time for the evening meal.

"You'd better fuck right off," Brahgen shouted. "Untie me and we'll see how loud you laugh with my dagger making mincemeat of your innards, you maggot-infested pile of boar shit."

The man turned as if to attack him again, but his comrades stopped him. Either they knew their friend was likely to kill the dwarf and leave them with nothing to show for all the effort to take him alive, or they had plans to return later when Samor would not be available to stop them.

At least the youth still had a little spirit in him, which was an encouraging sign. That would cause him to suffer a little more during the trip, but it would take considerable abuse to break him. And not only because his kind were mentally strong but because he was a step above most when it came to mental toughness.

When the rest of the crew were distracted with getting something to eat on the other side of the hold, Skharr managed to squeeze out of his hiding place and moved carefully to the upper deck. He would have to leave his bow behind for the moment, but it wasn't likely to be very effective while fighting on the ship.

For now, it was best to keep his presence unnoticed. Night falling would certainly help with that, as the crew kept their use of lamp oil low, both to conserve it and to avoid detection by other vessels. This was an old pirate tactic that was only effective if they had a sound navigator who had a good mind for where all the reefs were hiding.

The barbarian drew a deep breath of the fresh sea air. It had been a long time since he had simply enjoyed the scent of the open sea. He moved cautiously away from the stairs to the hold. A few of the crew remained at their posts but were more concerned with anything that came toward the ship than what was on it. He counted about twenty, including those who were eating below. With the group he was tracking, that was another eleven. Even with Brahgen with him, he doubted that he would be able to eliminate them all and if he did, how would he sail the ship?

He paused and glanced at the steps he'd used as the mercenary who had kicked Brahgen came topside. The man looked like he'd already eaten his fill and he belched loudly as he wandered to the side of the ship and undid his trousers.

The barbarian immediately recognized this as one way to even the odds. He remained low, drew a dagger from his belt, and inched forward while the man was distracted voiding himself.

Quickly, he covered the mercenary's mouth before he thrust the dagger into his back hard enough that he felt the spine crack against the blade. In a moment, any attempt to struggle ceased and he inched away and let him fall into the water when the ship met a small wave. As the vessel teetered on the low crest for an instant, Skharr caught sight of the horizon. Not because of a ship that came over it, fully lit as he might have hoped, but because flickers of light in the distance were quickly followed by rumbling, rolling sounds of thunder.

They were trying to circle to avoid a storm but he doubted they would be able to. From the way the lightning sizzled across the clouds, it looked like a summer storm had struck a few months too early.

It wasn't entirely unheard of in these waters. There was much that drove the weather to madness. He'd heard that the worst part of the Ancient Wars was fought in the region and things had been so terrible that sections of the continent sank into the sea.

Given that—and he did not doubt the veracity of most of what he'd heard—Skharr assumed that possibly hundreds of dungeons were built into those sunken landscapes whose magic influenced the weather and were probably filled to the brim with treasure as no one had the opportunity to delve into them.

The sounds from below told him that the evening meal was finished and the crew were returning to their posts. A lookout must have caught sight of the storm and the helmsman decided they wouldn't escape it.

The barbarian could already hear the groans from the assembled crew and even the mercenaries were pressed into service to help.

"We will need all hands on deck for this fucker," the captain roared. He was slim of build, although a thick, grizzled beard added to his stature, as did his inordinately deep voice. Rules on pirate vessels were easy to follow. If you didn't like how the captain ran the ship, kill him and take his place. That kind of simplicity came from true barbarism.

The myriad scars told how long he had held his position on the *Redress*, and it looked like the other pirates held him in high regard.

"We're not sailors!" one of the mercenaries protested.

"The sea will drown you whether you're sailors or not so you might as well try to avoid it," the captain retorted immediately. "All men to the rope decks. We'll stay above the water if it kills every single one of you. Where is Bayon? The dumb fuck had better not be trying to get out of work."

Skharr looked around the group from his hidden vantage

point and counted all the men he'd noted before. All except for Samor, of course. He'd never known the man to be involved in any kind of work, even if it was to save his life.

Which meant that only one man was missing—the one who had fallen overboard not a minute before. He smirked and sank lower in his hiding place.

"The lazy bastard might as well fucking drown if he's simply going to be a drain," one of the sailors muttered and shook his head.

"All hands to work now! We'll need to be ready for the storm when it hits us."

They would need considerable help to stop the *Redress* from capsizing. Skharr wondered if this was the point to show them that they had an extra skilled hand at their disposal.

Then again, he had no intention of fighting the storm while he was in the water himself which he might well be if they knew he was aboard.

As the crew set to work, he moved toward the steps leading into the hold. The lightning flickered again and illuminated the whole vessel in a flare of light a few seconds before the rumbling thunder crashed. Skharr felt it in his chest and the horses below had it even worse. They neighed loudly and tried to break free from their tethers.

He managed to sneak into the hold to where the horses stamped nervously. Even more of the lights flickered above followed by peals of thunder. It would be a storm for the ages and he had managed to slip himself into it.

Irritated, he shook his head. Why couldn't Brahgen have been captured by a group of forest nymphs? At least he knew how to keep them from killing folk.

It was time now and he moved through the hold but hunkered down when a group came to close the windows to prevent water from coming in. The waves rocked the vessel harder, and it wouldn't be long until rain whipped fast enough to sting any bare skin.

"Fucking gods…is that you, Skharr?"

The barbarian froze and looked around quickly, surprised that he was already near Brahgen and the dwarf had seen him.

Or seemed to think he'd seen him. Even in the darkened hold, there wasn't any way to mistake him for someone else.

"No, it can't be you," the youth muttered and shook his head. "I've…fallen asleep and you're…a spirit come to haunt me…for leaving you in that fucking cave to die."

"I would have thought you would dream of something else like dwarf ladies with thick beards and large breasts."

"I don't like dwarf women. And you've seen dwarf women. You know they don't grow beards. Most of them, anyway. My grandmother has started to and I don't know what to think about that."

"Keep your wits about you, useless dwarf. I'm here to help." Skharr dropped to his haunches beside him and his blood began to boil when he saw the bruises on most of his friend's body. Many were covered by his beard, hair, and clothes, but there were more than enough to make the abuse inflicted by his captors clear.

He also looked like he was about to vomit, and as the rocking began to grow more intense, the barbarian had a feeling that wouldn't improve.

"Is that truly you?" Brahgen whispered. His eyes narrowed and he leaned forward like he didn't quite believe it. "I thought I was going insane when I saw Horse boarding the ship but—"

"I can slap you across the face if you still have difficulty believing that I'm here," he stated cheerfully.

"I…uh, don't believe that will be necessary. Are you here to rescue me?"

"No, I came along because I fancied a short ship journey that ended with a freak storm. Of course I'm here to rescue you, moron." Skharr yanked him forward and used his dagger—still stained with blood—to cut the ropes that tied his hands behind his back. "Unfortunately, there is no rescue from what is about to hit this ship. We'll need to endure it."

"And then what? Swim to shore?"

"Can you swim?"

The dwarf opened his mouth and shook his head. "Not…not very well."

"And I doubt even I could swim that far, much less Horse and Jenny."

"Horse and—"

"Did you honestly think I would come this far to rescue you only to leave Horse in their clutches?"

"Huh. You make a sound point. So what do we do?"

"They don't know I am on board yet. For the moment, we wait the storm out. Hopefully, that will thin their number enough that we'll be able to kill the mercenaries ourselves."

"And what about the rest of the crew?"

"They'll be interested in reaching dry land as well. We have to hope that means that they won't kill us."

"Why?"

"Because I can't sail this ship on my own."

Skharr felt his frustrations over his inability to plan ahead bubble to the surface. Thankfully, the sounds of the storm from outside masked his voice as he struggled to calm himself.

"Do you have a plan?"

"Not as such. I've merely attempted to find you from the point when I left the fucking dungeon. Plans never had time to be made."

"Well, this rescue is going wonderfully, then."

The warrior narrowed his eyes. "Count your lucky stars that I came to find you at all."

"So we could die together instead of apart?"

"If it comes to that, yes!"

Both froze as the ship was rocked again but this time, the motion was contrary to what they felt from the waves. Skharr looked at the walls when they felt the impact again. It felt as though something was physically striking at the ship.

"Is that part of the storm?" Brahgen asked and frowned, his queasiness temporarily forgotten.

"No."

"Have we…uh, run into some rocks? Hopefully?"

It was a good thing that the dwarf at least recognized that something was well and truly wrong with what they felt, but the scenario he suggested was unlikely. He felt the ship shudder as if something had taken hold of it from the outside and wouldn't let go.

"No," the barbarian whispered. "But it's good of you to keep your spirits up. I fear you might need it. I'll head topside and see what it is."

"What do I do?"

"Stay there," he answered and handed him the bloodied dagger. "Act like you're still tied. If you see the opportunity, stab one of them with it."

Brahgen nodded. The lamplight in the hold was dim but Skharr could still see his face pale as he took the weapon.

"Hold fast to your courage," he said and patted him on the shoulder. "While we live, there's hope. There's considerable living you can do while you're still alive."

"You're godsbedammed useless at inspiring people, you know?"

"I always was better at killing them. Stay alive!"

CHAPTER SEVENTEEN

Rain lashed the deck. The droplets stung his bare skin as he emerged from inside the hold and swept his gaze around in an attempt to gauge the conditions the vessel was facing.

Lightning still flickered, and Skharr held onto a nearby railing as the *Redress* was rocked again. The waves continued to shake it but it felt like the ship was caught with its anchor down and was battered by the waves.

At least the captain seemed to know what he was doing. The sails were all down and the masts were secured against the whipping motion. The real danger, of course, was that something had grasped the back of the vessel—something large and heavy. The barbarian drew a deep breath and focused to try to catch sight of whatever it was, but there was no sign that it had come into view yet.

Some of the crew had reached the same conclusion. There was a danger that the waves would rip their ship to pieces, but the way to save themselves from that fate was, interestingly enough, the same way to prevent being dragged down by whatever had control of the ship.

A few of the crew members caught sight of Skharr. They immediately pointed and shouted at him, but they knew they had more to worry about than a stowaway.

Suddenly, a shrill scream erupted, loud enough to break through the constant rain, wind, and lightning. The barbarian spun and immediately realized where the noise was coming from. One of the sailors was being dragged across the deck by something thick and sinuous wound around her leg.

It didn't last long and with one final shriek, she was hauled over the edge and into the roiling waters beneath.

"Sailor overboard!" someone shouted into the rain, but all those on deck were more concerned about what was happening around them.

Skharr hated to even think it, but when he saw the captain still manning the helm, it provided him with the perfect opportunity to make sure that if they came away from the fight alive, they wouldn't be tossed overboard immediately.

He shook his head and held fast to anything that could maintain his balance as he inched toward the helm.

In one moment, the storm was no longer their greatest worry.

Thatch had been in dozens of storms like it, sometimes on lesser vessels too. He trusted the *Redress* with his life, of course, and all she needed him to do was to avoid making godsbedammed foolish mistakes that would see her dead.

That was his only job.

He'd heard about sea monsters wandering these waters. A few even used the storms to their advantage, folks said, and rose from the depths to drag vessels down that were already being battered by the sea. He hadn't expected to learn the lesson to not doubt the voices of caution, but there he was, struggling to keep control of his ship. Some great beast was climbing on from behind and it had caught the rudder to stop it from moving, which effectively negated any control he might have had over the vessel.

No one did that. Not even the mightiest of sea monsters.

"Draw yer weapons, lads!" the captain roared over the storm that lashed the vessel. "You'll have more to fight than treacherous winds and a little rain this night."

"We came on board this ship so experienced sailors would do the work."

He turned and narrowed his eyes as he searched out the culprit. One of the thieves he'd allowed aboard his ship was complaining. The man certainly looked miserable, drenched from head to toe while he struggled to keep his balance as the *Redress* was rocked repeatedly, no longer from the waves.

"Are you plannin' to die this day, you whining slug-brained idiot?" he snapped as he advanced on the man.

"Your people think they can pass the work off on us and—"

The mercenary's voice was replaced by a loud gurgling sound and the captain felt warm blood mix with the ice-cold rain. It flowed from his dagger blade and onto his hands as the man dropped to his knees and clutched his throat.

"Right then!" He looked at the other men on deck. "Do any others think they don't need to carry their weight in this time of need?"

There were no other takers and he waited for a moment while the rain washed the blood from his blade and hands.

"Then fling this worthless bag of meat overboard and we can get back to the battle of survival."

His men jumped into action immediately. Two of them took hold of the dead man's hands and legs and tossed him over the side of the ship.

The other mercenaries made no clamor about not wanting to work through the fucking storm and it was for the best. Thatch felt as though he didn't have the patience to deal with the rest of them. He didn't even have the time to hunt for Samor and drag him out to do his part as well.

Like it or not, the self-glorifying little asshole would probably kill any sailors who tried to make his pansy hands do any hard work.

He turned to the helm, grasped the wheel, and tried to force it to turn. The vessel had begun to be forced around parallel to the waves and if that continued, it wouldn't be long before it capsized and they were all dead.

Worse still, he could see more of the damn tentacles slither onto the deck. They reached out for his sailors, who already struggled to either bail the water that poured in, tighten ropes, or shift anything from the deck into the hold where it would act as something of a ballast.

A few had their weapons out and attempted to attack the tentacles as they swished from side to side, but it was clear that the monster was merely probing. It couldn't see what was happening on the deck and it used those appendages as eyes so that it didn't need to rise from the water.

His crew were hard workers, all having earned their place on his ship, and even the mercenaries now put their backs into the work when they could. More than a few still hadn't acquired their sea legs and found it difficult to remain on their feet.

This was only the beginning, of course. Once the sea monster had a mind to rip the ship apart, the main tentacles would make an appearance with suckers powerful enough that they were capable of tearing planks off of the ship's hull.

Thatch suddenly froze in place when something painfully sharp dug a little too hard into his back. For a moment, he thought it was Samor trying to make a statement about him killing one of his men. He liked to do that himself if the reputation spread about him was to be believed.

But a quick look behind him told a different story. A massive, hulking beast of a man was mostly hidden in the shadows and yet clearly not a part of either of the crews he'd brought aboard his ship.

"Hello there, Graves," a deep, gravely, and painfully familiar voice rumbled through his ears. "I hear you're calling yourself Thatch these days."

It took him a moment to link the voice to a face and a name but once he did, it all started to make a little more sense.

"Fucking, shitting, tit-sucking hells." The captain laughed as he turned and was only warned against any further reaction when the knife dug into his chest. "Is that you, Scourge? I did not think I would see you on a ship again. They said you only had legs for solid land. You're a sight I never wanted to see."

"Things change. I believe you and I need to parley for a moment."

Graves looked around the deck of his ship. "Does now strike you as the best time to have a pleasant conversation?"

"It gives me the most leverage, so yes. We can talk about the old days over a bottle of rum once the threat has been dealt with. For the moment, you need help to keep the *Redress* afloat."

"That does…sound accurate. What will you do?"

"I'll rid you of the creature."

Any other mortal would balk at the challenge of facing a sea monster. Graves would have laughed in the face of most who said that, thinking they were mad, drunk, or both. Probably both, in all honesty. Drink only served to emphasize the madness that was generally hidden beneath layers of civil discourse.

"This is a parley," the captain reminded him. "You're offering to deal with a threat to me ship and me crew. What would you have of me—unless you think to help us out of the kindness of yer heart?"

"Now what kind of business sense would that be?" The giant

shook his head. "I'll need your crew to get rid of the thieves and mercenaries who currently infest your deck."

"They're doing a damn fine—well, a decent job of keeping the ship afloat."

"Do you think they could kill the monster?"

The barbarian made a good point.

"Fair enough. But the leader will be a little more difficult. Blademasters are tough shits to crap, and this one is the prickly kind who won't go without causing pain to any asshole who fights him."

"I'll kill him. I owe him a long, painful death once the storm and threat passes."

"And if you can't?"

"Then I'll be dead and your ship will likely sink, with you and your crew painfully consumed by a monster of the depths."

They were running out of time. The sweeping tentacles grew more aggressive when the men tried to fight them. It wouldn't be long before the creature moved in for the kill.

"Make it so," Graves answered with a mad grin. "Parley done. We'll rid the seas of the useless slime-suckers. Fish feed is probably all they were good for anyway."

The knife was quickly withdrawn and the barbarian's eyes gleamed as a flicker of lightning crossed the sky. Time had driven the captain to forget how terrifying it was to stand across from the man when he had murder on his mind.

Thankfully, neither Graves nor his crew—who were of another generation and only knew him as Thatch—were those he planned to kill.

In a moment, the giant vanished from his sight. It was easy to lose him in the darkness, despite his size. Skharr had a way of moving that addled the mind.

Graves turned to the helm and laughter bubbled from his chest as he grasped the wheel.

"Fight harder, you worthless scum!" he roared and tried to

wrestle control of the ship from the beast. "You'll not see the inside of a sea monster's belly this night!"

Of course, once it was defeated, he would have to come to terms with having the Barbarian Scourge of the Waters on his vessel, but priorities needed to be attended to first.

CHAPTER EIGHTEEN

C ertain rules governed the process of killing a monster like this. Or, failing that, driving it off the ship and into the depths.

Skharr recalled the last few times when he'd been forced to act. He'd been a younger man then but everything still applied. The creature was looking for food. Wounds would attract other, larger beasts so they would pull away if the risks outweighed the benefits.

First things first, then, was to relieve it of its tentacles. There were a few civilizations that prized the meat of such mighty creatures. He had tried it once, mostly out of curiosity, and found the bitter taste and rubbery consistency of the meat unpalatable. It would do in a situation where he had no other options but was not something he wanted to eat every day. As far as he could remember, it had required a week and many bottles of rum to wash the taste from his mouth.

But he had learned a great deal more about monsters with tentacles rising from the depths. Memories of the beast in the lake and the undergod in the temple reminded him that all might not be well with a creature like this. He pulled the sword from his back, unsheathed it smoothly, and felt a hint of warmth from having the light blade in his hands.

If this monster had anything magical to it, he had a feeling it would not like the bite of his blade. He needed a name for the sword. It possibly had one once but it had been lost to time when it had rotted away in the damn tower for centuries. He would have to find a new name—a fitting name.

"God-Slayer does have a fine ring to it," he muttered, vaulted over the railing that separated the helm from the rest of the deck, and landed on his feet. He tried to keep track of what was now almost a dozen tentacles that slithered across the deck, looking for victims to drag away.

It wasn't long before one found its prey and he moved as quickly as he could to intercept it. He had been on land too long and finding his sea legs again proved to be something of a problem, but even on the deck slick with rain, he moved faster than the mercenaries.

The tentacle flicked around, almost like it had a mind of its own and it tried to pull away from the deck and into the water while still wound around one of the sailors, who called desperately for help.

A few of his comrades attempted to hack at it with axes and one even tried with a spear, but none were successful until Skharr rushed in and skidded over the slippery wooden planks as he slashed his sword upward.

The blade sliced through the flesh like it was nothing. The part that was still connected to the beast below whipped like it hadn't realized that a whole chunk of itself was missing. The part that was wrapped around the man's leg seemed to tighten, but its strength faded quickly and the sailor yanked it off in disgust, leaving large, sucker-shaped bruises on his legs.

There was no time to stop, of course. Skharr had a feeling that the beast had more of those coming. His instincts proved correct and while the smaller tentacles continued to move around, larger ones snaked over the hull of the ship, large enough to see even in the darkness, through the rain, and with the flickering lightning all around them.

The barbarian hefted his sword and adjusted his hold. The lack of any smoke rising from the limb he had severed said there was no connection between the creatures he killed in the past and this one, but the blade would still do damage when it bit into the creature's flesh. It was about all he could ask for as he fought to move to the other side of the ship where two of the appendages had caught the same sailor.

One snatched him initially and dragged him into the path of another that wound around him and began to pull in another direction like they didn't realize they had caught the same prey. It made sense if the monster still couldn't see what was happening.

He rushed forward and his blade gleamed in another flicker of lightning as he hacked into the closest fleshy appendage and sliced a chunk off almost without effort when he drove through it hard. The second one, suddenly not in competition with one of its fellows, had begun to drag him the other way, this time considerably faster.

"Son of a godsbedammed goblin-fucking whore!" Skharr yelled, vaulted over the railing the tentacle had needed to go around, and without a thought, flung his weapon into its path.

It was a mistake. He knew that almost as soon as he released the weapon. If he missed, there was every chance in the world that the blade would slide over the side and be gone from him forever. Or he might have struck the sailor instead.

But the blade flew true and sank into the pink rubbery flesh and even deeper to bury itself in the wooden deck.

The appendage writhed and tried to fight against the blade, but it was in too deep and all it was able to do was tear into its own flesh. He yanked out the ax hanging from his belt and hacked into one side before he drew the sword. Only a tiny sliver of flesh connected the chunk that was wound around the sailor, which wasn't strong enough to continue pulling him, even though it tried.

Skharr growled in disgust and severed it with his ax before he hooked the weapon into his belt and searched for more of them. He would need to attend to the larger ones that had begun to wrap around the ship as he could hear the creaking of wood under pressure.

"You!"

He whirled and looked at the man he'd rescued, who had already dragged the tentacle from his leg.

It was suddenly clear that he was not one of the sailors. The way he struggled to stay on his feet and the fact that his clothes were of slightly better quality should have warned him already, but he had been more distracted with the tentacle wrapped around him. The darkness and the rain had similarly kept the man from being identified immediately.

"Yes," he answered with a broad grin. "Me, you goat-fucking spawn of Janus' slimy scrotum."

The man reached for the blade at his hip, but Skharr lunged across the short distance between them with his sword in hand and thrust decisively. It was a short fight as the mercenary wasn't even able to draw his sword before he buried his into his chest.

It cut through the padded armor almost effortlessly and drove out the other side before the warrior even thought to draw it back.

And in that moment, he thought of a better purpose for the godsbedammed bastard.

"It might not be a god," he muttered with a grim smile, "but I'd wager it appreciates a sacrifice nevertheless." He heaved the dying mercenary at his feet onto his shoulder and carried him to the edge of the deck.

He hurled him overboard and watched him plummet toward the water, but something caught him before he could splash in. A writhing mass of the tentacles dragged the man to the back, where more of the larger, heavier tentacles had begun to slither higher onto the ship.

The creature was massive. The lightning that flickered and flashed around them as the storm grew more intense might have exaggerated it in his mind, but the beast attempted to climb onto the back of the ship and its weight had begun to drag it into the water. It hadn't quite managed to gain sufficient purchase and the larger tentacles slipped often but quickly reattached themselves.

There was no doubt in his mind that it would be able to drag the vessel down, especially once the larger limbs were able to reach the deck and wind around the mast.

More of the smaller tendrils flailed and writhed with increased determination to find something to take hold of. They began to wind around anything they could grasp and pulled until the wood strained under the weight of the monster.

That left only one possible option. The smaller appendages wouldn't be able to drag the creature up on their own. If he managed to attack the larger ones, it would need to sink into the water.

Hopefully, it would be enough to force the smaller ones to withdraw. It was a far cry from killing it, but perhaps something closer to its overall size would have a better chance at that. He had a feeling that such monsters were not uncommon in these waters and merely didn't bother to come to the surface due to the lack of food.

"Oh, this is not a good idea," Skharr muttered, moved to a coil of rope that was tied to the mast, and wrapped it quickly around his waist. He reinforced it with a loop over his shoulder and between his thighs. He was able to work uninterrupted as more battles had broken out when the sailors and mercenaries alike were driven away from their tasks to fight together against a common foe. They were in no immediate danger, and there was a greater threat for him to deal with while they were engaged elsewhere.

He knew he would regret this idea, one way or another. Either it would go wrong in the worst of ways, or he would be left with extreme tenderness in a place that was only meant to be treated well.

Whatever the outcome, he was now committed. The barbarian drew a deep breath, lurched toward the side of the ship, and looked down to where the closest of the larger tentacles still attempted to gain purchase on the *Redress*. He jumped before he could change his mind.

His descent was stopped less than three yards down when his feet caught on something thick, fleshy, and slimy. He realized that the appendage had already moved up from its original position and he tugged the rope to find better balance. It was difficult as his boots slid constantly on the slime but the rope afforded some measure of stability to stop him from slipping off entirely.

"Get...off...the fucking...ship!" Skharr roared and tried to adjust his position so he could do more than simply remain where he was.

His balance was threatened even more when something wound around his left ankle. He scowled at one of the smaller tentacles that attempted to drag him off. It spoke of the sensitivity of the creature, given that he was smaller than a gnat by comparison.

Almost without conscious thought, he retrieved his ax and swung it into the hull so the blade bit deep enough to provide a solid handhold. He swung his sword with his free hand to sever the tentacle and pulled himself into a more comfortable position.

His hold on his sword tightened as he looked around and tried to determine what he should do next.

"Get off the ship!" he bellowed at the creature when he finally decided to drive his sword down with as much power as he could summon. The blade met with more resistance and he felt something almost like tendons working within the fleshy appendage. Even so, the reaction was almost immediate.

A nerve had been struck and the entire creature twitched with enough power to knock him off his perch so he dangled precariously with only a single rope between him and the roiling, murky water below.

He groaned as the rope tightened painfully around his groin, but the blade had no doubt injured something because the beast jerked in pained response and tried to withdraw the affected tentacle while it maintained its hold on the ship.

"Don't you fucking dare, you godsbedammed slime-oozing bag of stinking troll shit," he warned and let the pain fuel his anger.

The rain had begun to lose some of its fervor and the wind seemed to have died down a little as well. This left him with nothing else to focus on but hacking the fleshy tentacle with his sword to open the wound even more until the beast finally tried to move away from his vicious assault.

"And where in all the hells do you think you're going, you gormless pus-pudding?" Skharr shouted and used the rope to maneuver himself to where one of the other appendages inched over the same portion of the hull. It didn't get far before he stabbed his sword deep into it.

This time, he was sure he heard a roar of pain from the monster. Lightning flickered again and the writhing mass of tentacles whipped wildly, torn between trying to hold onto the vessel and to determine what had caused it so much pain.

The barbarian thrust repeatedly and pushed his blade in as deep as he could—which wasn't as much as he would have liked due to his awkward position on the side of the ship—until finally, it fell away.

In the next moment, wood splintered as planks that were still grasped by the massive suckers were suddenly dragged free. The smaller ones retreated as well, and the vessel above him rose sharply when the weight that had dragged it down was suddenly released and it started to move normally again.

The yank tightened the rope between his thighs again and he groaned as he hung over the side of the ship for a few moments. He tried to recover by drawing a deep breath and turned his focus to where his ax was impaled in the side of the ship. After a few attempts, he managed to work it free and began to pull himself up slowly.

Some said that Samor was capable of sleeping through a storm. They were right about that, of course, but the exception was when their ship was being attacked.

The way the ship jerked from side to side was enough to wake him and almost upend him from the hammock he slept in. Something was wrong, that much was clear, and they needed his help to deal with it.

Of course they did. He was the only one aboard with sufficient intelligence, experience, and skill, after all.

He emerged from the hold and hesitated when he realized how large the problem was. The rain and the fury of the storm were what he'd expected, but it was far from the greatest threat. His hasty scrutiny of the scene revealed his men mixed with the sailors and he assumed they had banded together to fight a mass of tentacles that had begun to invade the deck.

Although he'd heard that these waters held numerous sea monsters, he hadn't ever thought he would have to deal with them himself.

"Son of a godsbedammed pox-ridden whore!" He growled, drew his sword, and rushed to the group that held most of his men. They were surrounded by three of the tentacles and attempted to drive it off with a collection of spears, hooks, and oars. Despite their concerted efforts, neither he nor the sailors would last very long given the sheer number of slimy adversaries they faced.

Without hesitation, he entered the fray. He vaulted over two of the appendages that tried to stop him, flipped smoothly, and landed firmly on the wet deck as he swiped his blade in a wide arc to sunder one from the body of the beast.

The remnant jerked in pain and withdrew quickly. Samor twisted and flicked his sword to his left hand as another of the ghastly limbs slid across the deck to catch one of his legs.

It fell away when he severed it deftly and left him clear to turn his attention to the two that were harassing his men.

"You godsbedammed useless pricks need me for fucking everything, don't you?" he snapped at them and sliced smoothly into the tentacles. His blade didn't quite cut them off but the wounds were enough to drive them away from the group.

Suddenly, the whole ship jerked forward and almost hurled Samor from his feet. He regained his balance and looked back to where most of the appendages receded from the deck, slid over the side, and left the men alone for the moment.

"There, you see?" he muttered as his gaze scanned the scene again. "All it needed was a quick lesson in the history of pain delivered by my sword. Whereas you bumbling fucking imbecilic incompetents need to learn how to fight the larger threats. How you survived this long is honestly beyond comprehension."

He turned, hoping to see his men standing in proper awe of what he'd accomplished when barely out of bed. Instead, his eyes widened when he realized that all but one of them sprawled on the deck and clutched gaping wounds. The last one screamed as something powerful launched him overboard.

The darkness was almost complete aside from a handful of lamps that were still hanging despite the storm, and the rain, while it didn't fall as strongly as it had before, continued to batter the vessel relentlessly.

It was only when a sizzle of lightning illuminated the deck that he realized another man was present. The veritable giant stood with a sword in his hand and appeared to be covered in blood. It looked quite black in the almost nonexistent light.

Of course, it could be only one man given the circumstances. Samor had assumed the barbarian was dead but in retrospect, there was no valid reason to believe that.

He hadn't seen the body, he reminded himself, which merely proved that he should never ignore one of the few rules he lived by—make sure the fucking bastard is thoroughly killed.

"You could have walked away," he pointed out caustically. "The world would have believed you dead and you could have moved on from it to a new life, but no, you had to return. And why? For a useless fucking dwarf?"

Skharr didn't answer, but in the silence, the mercenary stole another hurried inspection of the deck and finally realized that the warrior hadn't killed most of his men. Instead, the remaining crew had done the deed.

As he stared at the scene and tried to assimilate this information and determine what it might mean, the storm began to dissipate. A few clusters of stars appeared above them and shed a little more light on the ship.

The crew were already assembling, with a few still attending to the tasks needed to keep the ship running. The captain approached him but his demeanor distinctly suggested that he would be of no help.

"What the fuck is this, Thatch?" Samor demanded, his sword still in hand. If they intended to kill him, he would certainly take a handful of them into the afterlife with him.

"Justice," Skharr told him coldly.

He turned swiftly, ready to meet the expected attack, but the giant buried his sword in the deck, rolled his shoulders, and approached with no weapon in his hands.

For a moment, it seemed like it was a poor decision on the man's part, but as the mercenary swung his blade to slice into the barbarian's chest, his adversary's hand snapped out at an impossible speed, caught him by the wrist, and squeezed until he could feel bones grinding on bones and pain surged up his arm.

He tried to retain his hold on his sword but it was impossible and it clattered loudly onto the deck as he twisted and tried to throw a punch to push the large man back.

The blow landed but it didn't seem to cause any damage—not to Skharr's face, at least—and a small smirk touched the barbarian's lips in response. By contrast, Samor's hand exploded in pain as a massive hand took him by the neck, wrapped tightly around his throat, and with an almost effortless tug, lifted him off the deck.

There was unfortunately no time to draw and quarter the man, as tempting as the notion was. Besides, that kind of effort required far more than Skharr was willing to expend at this point, but he could still make Samor's death last. He could certainly make it a terrifyingly painful experience rather than a swift delivery of justice.

With a feral grin, he squeezed the man's throat and held him in mid-air until his struggles had almost stopped before he finally opened his hand and let him fall heavily with a painful thud.

The pirates laughed and seemed sure that it was as good as over. One had even claimed the sword Samor dropped. But the barbarian was not quite finished with him yet. The mercenary sucked in a deep breath of the crisp evening air and his eyes bulged as he tried weakly to drag himself away.

Skharr scowled, unhooked his ax, and moved to where the man lay prone. He twisted his fingers into a handful of the thick, golden hair the fool appeared to be so fond of and lifted him onto his feet to march him to the edge of the deck. Still holding him in a vice-like grip, he stopped where the railing had been knocked away by the tentacles that had invaded the deck not long before.

"You...you can't do this," Samor whispered. He stared into the water and his eyes widened as his fate suddenly became clear. "Captain!"

"You told me that you took someone who now appears to be a friend of the Scourge of the Waters," Graves answered with a chuckle. "That's a godsbedammed foolish decision—a lesson you would have to learn if you survive. Not that you will, of course."

The warrior smirked and thrust the ax blade into the mercenary's stomach until blood ran freely from the wound and the muscles beneath no longer resisted. Once that was done, he drew the blade across and more blood gushed from the gaping hole. The man's screams echoed across the water when his guts were exposed to the air, and after a few long seconds, they began to slide out.

Skharr took a step back and watched with grim satisfaction as the man tried to contain his innards, but they slid through his hands until their weight and the pain dragged him overboard. A second later, he splashed loudly into the ocean, although it was debatable how long he would be able to stay above water. If he was unlucky, he would be able to keep himself up until the sharks or one of the other sea monsters found him.

"Right!" Graves shouted and turned his attention to the remaining crew. "Get those godsbedammed coin-addled fucks off my ship to join Samor as fish food and clean this deck. And one of you lazy shits, find me the dwarf!"

CHAPTER NINETEEN

Revenge was not something Skharr pursued often. He'd been on that path already in the past and had learned the hard way that there was always an empty feeling afterward. As the adrenaline faded, his fingers felt light and trembled somewhat as he drew a deep breath and focused on the disaster around him.

The crew had begun to clear the debris left by the storm. A few of the more skilled sailors focused on the repairs while others used wooden buckets to bail rain and seawater from the deck. They would have to do the same in the hold, of course, but anything above would ultimately seep through and they preferred to work from top to bottom.

It was a blessing that the storm had mostly cleared to leave them with a light drizzle rather than a deluge. Perhaps the monster had brought the storms and used them to shield itself when it attacked vessels on the surface.

The barbarian smirked. The fact that it was far from being the craziest thing he had ever seen was an interesting commentary on his life.

The crew appeared to give him something of a wide berth.

While he was used to that kind of reaction when he was among the general populace, folks who were hardened fighters tended not to.

He had a feeling they might have heard of his reputation, which begged the question of which reputation they'd heard.

It wasn't long before shouts issued from the hold and a familiar voice berated any and all who came into his path.

"You rabid sea-swine shitheads had no issues with transporting me to my death, did you?"

"We did not know you were traveling with the Scourge."

That explained which reputation they knew him as, at least.

"Who gives a godsbedammed pile of stinking goblin turd who I was fucking traveling with?" Brahgen snapped. "Am I supposed to act like all is forgiven because you suddenly no longer plan to kill me?"

They emerged from the hold and the results of the argument were immediately apparent. The sailor clamped his hand over a wound on his shoulder, likely inflicted by the dagger Skharr had given his companion. The dwarf appeared to have been sick a few times while belowdecks and was in a foul mood as he approached his friend, who had begun to clean the monster and human blood that collected on him.

The youth paused and tried to not show any reaction at seeing him looking like he did before he shrugged, chuckled, and moved to where Skharr used a clean cloth to wipe his weapons.

"You look like you...uh..."

The barbarian nodded. "Like I climbed inside a monster's asshole and cut through to the front end. Yes, I've seen my reflection."

"I intended to say like shit, but I suppose yours might be a more colorful and accurate depiction, yes." Brahgen shook his head. "I have a question for you."

Once the weapons were clean, the warrior picked up the bucket of seawater he'd used and emptied it over his head. He spluttered as the cold liquid sluiced over his body to wash away most of the blood and grime that had collected on his skin. "Will you ask it or wait for the heavens to open and answer it for you?"

"Why do they call you the Scourge? I've heard the saying that the Scourge took him or something like that since I was a child, but I always assumed it was a particular monster of the sea."

"A monster, perhaps," he answered. "But not of the sea. At least, not exclusively."

Before more could be said, the captain approached. He looked a little the worse for wear now that the fighting was over.

"Why do you call him the Scourge?" Brahgen asked before Skharr could say anything.

"Because that's what he was—for a while at least," Graves answered honestly. "Barbarian Scourge of the Sea. It's been some time since I've seen him on the open water but there is no mistaking him. He hasn't aged a day either, I should add."

"This was not my finest hour," Skharr muttered.

"Think that if you like." Graves grinned. "Still, you came onto my ship, killed heaven knows how many of the godsbedammed mercenaries while fighting a fucking kraken, then paused to negotiate your passage in the middle of the attack, during a thunderstorm, and proceeded to not only to drive the kraken off but kill your enemy as well. If that ain't your finest hour, I'd love to see the moment when you climb to Janus' throne and kick him off it. I can conceive of nothing else that could possibly exceed what you accomplished tonight."

The barbarian smirked. "I might have told bigger stories in my day than the reality of what I did."

"You're on my ship, not in chains, and you say you might have stretched the truth? The last I knew, folk don't give a wagon-load of horse shit about the truth. You have to lie to make your reality believable."

"I had a friend in trouble," he answered.

Graves raised an eyebrow. "The dwarf?"

"Aye."

"Friend?" Brahgen asked when he realized that he was suddenly a part of the conversation. "No offense, Skharr, but you have an arrangement with my uncle."

"I told Ahverna you were my friend and one doesn't lie to a goddess," Skharr answered with a shrug. "At least, not to her face."

"You spoke to the goddess Ahverna?" Graves chuckled and shook his head as the warrior took another bucket from the crew who were still tossing water overboard. "I told ya, Scourge. Ya got to lie to make folk believe even half the truth, DeathEater."

"You spoke to the goddess?" the dwarf asked and narrowed his eyes.

"I have a feeling everyone's fallen under some kind of deafness spell," Skharr muttered. The slime from the kraken that had caught on his legs proved particularly troublesome to wash off.

"It's odd how she hasn't heard any of my words for decades and now, she's paid attention to me twice in the span of a month."

"I have a feeling she's listened to you a great deal more than that," Skharr interjected. "She merely did not need to answer."

"I needed her before!"

"Not this badly, I suppose. Still, she heard your prayers and healed me from whatever trap they left for us in the entrance with a little extra besides. I think she had a mind to see me hasten my pursuit because I didn't need to sleep until I was a day out of Tacham."

"I must assume that is how you managed to close the distance between us," Brahgen muttered and looked almost impressed as he glanced at the crew who kept to themselves and avoided the conversation like their lives depended on it.

Skharr could see the questions still welling in the dwarf's mind, but he immediately had the good sense to move away from them.

"Wait." The youth shook his head. "What happened to the trap they left outside the cave? They left it there specifically in case you survived whatever they poisoned you with first."

The barbarian shook his head. "I think she might have tripped it or disarmed it. I kept it, of course, and have it somewhere in my packs. It annoyed me that they felt the need to kill me again."

"Is that why you gutted him and fed him to the sharks?" Graves asked.

"You what?" Brahgen snapped.

He narrowed his eyes. "I was angry. And I did have considerably more planned that I wanted to do to him, but after dealing with the kraken, I was more tired than anything else."

"Gutting a man and tossing him into the water is what you do when you're tired?" The dwarf shook his head. "I almost asked what you would have done to him if you weren't exhausted, but I have a feeling I don't want to know."

"I planned to castrate him, gut him, and make him watch while I cooked his entrails over a brazier," he answered.

"See, that is why I did not want to know."

"That's nothing." Graves laughed with evil amusement. "The most interesting story I heard was when one captain captured him and intended to see him buried up to his neck on a beach and marooned there. The Scourge escaped and impaled the crew on their masts."

"And how did I get off the island?" Skharr asked.

"Hmm?"

"If I impaled the whole crew on the island using the masts, how would I have left the island?"

The man tilted his head and nodded. "But I suppose there is some truth to the tale?"

"I did impale the captain on the stake he wanted to impale me on," Skharr answered. "It was a long, painful process for him and the crew agreed to take me to the nearest port provided that I did not kill them in the same way."

Brahgen narrowed his eyes. "Impalement is when you sharpen

the stake and drive it up a man's…"

"Yes," he answered.

"Until it comes out the…"

"Indeed."

"Well then." The dwarf coughed. "I'm learning a little of what you're capable of when angry."

"Aren't you glad you're my friend?" he asked. "And that I did not take it personally that you tried to rob me when we met?"

"Yes…and yes." Brahgen grinned.

Skharr nodded and turned his attention to Graves. "How seaworthy is the *Redress*?"

The captain looked like he had dreaded that question. "Seaworthy might be putting it kindly. When that fucking kraken tried to mount her, it caused all kinds of damage that even I won't be able to fully determine until I see it for myself. We have holes in the hull that need repair and the rudder is damaged, which means we'll limp to the nearest port to see to those problems."

"I see." The warrior looked thoughtful for a moment. "And where is the closest port of call?"

"The Dragon Followers have established a small town at the cape that should be a decent enough haven."

"I'm sorry—the Dragon Followers?" Brahgen asked.

"Nothing like what you're thinking," Skharr interrupted when he realized where the dwarf's mind was headed. "They're a raiding group that works with pirates—brigands with a small fleet and every boat has a dragon's head carved into the bow. They attack fishing villages and the like up and down the coastline."

"Well then." Brahgen nodded. "I suppose that's our next stop."

"Right." He sheathed his sword. "Now if you'll excuse me, I need to feed Horse a few apples."

Graves sighed and shook his head. "Of course he smuggled his horse onto my ship as well."

CHAPTER TWENTY

"**W**hy won't the empire simply come in and deal with the fuckers?"

Skharr looked at where Brahgen still clung to the side of the ship, ready to hurl whatever food he had eaten during their morning meal. He had tried to tell him that he needed to continue to eat, even if he threw it up. It was simple logic. He would need any sustenance he could manage and not everything that went down would come up.

The slower movement of the ship and the comparatively calm waters certainly helped, but there was no immediate solution for the green hue that had suffused the dwarf's face. He wouldn't be comfortable until they were on dry land. While the barbarian felt bad for him, there was little he could do to help him.

"Well?"

The question pulled him from his thoughts and he tried to not smile at the way his companion clung desperately to the railing.

"Did you say something?"

"I asked why the empire won't come in and deal with the raiders and pirates once and for all."

"Why do you think the raiders and pirates settled in this location in the first place?"

Brahgen shook his head.

"This is about as far away from the imperial city as they can be," Skharr explained. "Most of their troops are committed to wars in the west and the north, which leaves this little corner of the empire to practically govern themselves. I doubt that a tax man has been through these parts in the last decade or so. As such, with nothing to hinder them, the criminals found a place where they could continue their actions without having to deal with imperial troops at all. And if the troops were to arrive, they would simply climb into their ships and sail to where the soldiers aren't."

The dwarf tilted his head, rolled his eyes, and looked a little less sick than he had a while before. "I will assume you know so much about it because you read a great deal during your travels. While you were saving innocent travelers and keeping the virgins pure and the monsters at bay."

"The…virgins were not kept pure," Skharr admitted. "But in my defense, they were not pure in the first place. And they asked me to…" He shrugged

"I see," Brahgen muttered. "You were one of these shits—raiding, killing folk, and transporting people to be killed."

"I wasn't like them," he muttered. "I was considerably worse. They don't call folk who are like the others anything other than a pirate like the rest of them."

"What made you stop? Why do you fight for the gods now?"

"I was…in an emotional state. When that passed, I realized I was taking my pain out on the rest of the world. From that point forward, I decided I would be a farmer for the rest of my life and grow things instead of killing them."

Brahgen looked around the deck and chuckled. "I'd say you're one shit farmer."

"Shut your hole, dwarf. A god meandered along one day and

told me he wanted me elsewhere. I doubt either of us thought I would survive a dungeon with a fucking lich in it, but I did and… well, I've tripped into one fucking pile of horse crap that needed fixing after another."

He didn't like being in the region any better than his companion did, although for vastly different reasons. Old memories of what he had done while sailing through these waters were unpleasant to think about. That time was truly as low as he'd ever been.

And the way the crew looked at him didn't help. Something almost like reverence gleamed in their eyes alongside the fear. They expected the Scourge to turn them into a story that was told by drunken sailors at the end of the night when all the good wine was gone.

"We are approaching the Dragon Followers, Captain," one of the crew shouted.

Skharr turned his attention to the small bay that had carved into the coast where a river finally delivered its water to the ocean. It was easy to miss, the kind of nondescript feature that blended into the landscape. More importantly, with cliffs rising from every point around it, the sea was the only way to approach it. Old imperial ballistae had been positioned on the rocks to turn any ship approaching into a smoking wreck. A determined attack would get through but not before the denizens inside had time to sneak away.

He'd always been of the opinion that the Dragon Followers had started as a small imperial fleet that decided to turn pirate, but over the years, so many of them had been killed that even their history was lost.

"The area is appealing," Brahgen muttered. "I could see myself living here after a while."

"I'm sure you could," Skharr responded. "Although they would ask you to repair their weapons, given that you're a dwarf. I doubt they would let you do much of anything else."

"Ah. I'd avoid this particular location, then."

"Good lad. Clever thinking."

The *Redress* still limped along, and it took effort to turn her into the inlet. It inched painstakingly slowly through the calm waters to where a group had begun to assemble on the white beach surrounding the village. The settlement looked fairly simple and there were many similarities between it and most military camps.

With that said, it looked like the original camp had been in place long enough to grow roots. While more than a few temporary-looking tents were in evidence, buildings had been erected on tall stilts to avoid the rising tide waters. Dozens of trees grew in the expanse between the water and the sheer cliffs above them, but their roots also acted as stilts.

Most importantly, Skharr noted an area in the cliff face where it seemed like they had tried to dig tunnels into the rock, only to have it cave in on them. It seemed probable that all attempts were abandoned thereafter.

They were raiders and pillagers, not engineers.

Brahgen chuckled when he noticed the same thing. "Bring in a team of my kin and they would have a small city built into the cliff face before six months had passed."

"Who would bring dwarves to this kind of place?"

"You."

The barbarian frowned for a moment, then nodded. "Well, you're right about that, I suppose."

The ship finally completed its slow approach to the dock and they were both pulled into the work required to move everything off the ship and unload it onto the beach while the Dragon Followers watched them with their weapons close but not at the ready. They clearly did not expect a fight to ensue, not over a ship that was taking water on by the bucketful.

It was hard work, and only once this was completed was it moved to a dock on the far side, where a rudimentary system had been created to draw it onto the beach at high tide. When the tide receded, the vessel would remain out of the water and repairs could be done.

Even he hadn't expected the damage to be so extensive. Massive chunks of the hull had been ripped out and more along the back and the bottom, where the creature had suctioned fast. Divots made by huge, spiny teeth were visible on the bottom as well.

"It'll take you a while to repair that," Skharr commented to Graves, stating the obvious.

"Aye, but she's seen worse, the old gal."

"Worse than a kraken chewing on her from behind?"

"Sure. Not while I was captain, of course, but you can see the scars in a ship that show exactly what she's been through."

The barbarian narrowed his eyes at him. Either he knew exactly what he meant or he was simply talking through his ass since he could see none of the scars he had mentioned. Perhaps a barbarian didn't have that kind of eye for ships.

"Will you remain here with us?" Graves asked. "Or do you have other plans in mind?"

"I need to take the dwarf to his family."

"In that case, you'll need to negotiate with the clan leader. When I was here last it was Neera Reed—and there she comes."

Skharr turned to study a lean woman who approached with a confident stride. Her hair was cut short and the right side was completely shaven to reveal a web of tattoos that traced down the left side of her face as well. He could see the burn scars the tattoos were covering and noticed that the flames had seared half of her right eyebrow away as well.

"Captain Reed," Graves called and moved to meet her. "I apologize for the suddenness of our arrival."

She smirked and didn't slow her approach, although she kept one hand on the saber she carried on her hip. A little taller than Graves, she was leaner too and walked like she was constantly off-balance. He recognized it as how folk tended to move when they were so used to moving on the sea that a lack of rolling waves under their feet felt unnatural.

It almost made it look like she was drunk.

"We saw the storm last night," she answered and her gaze focused on Skharr almost immediately. "And we assumed a few ships would come in for repairs. Although I didn't expect you to arrive, Thatch. I thought you were smarter than that."

"The storm struck a little too quickly," Graves admitted. "And the kraken equally as quickly. The weather would have been a breeze by comparison if the bastard hadn't found us."

"They follow the storms," she muttered and shook her head. "Godsbedammed scavengers. And sometimes, they cannot wait for the storms to sink their prey and choose to attack." She had not moved her attention from the barbarian. "This one is not part of your crew."

"He needed passage on my ship," Graves answered. "And I fear I will not be able to take him and his companion to his destination."

"I'm a sound sailor," Skharr explained. "And a good fighter. If you could provide us with passage, your crew would benefit from another skilled hand among them."

Reed looked at the other man. "Is this true?"

"I've not seen his like as a fighter," he answered. "As a sailor… well, he has some experience, at least."

"A ringing endorsement," the warrior muttered.

"I've heard many say that none are their equal as fighters," Reed answered. "I haven't seen it proven once."

"And you've seen many fighters, have you?"

"More than you could count, barbarian. I've killed my fair share of them too."

It wasn't a boast or at least didn't sound like one. She carried herself with a quiet confidence that made him wonder how many she'd killed and which of them had left her with the scar on her face.

His careful study revealed others. She wore light clothing and more than a handful were visible on her arms, shoulders, and legs. Her right hand was missing a finger as well.

And she didn't look like she could be a year older than thirty.

"You won't take Thatch's word, then?" Skharr asked. "We could probably trade our way out of here if you prefer."

"Do we look like a trading post to you? All those who board my ships must sail them and fight for them on equal standing. As for Thatch's word...well, I'll say his standards for fighting and sailing differ from my own. And my boys are in need of a little entertainment today so if you don't mind?"

She raised a hand and motioned for him to join her as the others began to follow them into the trees with the roots that kept them off the sand. They were high enough that even he could walk through them and they wandered to a small clearing where a small arena had been erected, supported by the roots.

"Wait here," Reed snapped and jogged lightly up the seats of the arena to where he could see a hut. It was built into one of the trees as well. She didn't bother to knock and simply pushed inside.

"I think they want you to fight," Graves said when shouts issued from the cabin. "I would say that is where their finest fighter lives."

A couple of women rushed outside the dwelling as the yelling continued, mostly from Reed.

"They want me to fight him?" Skharr asked as she exited the cabin again and looked angry.

"Yes," she answered.

"I wouldn't suggest it," he stated. "I wouldn't want to deprive you of a fighter."

"If you're injured, we haven't lost anything."

"Aye. And if your man is injured?"

"We haven't lost much of anything either. Did you think we would have you fight to the death?"

He regarded her with open curiosity. "Yes... Yes, I suppose I did think that."

"I don't gamble lives lightly, barbarian. A little fun and pain are all you have to fear from this."

Skharr focused on the cabin as the occupant exited. A tall man with broad shoulders, it was clear he was a skilled fighter, although he walked with bowed legs.

He did not appear to have just woken up and he seemed ready for a fight. Reed's shouting had no doubt riled him sufficiently and he had a freshly painted bright blue "X" on his chest. With barely a glance at the newcomers, he marched to the center of the arena.

"I'd say that X marks the spot." Graves laughed.

"Say I should beat him," Skharr said and turned his attention to Reed, "would you allow us passage on your boat?"

"And you needn't even pay for it." She smirked. "But you will be expected to work. You and the dwarf."

He looked at Brahgen, whose eyes were suddenly wide.

"That is fair," Skharr agreed. "But I'll need my horse to remain here until I return."

"That you would have to pay for."

It was a fair condition as well. He took a deep breath and turned his attention to the man in the arena, who stretched and rolled his neck while he waited.

"Right then," he muttered. "It's been a while since I've been in a real fight."

"You fought a kraken only a few hours ago," Graves protested.

"Krakens aren't intelligent creatures," he returned, shrugged his packs off his back, and removed the weapons he carried. "Throw them a handful of thieves and cut into their tentacles and they decide they've had enough."

The barbarian grinned before he shrugged and stepped into

the arena. A few dozen of the Followers had already gathered in the seats provided. Already, a few of them were casting bets as he approached his opponent, who looked like he was in the mood to start a fight.

"I hope we didn't interrupt anything important." Skharr cracked his knuckles.

"There were two women in there with me," the fighter snapped. "Do you honestly think I'm interested in trading blows with you?"

"You'll want it over as quickly as possible, then?"

"Aye. With you chewing on the sand."

He grinned. "We'll see."

The man was almost as big as Skharr was, but he was certainly stouter and his face and head were shaved clean. He certainly moved with the balance of one who had been in enough fights. The warrior, on the other hand, hadn't fought much on sand and tested his balance on the soft surface while he watched his adversary advance, draw his arm back, and throw a punch.

It was slow and obvious, but he decided to put it down to the man being angry and more in the mood to end the fight than win it. While he jumped out of the way, he didn't respond with a counter yet. To be honest, he wanted the fight to last as long as he could draw it out.

Having a good fight was a sound way to get the blood flowing again.

The other man recovered quickly and narrowed his eyes as he tried to determine how the barbarian had moved so quickly.

"Come on, then," he taunted. "I should be chewing on sand by now!"

His opponent rushed in again and this time, he stood his ground, blocked the punch thrown at his ribs with his elbow, and pushed down on it. He caught hold of the other hand aimed at his face, jerked his head forward, and drove his forehead into the man's nose. A loud crunch was audible, and the watching group cheered enthusiastically.

The fighter fell back, clutching his nose, as Skharr wiped a little of the blood that had spattered onto his forehead.

"You'll pay for that!"

"Until now, you've been all talk."

Another wild swing made the barbarian duck hastily and he leaned to the left as another followed, and another in quick succession. The man was large and put tremendous power behind those blows, but he had a fatal flaw in his style. He was too reliant on his size and power and had never bothered to learn technique.

"Come on, then," the barbarian taunted. "It's time for you to stop dancing and start fighting!"

The other man hissed in fury, lunged forward, and swung his fist in a wide arc to catch his adversary across the jaw. When Skharr moved out of the way, he suddenly realized what his opponent was doing.

The knowledge wasn't in time to stop him, of course, and the fighter dropped low and brought his other hand up in a quick strike that crashed into the warrior's groin.

An explosion of pain ripped through him as he was forced back and he sucked in a deep gasp that somehow never seemed to find the bottom of his lungs.

"Is that enough for you, barbarian?"

There was no point in calling foul, of course. The pirates weren't the type to follow conventional rules and the blow appeared to follow the accepted and unspoken rules of a brawl in their territory.

The pain had already begun to fade, but Skharr still sank to his knees like he had difficulty standing or even focusing on the fight. The reaction was one the man didn't question as he approached with a broad grin on his face and prepared to deliver the finishing blow.

The barbarian waited until he was close enough with his fist raised to strike before he lashed out.

His right arm came up first and his fingers closed like a vice around the man's genitals and squeezed them until all the fight evaporated from his eyes. He grinned as he grasped the fighter's shoulder next and stood, lifting him with a heave and grunt, and held him over his shoulders as he looked at the silenced crowd.

Dropping the man onto his knee would end the fight, of course, but it would also break his back. Among the Dragon Followers, that was tantamount to a death sentence on its own. He was angry that his opponent had gone a little too far but not that angry.

With another grunt, he flung the fighter onto the sand a few paces away, where he remained while he groaned and clutched his groin.

After a moment, Skharr followed the man's lead, groaned, and adjusted his balls, which were still sore from the strike.

"Fuck me," he whispered before he turned to the others. "Your friend will need help from your healers, provided you have any. And if he ever has the intention to fuck again, you might want to make it as quickly as possible."

Three men bolted up from the stands and hurried immediately to drag their friend to his feet as he still tried to shield the parts that had been handled so roughly.

Reed looked pensive as she wandered onto the sand as the other onlookers were leaving.

"You have a toughness to you," she said. "I can appreciate that. If you and your dwarf wish to leave this place, we have ten snekkar sailing soon. But we cannot keep your horse. Not for free."

"I'm not his dwarf," Brahgen protested.

Skharr looked around. "We have some coin that we could part with, but I have a feeling you prefer to trade in goods, yes?"

She nodded. "That sword?"

"No. But we have a donkey in need of a new home. She'll work hard and provided you treat her well, she'll work for a long time."

"We can't give them Jenny!" the dwarf protested.

"All our crew are treated with respect, even those that can't speak," Reed answered. "A good donkey is no good if she's angry and afraid."

"Jenny can speak." The youth shook his head. "But...Skharr is the only one who can understand her."

Reed looked at him in silence like she wasn't sure if he was right in the head or not, but she blinked and moved past it. "For the donkey...Jenny, we'll keep your horse. He'll need to work for his keep as well, however. What is his name?"

"Horse."

"Yes, the horse's name."

"The horse's name is Horse," Brahgen explained in exasperation. "Barbarians might be mighty fighters, great tacticians, and possibly even philosophers, but their creativity fails them when it comes to naming things."

"The horse is a royal beast," Skharr interjected. "What better way to name them than by their royal name?"

"That makes no sense to me," Reed muttered. "But if you plan to sail, I suggest you prepare yourselves."

CHAPTER TWENTY-ONE

"Another fucking storm on the horizon."

Skharr settled his gaze on Brahgen, who approached him in disgust. The smaller snekkar were more unstable on the water than the *Redress*, and yet the dwarf seemed far more comfortable. He still looked like the wrong twist would topple him over the side but was decidedly not as unwell as he'd been on the larger vessel. They sailed in the shallows but still moved smoothly over the water as the crew plied the oars to supplement the wind filling their sails.

"You look...well," the barbarian remarked suspiciously.

"I told one of the raiders that I got sick on sea voyages and he gave me a little of a plant, cut up and fermented, that has had a calming effect on my stomach."

"Hmm. Did he happen to share what it was and how you would be able to make more of it?"

"I'm afraid not. He said I could pay for it but he named a price too high even for me."

The barbarian nodded. "I had a feeling he would. Nothing ever comes for free from these bastards."

"And what about you? You went so far as to take a detour to

clear a dungeon during the journey. I didn't mind, of course, but I happen to know you don't need the coin."

"All the coin I've gathered is locked in a bank in Verenvan or in your uncle's hands. Out here, there are a few ways to gather the coin you need without having to carry so much as to make you a target for those with crime on their minds."

Brahgen nodded. "Well, it has been an adventure. I can't say I wouldn't have it any other way, however. Being captured and dragged along, thinking that you were dead and that I was about to die was not a pleasant experience."

"Adventures rarely unfold the way we want them to," Skharr answered. "Which is why the bards find a way to make them sound perfect. If you were to have the power to create a narrative, wouldn't you fix a few hundred details along the way to your benefit?"

"I suppose I would." The dwarf sighed and shook his head. "Thank you…for, uh, for coming to save me. Not many folk would have."

The barbarian narrowed his eyes. "Whatever the Followers gave you might be fucking with your head, I think. You do remember that your uncle went through considerable effort to make sure you were safe with me for this journey, yes?"

"He might have assumed that being with you does not necessarily mean safe," his companion muttered. "You seem like a magnet for trouble."

"That's true enough, I suppose. But then, so are you. And with me around, you have a better chance to come away alive."

"Which was why I was thanking you."

After a moment, Skharr placed his hand on the dwarf's shoulder. "I've come to see you as a friend and it is what friends do. I understand if you do not feel the same way. If you like, you can see it as me fulfilling my promise to your uncle to keep you safe."

The youth looked at him and grinned. "I like the idea of friendship better."

He smiled and shifted his gaze to the storm clouds that were still approaching. If the truth be told, he was about as disgusted as the dwarf had sounded when he'd complained about the weather earlier.

"I swear it's like someone is fucking with me personally," he muttered under his breath. It couldn't be a coincidence that this was the second time he was at sea and the second time they were hounded by storms. It wasn't even the season for them in this region.

Still, he doubted that even the gods would be capable of altering the weather to such a degree. Then again, he didn't know exactly how powerful gods could be. Perhaps he had offended a weather god or goddess who now exacted retribution. Given how many dungeons he'd raided, he was surprised that there were any gods out there who didn't want him dead.

"Knowing our luck, there is probably some kind of monster hiding in these storms too," Brahgen commented.

After a moment, Skharr nodded, moved to his pack, and retrieved his bow. Calmly and methodically, he began to string it.

"I was joking," the dwarf protested.

"And yet you are right," he answered. "It's odd how your humor has a truthful quality to it. You might want to consider taking your instincts a little more seriously."

The youth looked anxiously at him. "I...should probably go under...uh, belowdecks, shouldn't I?"

"If you like," he answered and strained as he tested the bow. "You might want to consider that if something were to attack us from below, that will be the first part to fill with water."

"Oh."

"Sometimes courage, going against every instinct, might see you charge directly into the area where there is the least danger by accident."

"How has that worked out for you?"

"Randomly."

Brahgen nodded. "So, you think I should pay more attention to my instincts yet sometimes act against them?"

"It's paradoxical, I know, but in the end, your mind and your body need to find ways to work together. You shouldn't give yourself over entirely to the natural instincts, but they occasionally have more to say than you might think."

He knew his advice might seem confusing to the dwarf, but the world was a bewildering place. It had taken him a long time, a considerable number of mistakes, and too many close scrapes to count to learn as much as he had—which, when he thought about it, wasn't a great deal.

Skharr drew a deep breath. The waves beneath them began to grow higher and the crew already labored to prepare the snekkar for the storm. They worked quickly to lower the mast and strap everything in while the men held to their oars.

None of them seemed to show any sign that they would try to avoid the storm, although he could see why they wouldn't want to be anywhere near the coastline where the waves might wash them into the rocks.

The rain soon fell in sheets but the wind didn't pick up the way he thought it would. He could hear thunder but no lightning streaked the sky, which meant all ten ships were still a fair distance from the center of the storm.

It wasn't long, however, before he caught the first sign of sizzling light across the dark gray clouds. He peered into the water when the snekke began to rock harder with the waves. Prompted by an inner certainty, he grasped the railing, narrowed his eyes, and was finally rewarded when a large fin broke the surface as the water troughed in preparation for another wave.

There was more than one creature under there, and the fin was long enough to tell him that whatever lurked in the water was long and slithered through it like a snake.

Skharr already had his bow in hand and took a few arrows from his quiver as the first monster rose from the depths. It was much larger than a snake—about as thick around as an oak—with fins that spread wide like wings when it jumped out of the water.

"What the hell are those?" Brahgen shouted over the rain, wind, and lightning around them.

The barbarian had no idea what they were facing. All he knew was that they looked like they were less interested in sinking entire ships and more in snatching the sailors off the decks.

They also had the body for it. The monster was a little too long to heave its entire body out of the water, even with a jump, but the wings allowed it to sail over the ship with its claws extended to grasp the wood while its jaws snapped viciously to claim one of the sailors. Before they could hook or spear it, the creature dove into the ocean.

While their attention was drawn to the stern of the ship, the bow was suddenly attacked by another beast with glinting blue scales. This one rose out of the water like it was waiting for someone to approach close enough.

One of the sailors did and it struck like a serpent, snatched the woman deftly, and tossed her high to clear the deck before it caught her as it submerged and took her with it.

The scales would be a problem, even for his bow. As was the rain and the rocking of the boat, but Skharr dropped to his haunches and spread his feet slightly to steady himself as he drew the bow slowly and waited for the creatures to show themselves again. If they were that large, they would not be satisfied with only one human each.

He drew a deep breath and tried to not let the rain into his eyes as another flicker of movement from the ship behind them caught his eye. He shifted and let his body direct his aim for him as he drew the bow back fully and loosed the arrow without so much as a moment's hesitation.

The projectile streaked away and slashed through droplets of rain for what felt like forever. The barbarian exhaled a sigh of relief when the arrow buried itself deep into the creature's back, pierced the scales easily, and embedded itself almost to the fletching.

It was a good shot, although it had struck a little lower on the creature's body than he had intended to, but the result was the same. It uttered a screech and looked into the sky and for a moment, it resembled a dragon when a flicker of lightning stabbed across the cloud and appeared to emanate from its mouth.

The monster might be close to a dragon but the similarities were thankfully limited. A dragon's scales were much thicker and more difficult to shoot through, although he surmised that thicker scales would not allow them to slip through the water as these beasts did.

Still, the screech seemed to stop the other one. In a moment, the slithering fins of the second indicated its approach and in the next, it was gone, hiding deep in the ocean where he could not reach it. The one he struck dove as well and chose not to remain anywhere near the surface.

Skharr had no idea if the creature would die or if it would be able to drag the arrow out and somehow survive the wound.

The rain continued and the other ships remained alert with spears and hooks at the ready in case the monsters chose to surface again and attack them.

After a few long moments as the storm began to intensify, there was no sign of the creatures. Instinct told him they wouldn't risk injuring themselves further, not if they weren't protecting something dear to them.

"Shouldn't you remain on your guard?" one of the raiders asked as the barbarian moved to take his place at one of the oars.

"They won't return," Skharr shouted in response and adjusted his strokes to follow the beat with the other rowers. "But if we don't leave this fucking storm behind soon, more will come. They will be hungrier and more determined, too."

The sailors heard his words of warning and soon, the snekke drew ahead of the rest and rolled smoothly over the waves. A few of the crew dedicated their efforts to bail the water out and Brahgen joined them. The others plied the oars with firm strokes in unison.

It wasn't long before the rest of the ships increased their pace as well, although the one that they were in moved a little faster than all the others.

Finally, the wind abated somewhat but the rain continued. Rowing was hard work, the kind the barbarian was no longer used to. Years before, he could spend up to a full day on the bench but his stamina for the work had diminished. Perhaps it was rowing through the hostile waters that sapped his strength, or maybe he had simply spent too much time away from the sea.

He didn't like it but he could feel his powerful muscles strain more and more. Keeping pace with the rowers grew increasingly difficult and he finally motioned for one of the others to take his place.

It didn't matter that he was far from the first to need relief on the bench. He hated that he wasn't the last and that he needed relief at all.

In that moment, the rain stopped and shortly thereafter, the sky began to clear and slivers of sunlight gleamed through the gaps in the cloud cover.

His eyes narrowed and he looked around while a few cheers issued from the sailors around him. They'd survived another storm on the high seas and it was always a reason to celebrate, but he couldn't help feeling like there was another reason for how quickly the storm dissipated.

Skharr doubted that he was right, but there was no denying the fact that the storms lost intensity the moment the monsters moved away. Listening to his instincts was something he'd recommended Brahgen do, and he heard something from his as well.

It was nothing specific, of course, but still enough to raise his hackles.

"How far are we from our first stop?" Skharr asked, rubbed his arms, and winced when feeling returned to his fingers with a sharp tingle.

The helmsman pointed into the distance, where campfire smoke rose like pillars into the sky.

"A whaling village," the man said and shook his head. "It has no real name as far as I know. They have meat the Followers need and a way to preserve it so that it'll keep for a long period."

That was good enough for him. The barbarian looked at Brahgen.

"We disembark there," he stated and glanced at the crew. "Will he need to be marked?"

"Aye," the helmsman confirmed.

"Wait…marked?" The dwarf looked worried.

"It's merely a small reminder," Skharr told him. "And to make sure the Followers don't attack you in the future."

He lifted his red hair and pulled his ear forward so the dwarf could see the small mark of the dragon hidden behind his ear.

"Oh." Brahgen tilted his head. "Will we do that now?"

"Yes. Before we land."

It would always happen while they were still on the ship. Skharr couldn't help but smile when his companion showed a little discomfort with the mark they left on him. It would heal before too long and it would prove to be the kind of injury that would no longer bother him after a day or so.

The ships were pulled onto the beach outside the settlement, where the villagers were waiting for them. It wasn't the warmest of welcomes as almost two dozen of them stood with weapons in their hands as if they expected some kind of trouble.

He couldn't blame them. The Followers weren't the type to pay for what they wanted with coin, but a tenuous alliance had been reached and it wasn't long before the group were negoti- ating what they needed from the villagers.

"Why are they trading with them?" Brahgen asked as Skharr gathered their supplies from the ship.

"I would assume it has something to do with the whale meat," he answered. "And their preservation techniques. The villagers managed to negotiate peace as long as they continue to sell it to the Followers. And they won't sell the process of preserving the meat as a way to keep them honest."

The dwarf nodded. "And I suppose that keeping the Followers fed can't be done with them raiding every little corner of civiliza- tion they can find."

"True enough. Eventually, they would run out of villages to plunder."

"I suppose you would stop them if they tried to raid this one. They would have the mighty Barbarian Scourge of the Seas to help them." Brahgen tilted his head. "Although I suppose the question remains of who the mighty Scourge would side with."

He opened his mouth to reply but paused and looked around. A handful of the Followers had heard what the dwarf had said and immediately started to spread the gossip to the rest of the group.

"Well...that secret didn't last," Skharr muttered.

"Why were you keeping it a secret?" his companion asked. "I would have thought it would have meant you didn't need to perform for our trip like you did for Captain Reed."

"Because sometimes, the past needs to stay in the past," he answered and tried to ignore the fact that many more gazes had settled on him, followed by the inevitable whispers. "Those stories were about another side of me—someone I'm trying to not ever return to."

"Why?" The dwarf shouldered his pack again and noticed that they were still being spoken of in hushed whispers as they walked slowly out of the village to the road. "Are you...uh, trying to atone for something you did?"

"Atone?" Skharr countered. "Do you mean repent?"

"That's more religious than I intended but it will work." Brahgen grinned.

"I don't repent." He shook his head. "I did what I did. There can be no way to change that. All I can do is change what I do from this point forward and leave the mistakes of the past in the past where they belong. They become lessons, to my mind, of what I should never return to."

CHAPTER TWENTY-TWO

The weather continued to grow warmer the farther south they traveled. While it certainly quelled any anxiety they might have about the cold, Skharr discovered that other problems arose from it.

What annoyed him most were the insects and other creepies. Mere nuisances in Verenvan, even in the summer, they soon became true threats as their path wound closer to the jungles in the south. Centipedes, scorpions, and spiders began to make regular appearances and the barbarian soon learned that he couldn't abide them.

"They aren't that bad," Brahgen said as he cautiously allowed one of the spiders to climb onto his hand. "The way you treat horses...well, I think I can communicate with the smaller crawlers in the world."

He couldn't help a gentle shiver that trickled up his spine at the sight of the furry, eight-legged creature climbing up his companion's arm.

"You truly are afraid of them." The dwarf narrowed his eyes. "I can understand that a few are a little more unfriendly than we might like, but you do understand that they are more scared of you than you are of them, don't you?"

"You'd be surprised," he retorted and tried to not look at the spider. "Besides, I've had the pleasure of encountering their larger cousins in the mountains and even in a few forests. I wouldn't say I fear them, but…well, I have a healthy respect for creatures that can kill me with one bite."

"This one can't," the youth answered although he kept the monstrosity away from his friend. "Brown spiders have poison in their fangs but not enough power in them to bite into human skin. They prefer to eat other insects and in some cases, they even attack slugs when they can. There are more than a few farmers in the Southern Kingdoms where they bring in the spiders by the barrel to keep slugs and snails away, as well as other pests."

Skharr nodded. "While I can appreciate that, I think it would be best to appreciate it from a safe distance."

Perhaps the dwarf would feel a little more comfortable in the south. As the weather turned warmer, his mood appeared to improve, even when a warm rain fell practically every afternoon. Or maybe he felt better the farther they moved from the sea and closer to the mountains in the south.

The peaks were massive but no snow capped them, which was an oddity in its own right. More than a few dwarf clans had made the region their home, especially since they discovered that they could span their cities across multiple mountains. There were even stories about underground paths that led from one dwarf city to another.

He hadn't seen anything like that himself yet, but it seemed like it might hold at least some truth. The only reason dwarves in the north tended to temper their exploratory digs was for fear that they would emerge near a troglodyte or goblin tribe—or worse still, along the feeding path of a wyrm.

Perhaps there were fewer of the larger creatures in the region.

It would balance the scales, given how many of the other pests crept and scuttled through the forest. Unfortunately, the hope that Brahgen would be able to talk the crawlers away for a night didn't work out the way he hoped it would. After another night during which he barely slept thanks to the heat and having to slap his skin every few minutes, Skharr decided he'd had his fill of the southern regions of the continent.

Verenvan felt like a distant, pleasant dream as he meandered along the dusty roads.

It wasn't long until they passed through the first set of defenses outside the mountain city. It didn't look like it was in disrepair and there was no sign that the inhabitants had been killed. A small moat had a river running through it and spikes on either side.

A few campfires in the area told him that they relied on scouts in the outer reaches to warn the city. The chances were they already knew that the two of them were approaching.

A short while later, heavy hooves thundered toward them. The barbarian put his hand on Brahgen to stop him but the dwarf laughed and shook his head.

"If we're in danger, there will be no saving us."

Skharr still held himself ready as a group of battle rams galloped into view. They were nowhere near as fast as horses but they were certainly faster than a human could run and appeared to wear full plates of battle armor without breaking a sweat. He had a feeling that any infantry troop would be hard-pressed to hold their formation when those spears and ram horns collided with them.

The fifteen dwarves came to a halt before they ran the two travelers over, and a few spears remained pointed at the barbarian.

None were pointed at Brahgen, however, and the leader slid from his saddle and pulled his helm off to reveal a proud, thick, black beard complemented by a bald head. He marched to where the youth stood. He was taller than most dwarves—a few inches over five feet—and filled his shoulder pauldrons better than the rest.

"Brahgen fuckin' AnvilForged, what the fuck are you doing here?" the dwarf demanded before he uttered a deep, hearty laugh. "I'm jokin'. Your uncle sent us word that you were comin' and that you were being escorted by a beast of a human. I don't know why they thought this'un would pass for that, but I guess any human that's taller than average would look like a beast to old Throk."

"Hello, Uncle Fas," the youth grumbled.

"That's Uncle Fasenroar to ye, laddie." The dwarf turned his attention over to Skharr and tilted his head awkwardly to look at him. "What do they call ye, big-un?"

"Skharr DeathEater," he answered. "Fasenroar AnvilForged?"

"Nae, GoldHoard. The boy takes his father's name but needs his mother's clan to keep him alive. We should have guessed that was the case."

"And yet you still ask my father's clan for all the steel needed to armor your troops," Brahgen commented with a grin.

"You learned more lip than I remember. I guess that's what comes from traveling with an overgrown troglodyte."

Before the barbarian could counter the offense, his companion had already stepped closer and threw a hard punch to knock Fas back a few steps before he stumbled and finally landed on his rear.

"If that's how you react to a half-pint giving you what will surely be a black eye, you might want to reconsider insulting Skharr DeathEater." Brahgen approached his uncle and helped him up.

The whole troop behind him erupted in laughter, and while the older dwarf looked like he was about to vent his anger for a moment, he began to laugh as well. He took his nephew's hand

and grunted as he rose to his feet and rubbed the place where the blow had met his eye.

"I don't know who you are, but where is Brahgen AnvilForged and what have you done with him?"

Skharr smirked as the others laughed.

"We'll escort you to the city walls," Fas stated, mounted his battle ram, and gestured for his troops to turn. "After that, we will continue our patrols."

That seemed reasonable and the group continued toward the mountains that towered against the sky.

Oddly enough, the city that rose above them was practically invisible from a distance, yet as they approached, Skharr wasn't sure why he hadn't seen it before. The walls were built high and into the mountain face, with massive statues of mighty dwarves of the past holding the gates that were lowered slowly when one of Fas' men blew a horn to announce their arrival.

Most of the dwarven cities the barbarian had been in before were the types that were built deep into the mountains and mostly isolated from the world, but this one was half out in the open. He could see that the city had been carved into the mountain itself like it was in one massive cave, and as the sun was setting, it cast light within to reveal that it was supported by hundreds of columns across the city.

These pillars provided housing for the dwarves inside.

This was a city to almost rival Verenvan in sheer size and scope, and all the more impressive due to how much work had gone into creating it from a barren mountain face.

The forests growing into the sides of the mountain extended beyond the walls as well and even into the city, which explained why it was so difficult to see it from afar.

"Your mouth is hanging open."

Skharr coughed and snapped his jaw shut as he glared at Brahgen and tried to ignore the arrogant grin on the boy's lips.

"Have you been here before?" he asked, desperate to change the subject.

"In my younger years. I suppose it is less impressive if you've been here when you were a child. In the end, you see most other cities as inferior and this as the median standard."

"What standard?"

"The...well, the average."

"Ah." He couldn't understand that. A city like this seemed like it was practically the stuff of myths and legends, like the City in the Clouds that he'd heard tell of so many years ago. "So why did you leave?"

"I'd acquired a few... bad habits," Brahgen admitted and raised his hand to reveal a hefty, viciously curved dagger—one he hadn't seen him with before.

It took the barbarian a few moments to realize where he'd taken it from.

"You truly cannot control yourself, can you?"

"I've never needed to."

"Have you thought about the fact that if you had, you wouldn't have been sent away from your home? And then sent away again?"

"And I would never have met you and gone on our adventures together."

That was a fair point, although he would have thought that anyone would prefer to have a nice, safe home to live in rather than travel the world and run face-first into a myriad of dangers, almost without pause.

The gates were open and as they crossed the bridge to reach them, the group on the battle rams rode away in the direction they'd come from, likely to continue their patrols.

"How long do you think until Fas realizes that his dagger is missing?" Brahgen asked as they passed through the gates and immediately headed through the city like he knew every inch of it.

"I would say he already knows and didn't want to make a scene about it in front of his men and subject himself to more mockery. Which means he'll approach you about it later if he knows where you are going. Which—do you know where you are going?"

The dwarf smirked. "My family has a large house in which almost every section is filled by the various branches breaking away from it. In fact, it is said that they created a new section whenever a new family was joined to ours. I think we might have run out of space eventually, but you can see the house. A city inside a city, my mother used to call it."

Skharr looked at where his companion pointed and had to concede that he was right. The house was built into the inside of the mountain. He'd almost missed it, thinking the mansion was merely the wall of the cave the city was in.

A wall had been built around its entrance as well, with a handful of guards already waiting for them, along with a tall dwarf woman.

She approached as soon as she saw them and led the guards forward before she stopped in front of Brahgen.

Her stern look softened as she stepped forward and wrapped her arms around him. "Welcome home, Brahgie."

The interesting nickname made Skharr immediately raise an eyebrow.

"I've missed you too, Mother," the youth whispered and returned her embrace.

She moved back, held him at arm's length, and brushed her fingers through his beard. "You've changed, my boy."

"I suppose I have."

The smile on her face vanished when she looked at Skharr who stood in silence nearby. "I see you've been messing with barbarians of late as well."

"He is my friend," Brahgen interrupted. "I love and respect you but you won't speak ill of a friend who has saved my life already."

The woman walked to the warrior and stood at a distance that allowed her to scrutinize him carefully without having to strain her neck.

"Do you have a name?" she asked finally after she'd completed her inspection.

"Aye," he answered.

"AnvilForged has a high opinion of you if he tasked you with protecting my son. Perhaps he's merely impressed by any human who is taller than average. Do you know how to use that sword you carry?"

Skharr narrowed his eyes. "I might do."

He could see Brahgen trying to hold his laughter in check when his mother started to display signs of frustration.

"Do you know how to speak in proper sentences, or do you merely grunt through any conversation and hope no one notices?"

"Perhaps."

Finally, she turned to face her son instead. "Please tell me he can speak better than this. Or are you so desperate for companionship that any old shit with nothing between his ears will do?"

"That's going too far, mother," Brahgen stated firmly and his tone took on a slightly arrogant edge. "This is Skharr DeathEater, Barbarian of Theros and respected client of Throk AnvilForged who recently completed the Ax of Skharr DeathEater and has been tasked with delivering it to the DeathEater Clan."

She turned to face the warrior and her face turned red. "Skharr DeathEater? Known as—"

The warrior raised a hand to interrupt her. "Merely Skharr will do. I would prefer to leave any other titles and monikers I might have in the past where they belong."

The youth narrowed his eyes. "You have more names? Unbelievable."

"Folk like to put their preferred titles on those they feel deserve it," he muttered.

"Do you call my son friend?" the woman interrupted before Brahgen could ask for more details.

Skharr nodded. "Aye. I've called him such in the presence of a goddess as well and I know better than to displease her by lying."

He could tell she wasn't entirely sure what to make of that statement, but she appeared to accept it, shrugged, and gestured for the guards to return to whatever duties they were required to do.

Once they were gone, a small tear trickled down her cheek as she wrapped the youth in another hug. "My son...you've become a man, and such a mighty one at that."

More members of the family began to show themselves and approached the group to greet Brahgen and congratulate him on his return. The barbarian inched back, reluctant to have to explain his presence to every one of them.

Even so, it was good to see that the young dwarf had received such a warm welcome to the home of his ancestors.

CHAPTER TWENTY-THREE

Brahgen had not been lying when he said the family had built a small city inside the city of Tuan—the name had only been told to him later but it came as no surprise.

Skharr had not missed the fact it was simply the dwarven word for city, which was an interesting commentary on how the dwarves viewed it. It was almost like the DeathEaters saw their clan as The Clan and having a name beyond that was rather superfluous.

He was escorted to a room that would be his for the duration of his stay, where he was told to prepare himself.

"A feast is being held," one of the dwarf guards noted. "Brahgen is being prepared as a guest of honor, and he said he would not attend without you there as well. It is not a common thing for a human to be present at our feasts."

He shrugged. "I've attended one before among the Anvil-Forged clans. I recall they are able to host a momentous occasion when it suits them."

The dwarf smirked. "Of course, AnvilForged are desperate for companionship and willing to let simply anyone join them. You will find our city's feasts to be something else entirely."

"You take considerable pride in being somehow better than your cousins in the north," he noted.

"That's because we are."

"In my experience, if you have to claim as much, you might be caught in a lie."

The guard narrowed his eyes. "Well, I suppose we shall have to see whether I tell the truth or not."

The barbarian winked. "We shall indeed."

The door was closed behind him and he paused for a moment to inspect the room.

It was nothing like the combination of wood and hay he had become used to at the Mermaid. In fact, the room was about the size of the common area of Verenvan's inn, with a hefty bed built into the stone and padded with down mattresses and blankets.

Either dwarves enjoyed having a great deal of space in their beds or this was a room reserved for when humans visited, as the bed was more than large enough to accommodate him.

There was a table, also made from stone although the chairs were made of wood. A jug of what smelled like watered wine and a couple of goblets, as well as a tray with fruits and snacks, were laid out for him.

All appeared to be freshly delivered as well. He wondered how long they had known that he was coming and how quickly they had been able to arrange the room.

Most notably, to his mind at least, was a large tub in the corner of the room. It was carved into the rock with seats inside and steaming water poured in to fill it. All that prevented the steam from collecting in the room was a small vent above it that appeared to suck it out.

In all probability, an entire intricate system had been laid through the entire building. He guessed there were likely similar systems to deliver water and remove steam from all the rooms in the building.

Skharr had no idea how they'd managed it, but they had

clever minds for this kind of thing. Besides, he doubted that he would be able to decipher their systems even if their experts explained it for him in detail. Like magic, engineering was something he had no mind for.

After a moment to explore the large, square room as well as peek through the large windows that gave him an interesting view of the city with the sun setting over it, he realized that he needed to prepare himself. If Brahgen wanted him present for whatever this feast was, he didn't want to be late.

"Horse wouldn't want to miss this," he muttered and shook his head as he moved to where his pack had been placed.

Clothes for a real feast weren't the type of thing he liked to carry around, and the dwarves wouldn't have anything that would fit him. It was an interesting conundrum but hopefully, they would appreciate his predicament and not judge him too harshly for his lack.

"And now you care about what dwarves think of your clothing." He shook his head and retrieved clean clothes from his pack. "You have come far, Skharr DeathEater, and fallen fucking far as well."

There was a time when he would appear in his common robes when invited to a feast like this, which then resulted in fewer invitations. He always told himself that he didn't care enough to impress others.

And now, the best he could produce was clothes that were clean. Before he put them on, he moved to the tub and discovered that a cloth and soap had been laid out for him as well.

He hurried his ablutions, even though the warm water tempted him to simply sit and soak for a while. The suds created by the soap floated and were soon drawn to where the water drained out slowly. He should have guessed that such a thing would happen, given that a steady stream of the warm water flowed in.

Once he was clean, Skharr climbed out again, dried himself

roughly, and took a moment to comb his hair and beard before he looped the former in a rough ponytail with a leather strap.

Some lordlings liked to braid their hair and beards when they were expected to make official appearances, but he had no idea how to create those. It was why he always tied his hair out of his face, even if he went into battle.

He pulled his clothes on and smoothed the wrinkles carefully, annoyed that he put himself through so much effort to impress folk he didn't even know. Folk, he reminded himself, that he likely wouldn't be around for very long.

The finest piece of clothing he carried was the belt presented to him by the emperor. Thick silver and gold threads were woven through it with scabbards for his sword and dagger, which had matching blades with snakes with emerald eyes on the pommels.

Perhaps that would be enough. Skharr shook his head and stepped out of his door where a guard already waited for him.

Or maybe still waited for him. He couldn't recall if he'd seen her earlier. She didn't say a word and merely nodded for him to follow her.

The mansion was a godsbedammed maze that he would need a fair amount of time to learn to navigate. Thankfully, he was led swiftly through the winding hallways and staircases until they finally reached a massive feast hall created in the open. The sun had already disappeared below the horizon, which left only the light of hundreds of torches and dozens of braziers to illuminate a gathering of almost a hundred dwarves.

A few of them looked and pointed at the barbarian who had been invited to the event, but he got the feeling that most had already been warned of his presence and didn't think it as uncommon as he was led to believe it was.

It wasn't long before Brahgen ran to where he stood.

Unlike Skharr, he wore clothes that were more appropriate for a feast, probably prepared beforehand when they were informed of his imminent arrival.

"Look at you." He smirked as the youth punched him hard in the shoulder. "You look like a little princeling—about what I imagined the emperor looked like when he was ten years old."

"And you look like a troll covered in face paint and dressed in clothing," his friend countered smoothly. "Who someone tied a fake beard and hair to."

"Trolls do grow hair and beards, although they are mostly gray," he told him. "And putting face paint on one would be mighty difficult, even for me. Unless it were dead."

"Have you fought a troll before?"

Skharr nodded. "It came fucking close to killing me as well. They are large bastards but they have little in the way of a sharp mind for battle. They charge at anything with their head lowered like a bull."

"You've fought a bull too?" Brahgen laughed. "Fucking hells, barbarian, is there anything under the sun that you haven't crossed blades with?"

He paused and inclined his head in thought. "I've never fought sheep before."

"Goats?"

"I've fought a goat. But, in my defense, the goat did start it. And even I know better than to pick a fight with woodland fae. Those bastards could leave you suffering from ill-luck for decades even after they are killed."

"Are you sure? It might merely be a myth."

"It could be. But would you truly want to risk ten years of bad luck when you can simply negotiate your passage through their woodlands?"

"Wait—you've met a woodland fae?"

"A long time ago. I was still a young barbarian then. He asked that I help him carry his pack. He'd been wounded and had difficulty walking. I assisted him with his burden and left him with food for the rest of his journey."

Brahgen narrowed his eyes as they moved through the crowd

that grew larger with every passing minute. "They are said to give good luck to those who help them in a time of need."

"True, but I was soon involved in a war that compelled me to kill one of my best friends immediately after, so I assumed he forgot to provide me with whatever fucking blessing he meant to."

"Or his luck was for you to survive the war. I can imagine there are a great many who didn't."

Skharr couldn't argue with that, although he didn't like to think the same luck that ensured his survival was what caused him to bury his sword in Tristan's chest.

Most tales insisted that there was a twisted humor in all agreements reached with the fae. Perhaps he would find himself in the presence of that little fucker again and if he were responsible, he would see him dead, bad luck be damned.

"Brahgie, come!"

The barbarian turned where his friend's mother called for his attention again.

"Not…a fucking…word," the youth muttered.

"As you say, Brahgie."

"Fuck you."

She looked like dwarvish royalty with her thick brown hair bound in an intricate braid, a bright red dress, and a flowing silk cloak draped around her shoulders and held in place by a silver broach with a sapphire in the center.

"Skharr, you are welcome to join us at the head table," she stated, although with considerably less affection in her voice. "You must tell us more about your travels. Throk said you would be arriving almost a week earlier."

"We were delayed," Brahgen interjected quickly. "We needed to circle a little more than planned and were in need of coin on the way. Skharr used his membership in the guild to find us some."

"Some work, aye," the warrior said as he slid into the seat he was offered at the main table. It was a little smaller than was comfortable and Skharr needed to pull the stool away for him to be able to sit on it. "We were contracted to clear the dungeon on the Groll Oak Orcs' Isle. Brahgen was able to communicate with the orcs and arrange safe passage to the dungeon that was being guarded by a handful of swamp hags."

"A story about how Skharr conquered a dungeon?" one of the dwarves called. "And before the bards get around to butchering it and removing all the good violence from it. This has the makings of a good story."

The barbarian laughed. "In all honesty, I had less to do with it than I have had in the past. I managed to eliminate a small clan of lizardfolk that the hags used to protect themselves, but when the crones revealed themselves, I was easily bested. A little too easily for any of the bards to like if they've made their coin by telling folk how powerful a barbarian I am."

The dwarves all shared a round of laughter at that, and he realized that he had an audience of at least three dozen listening to what he had to say.

"As the hags tried to drag me to their cauldron—there was considerable mention of how sweet my blood would taste and how stringy my muscles would be—Brahgen picked my bow up."

Every gaze turned to the young dwarf, whose eyes were wide, and Skharr could see that his mother studied the two of them with a disapproving glare. He realized that he was already drawing to the end of the story and he needed to make it last a little longer. Years of entertaining fellow soldiers with tales told him more detail was required.

"He knew in that moment that even if he did manage to shoot the bow and kill one of the hags, the other two would capture him as easily as they did me, so he devised a clever plan. In my quiver, he found one of my arrows that had a small load of blasting powder. He took it and the bow and fired the arrow into the fire over which the hags intended to cook me."

A few gasps issued from the young children in the audience.

"In that moment, a loud explosion filled the cave," the warrior continued. "And Brahgen drew his dagger and attacked the hags, who had no idea what had happened. He slew one almost before she realized he was there and gutted the next with a keen slash of his dagger. It was an impressive strike that I must take credit for teaching him."

That drew a laugh from his audience.

"Unfortunately, the third gathered her senses, moved to attack him, and forced him back. Before she could deliver the killing blow with her venomous claws, however, I reached out, still struggling to breathe from the spell they cast on me. It was not much but it was enough to distract her as Brahgen lunged forward with a dwarven battle cry I could not understand on his lips, slashed the hag's throat open from ear to ear, and broke the spell they had cast on me and saved my life in a single stroke."

The dwarves all cheered at the ending and a few of them uttered bellows of "GoldHoard," possibly imagining that was what the youth had shouted.

The matriarch grinned and shook her head as the attention moved to the other side of the room where a song had broken out.

"I saw the bow you carry, barbarian," she stated. "I know for a fact that Brahgen would not be able to draw it. So, what truly happened?"

"There were no lies in my tale, milady," Skharr answered.

"Salah," she answered smoothly. "And if there were no lies, how did he loose that arrow?"

"I used my feet," her son answered and pushed his stool back to demonstrate. "I put the bow on my feet and pulled the string with my hands. I missed the first shot too."

Salah chuckled but still looked dubious. "You would have me believe that my son is a mighty warrior now?"

"The mightiest warriors fight with their heads before the first blow is struck," the barbarian said. "I think in that, your son is a better fighter than most would give him credit for. With a few years of proper training, he might well be one of the greatest ever to be produced by the GoldHoard and AnvilForged clans."

He turned to Brahgen but the young dwarf had been dragged away from their conversation by a group of young women already trying to gain his attention by listening and hoping for more stories from him.

"I suppose this is one of those times when a mother must stop doting over her son," Salah muttered. "I had hoped he would want to spend more time with me, but I should have known that the young women of the city would be on his mind as well."

"I would say he's had the attention of his mother all his life," Skharr told her as heaping piles of steaming food and massive barrels of mead and ale were served. "And the attention of the womenfolk is a little foreign to him."

She laughed. "Well, I suppose I should leave him to it. Especially if I have a desire for grandchildren."

That was a little more than he cared to know about Brahgen's family and he raised a flagon full of ale quickly to his lips. Thankfully, she was requested to speak to a few others of the clan, likely on important business that had nothing to do with him.

A heaping plate of smoked sausages, salted pork, potatoes, and what looked like rice but was thick, yellow, and smeared with butter was placed before him, and he could smell the spices that had been sprinkled over it. They made him think of home. Dwarves had a taste for spices and the tolerance for those that would have humans who weren't used to them shitting blood.

But DeathEaters had mingled with dwarves for many a generation, and he most certainly had a taste for them too.

When he realized that a few of the dwarves were watching him, he guessed that they expected him to react violently to the heat of the food. He grinned as he took a bite of one of the sausages. The familiar heat filled his mouth and made his cheeks feel flushed, but he took another bite eagerly. Of all the things he didn't miss about home, food was not one of them. He was a decent cook in his own right but far from the skill of those who did so more often.

There was a taste of home in the richly spiced food, and he raised his flagon to those who were watching him before he washed his mouthful down with ale. They cheered and drank as well.

After he had finished the first plate, Skharr leaned back in his seat and took a long sip of the ale to cool his tongue. More plates were brought, this time with a heavy cauldron of stew poured over thick cuts of salted pork belly and spiced rolls of deboned chicken thighs wrapped around roasted asparagus and carrots.

The barbarian glanced at Brahgen and immediately noticed that while a few young female dwarves had gathered around him, his attention was drawn to one seated across the table from him. The young woman wasn't quite a dwarf, he decided. Perhaps there was dwarf blood in her but she was slim and taller than most of the dwarves at a little over five feet tall.

Most notably, she had no hair on her head, an oddity that didn't do anything to detract from her beauty.

She noticed him staring, grinned, and motioned for him to join them.

He circled the table and approached her as she stood, and they moved aside to where they could talk.

"You're no dwarf," Skharr stated.

"It is a good thing barbarians can see the obvious," she said with a soft laugh as her warm auburn gaze drifted across the revelers. "I suppose I should state that you are not a dwarf either. Would that be polite of me?"

He laughed. "You do have some dwarf blood in you."

"My mother was of the GoldHoard clan and she married a human. I was the result, although she passed when I was merely three years of age. My father is a traveling merchant who could not raise me on his own and brought me here to live among my kin. He visits regularly and pays coin to ensure that I want for nothing. I have been here twenty-three years, learning the merchant trade from Salah GoldHoard and the art of combat from the warriors among the clan."

She looked a little younger than twenty-six, although he put that down to her lack of hair.

"I spent time in my youth with the dwarves of the Anvil-Forged clan myself," Skharr commented. "It was a long time ago, granted."

She laughed. "How old are you?"

"Older than most humans ever live to see, even in decrepit old age. DeathEaters have lives that match even dwarves in longevity. Have you a taste for menfolk?"

Her eyes narrowed and she studied him closely. "I do, but you are…a little too large for me, I think."

He cleared his throat. "I did not mean for me, but…my companion." He tilted his head subtly toward Brahgen so she would look without being obvious about it.

"He is about my size," she noted after a brief scrutiny. "But what makes you think he's interested in me? I am not quite…well, what a dwarf would be looking for."

"Neither would he be if we're honest," he replied. "And I have it on good authority that an untraditional beauty such as yours would be more appealing to him."

She grinned. "Well, I suppose we can see about that."

He nodded. "Wait here, then, while I have a word with him."

CHAPTER TWENTY-FOUR

"I do not talk shit, I promise," Brahgen stated and laughed. "I was on the godsbedammed ship when the kraken attacked. I could see it bend the wood at the stern and pull chunks of the hull out before my very eyes."

"But krakens are myths."

"No, but they are not large enough to sink a ship. In fact, my cousin out near the water says they cook the little ones over a fire for food."

He had begun to understand something of the difficulties that surrounded Skharr. People who didn't travel much in the world only knew about the rest of it through myths and legends. These were mostly the type they generally disbelieved as being the construct of an overly active imagination and a need to embellish by the bards who spread the stories.

Captain Thatch had been right in saying that a few lies were needed to make his stories a little more believable. He was fairly certain that there were still those who didn't quite believe the story the barbarian had told them, although none would be so brazen as to say as much to his face.

And it had been an entertaining story too, the kind he didn't see much among dwarves and hadn't heard much of from the barbarian himself.

The young women around him began to argue over how large they thought krakens were and ignored him for a moment as he looked at where Skharr was seated.

He frowned when he realized he had stood, walked to the other side of the table, and was talking to another of the young dwarves he had seen and even felt a little drawn to. He had tried to think about what story he might tell that would gain her attention.

Of course, he should have known that all he needed to do was walk around and talk to her. The warrior was likely to make some kind of lesson over it after he and she had finished a night of vigorous fucking. The sheer size difference between the two would be interesting. She was barely five feet tall and her bald head barely reached his chest.

Perhaps that was the kind of thing women liked. The bigger the better.

Brahgen realized that she was looking at him and he shifted his gaze quickly to the others, who had finished with their argument.

"Did you truly kill those hags on your own?" one of them asked.

"Well, no. I killed them all with my dagger but I needed a little help. First, when Skharr eliminated almost a dozen lizardfolk that were guarding them and when the last one tried to kill me, he managed to stop her."

"I thought he only added that to make sure it didn't sound like he was completely useless in the fight."

"Aye, he wanted a little recognition instead of giving all the credit to a dwarf for saving his life."

It honestly felt like he was talking to people who had no intention of listening to his version of events.

He frowned when he realized that Skharr had moved away from the young woman and approached him instead.

"How does the life of the party feel, Brahgie?" the warrior asked with a grin.

"It is not as much fun as I might have thought," he answered honestly. The group had wandered off to get more drinks and would probably return soon. "It is an interesting feeling, however. None of them would have given me so much as a second glance before."

"Are you sure you want the attention of those who are so shallow that they must needs dole it out?"

The dwarf shrugged. "It isn't like I have much choice. And I might as well enjoy it. Soon, I will no longer be the life of the party and they'll move on to bigger and better things."

Skharr nodded. "You might want to consider that they are more interested in being the sole focus of your attention as the night wears on. Or you might want to find a way to choose which one's attention you want for the rest of the evening."

He winked, clapped him on the shoulder, and retreated as the young women began to return, once again arguing something.

"Hmmm," he muttered as an idea formed in his head. The barbarian was right. He didn't want to be that kind of dwarf and he doubted they had much interest in him aside from the brief moment of fame his recent return had garnered him.

And if he had to spend much time with any of them, he wanted it to be doing something they both shared an interest in.

"Basted like a goose," Skharr whispered as he approached the young woman again.

"How do you know he'll make thievery a point of interest?" she asked.

"I've spent enough time with the lad to know he has many

interests, but most revolve around his ability to take items from folk who don't pay attention." He looked at her again and noticed that she had tugged her dress down so the fabric hugged her curves a little better. There was certainly dwarf blood running in her veins. Most humans didn't have the perfect shape of an hourglass that generally appealed to him.

"Evanessa," she said.

"Hmm?"

"The woman under the dress you're admiring. Her name is Evanessa."

He nodded. "My apologies. I did not mean to stare."

"All it means is that others will stare as well."

"You'll want to reveal a little more," he commented. "You want him doing more than staring by the end of the night. Not all your skin but enough to make his imagination run wild."

She narrowed her eyes. "I have no hair on me, sir."

"Yes." He tilted his head. "That is a point of some embarrassment for you, I take it?"

She glowered at him and rested her hands on her hips.

"Have you ever considered that it might be one of your finest assets?" he suggested. Her eyebrows raised and her gaze shifted to where Brahgen was still dealing with an onslaught of questions.

"I see." She thought about it for another second before she tugged her dress a little lower to reveal more of her cleavage and slid her sleeves down so her shoulders were exposed as well.

There was truly little left to the imagination. Skharr knew Brahgen would have trouble finding proper words to greet her with and thankfully, that would be for the best. Him talking would be a problem. His mind would be gone and what was voiced without its interference would be about as honest as the young dwarf would ever be.

"Right then," Evanessa muttered and rolled her shoulders. "I don't think he'll see this coming."

On that, they could agree.

What was the point of telling a story if every word he said would be picked apart, analyzed, discarded, and replaced by what they wanted to be the truth?

Brahgen tried to not show his annoyance and drew a deep breath.

"No, they don't follow any dragons," he stated when he heard someone suggest as much. "They're called the Dragon Followers because their standard from when they were in the imperial army was a dragon."

"But you said there were dragons in the water," one of the women commented. "And they were pirates that sailed on those waters so they followed the dragons in the water."

There would be considerable misconceptions about the damn pirates by the end of this. He had a feeling that the pirates wouldn't mind that their legend was growing. Stories about them fighting alongside the sea dragons would spread now, unfortunately.

"Do you have any more stories?" one of them asked and flipped aside her bright red hair that had begun to fall over her face.

"Oh...yes, I suppose I do. A little more recent. I suppose you all know my uncle Captain Fasenroar, yes? The man who rides around on a ram all day long, telling the youths of the city to get back into the city walls before nightfall? I assume he's not a popular character among you?"

The general utterance among the group was that Fas was, in fact, not a popular dwarf with the youths of the city.

"I suppose that if someone were to have delivered a blow to his face, it would be a story for you to tell for a while, yes?"

"Sure, but none of us will believe that happened or he would barge in here to demand satisfaction from your mother."

"Perhaps he's a little too embarrassed because, while I laid him flat on his ass, he was too distracted to notice that I'd lifted something from him."

Brahgen took the dagger from where he'd hidden it inside his cloak. It was an item of some pride for Uncle Fas, as he recalled, a battle trophy collected from a goblin chieftain, who had in turn stolen it from one of the dwarf kings of old. It was almost long enough to be a short sword, with a burnished silver sheen to the wickedly curved blade and bronze on the pommel polished to look like gold. Three large rubies formed what looked almost like a mace as the base of it.

"I'll tell you what," he stated as the others began to inspect the weapon thoroughly. "If anyone manages to take it from me, I'll relate the whole of the story to them. In private."

That was a good way to make sure he could escape without injuring anyone's feelings and be able to spend the evening with someone he genuinely wanted to be with.

"How are we supposed to take it?" one of them asked.

"You'll have to steal it, of course," he replied. He reached up to grasp the handle to draw it out but his eyebrows raised sharply and he gaped when all he held was the scabbard.

"Won't you have to negotiate to get it back, then say someone can take it?"

The woman's voice caught his immediate attention and he whipped to face her. Something was different about her now but he couldn't put his finger on it. A distracting amount of skin was showing and she stood next to one of the braziers, tilted her head, and grinned cheekily.

Brahgen almost didn't notice that she held the weapon in her hands until she flicked it up and caught it. A smile still played on her lips, one that looked like a leopard about to pounce on a gazelle from the treetops while she licked her chops at the prospect of a good meal to come.

"Well…" He needed a moment to clear his throat and drag his

mind back from where it tried to decide how low she could get her dress without it sliding off. "Well…"

"You said that already."

"So I did." He nodded. "I'll be buggered."

"You don't seem the type who would enjoy that kind of thing," she countered smoothly with a smirk. "But if you're interested, I'm sure we can find the time. The night is still young, after all."

Everyone around him laughed and his cheeks turned bright red, visible even in the firelight.

She took a step closer and made sure that no one was stepping in the way before she tossed the blade to him with a flick of her wrist. Pure reflex saved him from being pierced by the weapon and he reached out reflexively to snatch the dagger from the air without so much as a single thought about the dangers involved.

Thankfully, he grasped the handle instead of the blade itself, which meant his fingers weren't sliced off, but he realized that his heart pounded a little too hard in his chest with something close to disbelief that he'd been able to catch it.

After a moment to collect himself, Brahgen managed to hide how his hands were shaking by sheathing the dagger.

"It seems I owe you for a wager," he said, surprised that there was no tremor in his voice. "But I never did explain what the reward might be."

"Then I suppose you'll have to negotiate rather hard, wouldn't you say?"

The young dwarf cleared his throat and felt something odd happening simply from seeing her gaze locked onto him like that. It wasn't that he hadn't felt it before but never quite so intense or as quickly. His mouth was dry and blood rushed from his head directly to his groin.

His intentions as to how he would settle the wager would be all too apparent in no time at all.

And she could see it as she stepped a little closer than was comfortable, placed her hand on his shoulder, and leaned forward so he could catch the hot, sweet scent wafting from her neck.

"Don't you worry. I'll go easy on you this first time."

A small grin slid across his face as her fingers traced over his cheek. He barely noticed Skharr standing nearby. The barbarian grinned like he had planned it all from the beginning.

But there was no time to think about that. His mind would certainly be elsewhere and he made no protest as she slipped her arm into his and pulled him away from the festivities.

CHAPTER TWENTY-FIVE

S kharr felt as though he had done the boy a good turn. Evanessa seemed like a nice enough young woman and between the two of them, he was sure they would find something to do together.

She was something of a natural when it came to thievery, which meant Brahgen was already watering at the mouth.

He shook his head as they wandered to another corner of the hall, sat, and began to talk. Salah clearly had some reservations but gave the two their privacy. Her time with her son would have to wait a while.

For the barbarian, the day had already been long enough and a good night's rest began to sound more appealing by the moment. The celebration would likely last into the small hours of the morning if he knew anything about how much dwarves liked their feasts, and he simply did not have the energy for it.

After a few toasts were raised and a few more plates were served, he asked to be excused and a guard led him through the maze of hallways and what he assumed were technically tunnels to the room he had left a few hours earlier.

"No one can say that dwarves don't know how to have a

good time," he muttered as the doors closed behind him. Skharr took a moment to stretch lazily, rolled his shoulders a few times before he unbuckled his belt, and placed his weapons carefully across one of the chairs to be tended to in the morning.

Except, he reminded himself, they didn't. He still needed to get used to the fact that neither dagger nor sword needed to be oiled or honed regularly, and he assumed that had something to do with the magic that was supposed to be infused in them. It annoyed him to have to remind himself of it. But he would need to tend to his other weapons. His ax, other dagger, and his arrowheads would need attention.

Once he returned to Verenvan, he would have to buy a few more arrowheads to replace those he had lost. He only had fifteen of them now.

He pulled his shirt off next, tossed it onto the same chair, and followed it quickly by kicking his boots off and finally, his trousers and undergarments. Having a wash before bed was probably a good idea.

"Well now, that is not something a goddess sees every day."

Skharr spun with no weapon in hand but his fists raised and ready to attack. He froze when he saw Ahverna seated on a nearby chair, her legs crossed as she raised her hands to clap slowly.

"I did have high hopes for what I would see here today and you have done nothing but impress, barbarian."

He cleared his throat and straightened. "Well...I've managed to bring your follower in safely and delivered unto him a night I doubt he'll forget. Or remember, depending on how much ale he's ingested by the end of it."

"So I've heard." She stood smoothly, walked closer to him, and ran her fingers lightly over his shoulders. "You know, I've had two more dwarves praying to me this night alone. I might find myself in a similar position as Janus and Theros before too long."

The barbarian smirked and shook his head but he didn't move away from her hand or the chills it sent up his spine.

"I did not know that," he answered as she circled him without letting her hand leave his bare skin. "Perhaps you have Brahgen to thank for it."

"Perhaps I do," she admitted. "Or perhaps I should thank the famed Scourge of the Waters? Or was it Dragon Bane? Or did you prefer Barbarian of Theros?"

"I generally prefer Skharr DeathEater," he stated firmly and didn't look around as her fingers moved away from his shoulders and instead, traced down the valley of his spine. "It's far simpler and easy to remember."

Ahverna laughed and he stiffened a little when her hand cupped his exposed ass and squeezed it gently. "Are you saying you don't need the accolades?"

Skharr turned, let her hand remain on his rear, and allowed her to see the effect her touch had on him. He was sure there was a trace of magic in it as well as he could feel his arousal growing more enthusiastically than it had in the past.

"Well," he said and his voice sounded a little breathy as her fingers moved and her nails dragged over his thigh before they settled at his groin in a more intimate caress. "I've never been tested by a goddess in the past. It makes a man wonder if he has what it takes to rise to the occasion."

She smiled and slid one hand over his chest to send tingles of sensation rippling across his body as she leaned a little closer.

"I think we both know that you've already risen to the challenge," she whispered. She brushed her lips lightly over his skin as she snapped the fingers of her free hand.

In response, all the buckles of her clothes fell away almost immediately and in seconds, she was as naked as he was. Her tongue brushed his flesh while her fingers continued their exquisite torment.

"I'll need to take your word on that," Skharr noted. "And if that is all that is needed to impress you, I suppose it bodes well for the rest of the night."

The goddess laughed and let her teeth score over the hard planes of his chest as his hands started to rise, brushed lightly over her waist, and moved higher to tease and knead her flesh.

"Well, it remains to be seen if you possess enough stamina to match a goddess. It would be my pleasure to judge how far a man can measure up to divinity."

Skharr smirked, moved his hands to take a firm hold on her hips, and lifted her effortlessly off her feet. She laughed, wrapped her thighs around his waist, and draped her arms around his neck as she pulled herself in close to press her lips hungrily to his.

Mentioning that he was tired from a long day of travel felt like making excuses at this point. All he could promise was his finest effort, and that was what she would be given.

There was certainly some magic afoot, as he felt a rush of passion course through his body—the kind he couldn't resist indulging in.

She squealed delightedly as he tossed her onto the bed and followed her to stretch beside her. Ahverna welcomed him hungrily and their limbs tangled and hands explored one another. The same passion he felt gleamed brightly in her eyes as he claimed her and she gave herself willingly to his mastery.

"Yes!" she screamed and her back arched as her hands twisted into the sheets around her. They rode the tide of their passion together, two moving as one until reality faded and all that was left was the power of their joining.

"Skharr! Yes!"

There was no time to wonder if someone would overhear her cries. He honestly didn't care if anyone did.

The water had gone everywhere.

After a few moments, Skharr realized that the whole floor was tilted so that any water that escaped the bath would collect in the same place all the water continued to flow out of. It wasn't a foolproof process as a few puddles remained, but they would be quick and easy to clean once someone had the time.

He most assuredly did not. He was more than willing to allow the mess to remain for a moment as he leaned back against the edge with the warm water still lapping gently at him and the woman-goddess on his lap.

She clutched his arms, pressed against him and her legs wound tightly around him so not even an inch of space remained between them. He could feel her hot breath on his cheek and her chest heaved gently as she sucked in deep breaths.

He knew the feeling. Breathing didn't come easily for him either. It felt like his whole body was being drained dry of everything it had, and fuck it, he wanted it to continue until there wasn't a drop left in him.

"Oh, fuck..." he whispered as her body loosened and she relaxed slowly against him. She slid down his lap to lay her head comfortably on his chest and listen to his heartbeat.

"I should find a way to turn that into praise to my name," Ahverna whispered softly and ran her fingers lightly over his chest. "So I'd hear it every time you said it."

"As..." he paused, still struggling to catch his breath. "I use it as often in my regular day as I do during sex. You might find yourself being summoned when I handle a handful of foolish highwaymen."

"I merely like the sound of you saying it, no matter the reason." She pushed carefully off his chest and looked into his eyes. "How many times was that? Six? Or seven?"

"Seven, I think," Skharr said uncertainly. He'd lost count about the time that they moved away from the bed and into the tub in his room. It had been an interesting transition that required an entirely new set of muscles to keep her filled and screaming his name.

Ahverna rose from his lap, tried to stand, and winced. She shook her head. "Oh...that still hurts a little."

"Is something wrong?"

She smirked as she settled onto the seat next to him and rested her head on his shoulder. "As if you wouldn't know what a woman feels like after your particular brand of lovemaking."

"It would have thought a goddess would be immune to that kind of thing."

"After the first three or four times, most certainly." Ahverna tilted her head and smiled. "Yes, definitely seven times."

That did touch his ego somewhat, although he felt as though he would have a difficult time walking himself. His knees were a little wobbly, and he would need water and a moment's pause before they began again.

"Another round then, barbarian?"

He turned to look at her as she pressed her lips into his shoulder and moved hands teasingly down his body.

"A barbarian would never dare disappoint a woman such as you."

His voice spoke with a confidence that his body wasn't sure it could match, but damned if he wasn't willing to at least try.

"Truly?" She laughed and her movements turned from light teasing to tantalizing insistence. "Do you have it in you?"

Her answer came when his body responded reflexively to her intimate caress.

"Unbelievable," she whispered, shook her head, and narrowed her eyes at him. "Unfortunately, I feel as though I would need to heal myself to continue, and that would break the spirit of this test."

"So you would instead stir my passion and leave me with no satisfaction?"

"I am sure you could fulfill that yourself with the mere

thought of filling my body in any way you deem most satisfactorily," she commented, pushed up from the seat, and climbed gingerly out of the bath.

She looked for a moment like she might fall, but as she stroked her body lightly, Skharr could see a decided difference in her gait. Whatever aches he might have caused, she was more than capable of healing them. He shouldn't have felt in any way surprised by that.

Before she'd gone three steps, she tilted her head, looked around the room, and snapped her fingers again.

This time, the reaction was considerably different. The water on the floor gathered itself and poured into the drain. The bed neatened as well, with the sheets carefully tucked in to make it seem as though there hadn't been people laying fucking on it.

And, most disappointingly, her dark clothes wrapped around her again like armor.

"Yes," she whispered with a small smile. "I feel two more followers and...oh my."

Skharr looked up from openly admiring her form. Even covered, it was a thing to behold and brought back memories of his hands running over her bare skin. Among other things.

"What?"

"I would appear that Brahgen has found someone and has been thoroughly thanking me for bringing her into his life. But I had little to do with that. Was it your doing?"

"I might have...influenced events," Skharr conceded. "Both were trying to come up with effective and clever ways to approach each other and I indicated that such frivolities were not necessary."

She turned to face him as he climbed out of the bath as well and found a nearby cloth to dry himself with.

"We will not speak of this night," Ahverna said in a tone that would not be ignored. "I have no desire to talk to my brother about bedding his barbarian. He is…possessive of the humans that follow him."

"Bedding his barbarian seven times," he reminded her.

She smiled. "Perhaps another time, we can try for eight. I know you were exhausted already from a long week of traveling and little sleep, so I look forward to encountering you at full strength. But for now, I find myself amidst new responsibilities."

"If you insist," Skharr answered with a smile and looked around to find another, drier cloth that could absorb the water from his skin faster.

"It has been a pleasure, DeathEater."

"The pleasure was…" Skharr paused when he realized that he was alone in the room. He shook his head as he moved to the bed, sleep suddenly on his mind as he finished drying himself.

He climbed onto the bed again and rested his still-wet head on the soft pillows, and his eyes closed almost of their own accord.

"The pleasure was all mine, goddess," he whispered, unsure if she was still around or if she could even hear him. Still, it felt like the right thing to say as he was drifting off into what he knew would be a dreamless sleep.

CHAPTER TWENTY-SIX

" **A** re you sure you need to leave?"

Skharr narrowed his eyes to study Brahgen. He and Evanessa seemed inseparable. In the few minutes since they had arrived in his room, they hadn't stopped touching each other. She was the most affectionate and constantly kissed his cheek, ran her fingers over his shoulders, and hugged him.

The youth seemed to thoroughly enjoy all the attention, which begged the question of why they were in his room and not somewhere else, enjoying each other's company in privacy.

"Yes," he answered briskly. "Quite sure."

"Why?" Evanessa asked without looking at him.

"For one thing, I doubt Salah would want me to remain and leech food and supplies from her while I don't contribute anything to her clan." He raised an eyebrow and watched the two of them with smug satisfaction. "She might feel indebted to me for having brought Brahgen home safely, but I have learned that one must never overstay one's welcome."

"I'm sure we could find work for you to do here," his friend commented and blushed as Evanessa ran her fingers through his hair. "You should find more than enough killing that needs doing in this region of the world to keep you occupied."

"Perhaps, but my second reason is more compelling. I need to retrieve Horse before the Dragon Followers decide their time is better spent killing and eating him. And from there, I should return to Verenvan to see if everything that plagued me there has cooled enough for me to be in the city again."

"Well, I cannot argue with that," the dwarf muttered. "Tell Horse I send greetings. And that...I miss him, I suppose."

Skharr smirked, slung his pack onto his back, and approached him. "I will, my friend. He will probably not return the feeling, but I'll certainly tell him."

Brahgen laughed and disengaged from his new paramour for a moment to stand in front of the barbarian. "I'll miss you too. And not only because you are quite skilled at dragging me out of trouble."

"Although I am sure that does factor in."

The dwarf nodded and after a moment, he stepped forward and hugged him.

It was an awkward embrace, and the warrior was only able to pat him gently on the back until they drew apart.

Skharr cleared his throat and looked away for a moment before he spoke. "Remember what I taught you. And don't wander blindly into danger. That is for me to do and me alone."

"Understood."

He moved around them and descended the steps that took him out of the compound mansion the GoldHoard family called their home. Although no one spoke, he knew that Brahgen and Evanessa followed him every step of the way.

Salah waited for them at the gate with her arms folded over her chest.

"You could stay for a little while longer," she said but he had a feeling her offer had more to do with Brahgen being in earshot than any genuine hospitality. "You've only rested for a few days and your trip has been an arduous one."

"Unfortunately, it must continue," he answered smoothly. He knew his manners all too well and could, when necessary, respond with a gracious refusal. "I have business to attend to on my way back to Verenvan that cannot wait."

"Well, may the gods guide your path," she said and patted him on the arm.

Fas stood not too far away, his eye blackened from where Brahgen had struck him. He must surely know the youth now proudly carried his dagger around the city like it was his own. The fact that he hadn't reclaimed it yet was a matter that required investigation as he no doubt had a good reason for that—possibly even one that included retribution of some kind. The barbarian might have said something but he could already see the dwarf staring daggers at Brahgen. Perhaps his interference wouldn't be welcome.

Still, he paused next to the guardsman and rested his hand on his shoulder. "You do know your dagger helped the boy considerably, yes?"

The dwarf scowled at him, his eyes narrowed.

"Aye."

"And you wouldn't want to ruin it for him. Besides, you now know he is as capable of putting you on your ass as you might be of returning the favor to him."

"Why do you think he still carries it?" Fas shook his head. "I only wish he weren't so…blatant about it."

"He's young," Skharr reminded him. "He'll soon learn that keeping friends like you is an important advantage and you'll have the dagger in your possession in no time. Likely with an apology as well."

A somewhat disbelieving snort followed. "I admire your optimism."

"Give the boy a chance. He truly is not the same child the GoldHoards sent away the first time."

He doubted that he'd convinced the older dwarf but it was the best he could do in the little time he had to hopefully avoid any future confrontation between the two. With a small shrug that suggested he knew he'd be proven right, he adjusted the pack on his shoulder again before he raised his hand in one last, silent farewell to Brahgen. The youth probably wouldn't see it as Evanessa was whispering something in his ear that turned his cheeks a bright crimson.

He knew Fas was there to escort him to the city gates, which meant no confrontation would occur soon. Still, he had a feeling the younger dwarf would be able to stand his ground in any fight by this point. Coddling him would do him no good.

"Of course he missed you. He said as much himself. Why would I lie?"

Horse didn't look convinced and Skharr rolled his eyes.

"Well, if you want to believe otherwise, far be it from me to convince you. But he has his family to deal with. That is the only reason why he didn't come along to say his goodbyes in person."

The barbarian had a feeling Horse would not be happy to see Brahgen again, but the distance between them and the matters each had to focus on made it a moot point. A short boat ride had brought him from the coast to the Followers' camp, and from there, after a short stop, they traced the river to the lakeside town.

He'd deliberately chosen a route around the Druums Woodlands now that he wasn't in any hurry and although it was a little longer, the road was easier and he would soon be in Verenvan.

"Have it your way," the warrior growled. "But if you're rude to him should we meet the dwarf again, it will be no more apples for you. For at least…a week."

That certainly wouldn't convince the stallion of anything. It was an empty promise and they both knew it.

"I would have thought someone as brave as you would take the shorter road through the woodlands," a voice called from behind them.

Skharr's hand was already on his ax, ready to draw it and prepared for a fight, but he knew it wouldn't be necessary. If Theros had a mind to kill him, there wouldn't be much a simple ax could do to stop him. Perhaps the sword or dagger he carried would help, but it was unlikely.

He narrowed his eyes at the old man, who leaned heavily on a walking stick and was followed closely by a foul-tempered donkey. There hadn't been much call for the god to reveal himself to him lately, and when he did, it was usually in his dreams.

A quick look around said this was not a dream, although he decided it was probably a sound idea to remain aware of any indications that might change that opinion.

Finally, Skharr shrugged. "There is a difference between being brave and being stupid. I could make my way through the woodlands but as I have no pressing concerns weighing on my mind, it would be a pointless risk to wander through there."

"I suppose that makes sense," Theros said and patted Horse's neck in passing.

"So, what are you doing here?" he asked as he began to walk again. "I'll admit I did not expect to see you anywhere around here. Is there a problem?"

"It is rare that I seek one of my followers out merely to hold a conversation," the god admitted. "I think we should stop to camp. It will give us a moment to speak."

"Can't you talk while on the path?"

"Why would I? In this body, there are certain aches and pains that distract me. So, camp?"

The barbarian shrugged. "Why the fuck not?"

They stepped off the road and Theros immediately lit a small campfire and positioned a kettle full of water over the flames.

"I don't suppose you'd like a bit of koffe, would you?" he asked and groaned as he sat on a nearby boulder.

Skharr's eyes widened as he sat. "It's been a while since I've tasted the brew. I suppose, for Abirat, I might have a cup in his memory."

"Abirat?"

"The redhead who died in our battle against the elder god," he reminded his companion. "It is odd that I would have to remind you of the folk who died in your name."

"Ah...yes. In my defense, there has been a great deal on my mind."

"I see." He regarded the old man with a teasing smirk. "I like to think I would remember the name of every warrior who died in my name."

"Give it a few hundred years and a few thousand names," Theros countered.

A sound point, Skharr thought as he was offered a wooden cup with the thick, bitter liquid.

"So, I assume all this is because you need something from me?"

"Aye, and it would be enough weight on your mind to perhaps drive you through the woodlands, but it is a little too late for that. For the moment, we can enjoy a beautiful day and a cup of something warm to drink."

It was warm with the perfect amount of bitter but there was a sweetness to it as well. It wasn't quite enough to be cloying but it took the edge off of the bitterness in a way he wasn't overly fond of.

"It's Cassandra," Theros stated finally and looked at him over the lip of his mug.

The barbarian had already finished his warm drink and placed his mug beside him. "What is?"

"I need help with my paladin."

He raised an eyebrow. "Is she injured?"

"Her body is in as fine a form as it was when you parted ways." The god shook his head. "I could resolve that myself. Her heart is…another story. She had a particularly difficult quest in my name. It came immediately after the situation she was in with you."

The lord high god looked off into the distance with a small, wistful smile visible amidst his gray beard. "She returned light-hearted—as happy as I've ever seen her. She did not give me too much sass when I needed a priest to ask her to investigate a problem. And that was when things went…horribly wrong."

Skharr narrowed his eyes. "What did?"

Theros sighed, shook his head, and put his mug down. "That is her story to tell."

"You'll need to tell me something."

For a moment, he could see the flash of the deity hiding inside the shriveled body of an old man in his eyes. It disappeared quickly but it was an effective reminder of who he was dealing with.

"Suffice it to say that…well, three paladins were sent to complete the quest and she is the only one who returned alive. That kind of fight has a way of weighing on the mind, and her mind most of all, I think. She was always an incredibly empathetic being."

The only sound that followed was the crackle of the fire as the two companions both stared into the flames. Skharr knew what that felt like. It was a shit feeling, no doubts there, and yet he wondered what he could do to help.

"Will you help her?" Theros asked finally and broke the silence between them.

He shrugged. "I would die for her, so I don't know why admitting that I am willing to help her would be any worse than that."

The god shook his head.

"I cannot make any promises, of course," he conceded. "I know she's always had misgivings about being a paladin."

"Self-doubt is possibly one of her most admirable qualities. She never evidenced the arrogance that others in her position were notorious for but was always able to summon the confidence to assume her role when it was needed the most. And yet in my effort to be godly, I failed to see her spirit and how fragile it is. Now…she is broken. I owe her more than that, DeathEater. I think the last time she smiled was when she worked with you. Which is why I thought you might be the one to help."

"She won't appreciate me coddling her," he commented.

"That should not be a problem." Theros tossed the rest of his koffe into the flames.

Skharr narrowed his eyes as his mind churned through the possibilities and finally, he could see what his companion was leading to. "You have another quest."

"Of course."

"Dangerous?"

"Obviously."

At least he was being honest about that. It wasn't something one could always count on from the gods.

"I suppose it also comes with the chance of dying?" he asked.

"When have you ever known a quest from a god not to?"

It was a fair point, one he didn't have to think about much and could simply agree with.

"Am I required to save the world, then?"

"Only a part of it." Theros smirked and raised an eyebrow. "There will be no elder gods standing in your path this time."

Skharr drew a deep breath. "How bad is it, precisely?"

The lord high god shrugged casually. "Enough that you should expect to die."

That didn't answer anything and he suppressed a sigh and reminded himself that he was dealing with a god he was supposed to be on good terms with. He had a feeling that many out there wouldn't mind seeing him dead, so it was a pleasant change of pace to be able to face it squarely. If that changed, he already had the attention of far too many of his as yet faceless enemies for it to be a comfortable situation.

Janus would probably be the first in line to try to kill him, no matter what favors had been done for him.

He paused to pour a little more koffe into his mug. The brew was oddly addicting, even if it was sweeter than he would have liked.

"Well, out with it," he said gruffly. "What do we have to face this time?"

Theros looked at him like he had dreaded coming to the point from the very beginning. There was no escaping it now, however.

"A dragon."

The two words made the barbarian's blood run cold as he paused in mid-sip, narrowed his eyes, and shook his head. After a moment, he also flung the contents of his mug into the fire.

"Well...fuck."

AUTHOR NOTES - MICHAEL ANDERLE
MAY 12, 2021

Thank you for reading both this story and these author notes at the end.

We are in book 06 of a larger story arc about this world.

Right now, we have the 7th book of Skharr DeathEater just turned into the beta readers (go gently on us!) and are just about to have the second book of *War Axe* by Aaron Schneider and me into the beta readers as well.

Once those four books are out, you will see the first book of *The Barbarian Princess* hit the 'Zon.

At that point, our first thirteen books will have been released on Skharr's side of the world. However, hints about how magic arrived "over here" have been placed in the stories, and we will turn our focus to the other side of the world.

And the story of the twin peaks.

These stories will be much larger, with a minimum of 150,000 words, and we are trying our very first hardback for the release of book 01 at the end of this year.

That story, revolving around a young thief who has a heart too good for her own future, is more a fantasy story since it focuses on a young mage who throws away a chance to live a mundane life for a shot at greatness.

Or death... *Yeah, probably death.*

During those releases, we will come back to Skharr DeathEater with Skharr 08.

So, I can tell you that LMBPN has planned a minimum of fourteen regular-sized books and six massive fantasies, all evolving on this same world.

The world of a canny barbarian, Skharr DeathEater.

AUDIO ROCKS!

So, I just got through with the first audio production of Skharr DeathEater #1 (Amazon link) last night while packing for my trip.

I'm presently at 31,500 feet, heading towards Texas for our son's graduation.

I mention this because I've now read that story at least three times, twice before publication and at least once after.

Yet I still loved the audio version.

I admit I was a bit annoyed to find out the second book wasn't out yet on audio. To all of you who (like me) are impatiently waiting, thank you for supporting LMBPN's audio efforts with our partners.

Your support in listening to our audio helps a lot!

What if Skharr goes to tv or movie?

I'd love it.

While I admit I'm not as much of a film or tv (cable) viewer as most, I still enjoy certain stories. I am aware that Conan and Red Sonja are both slated for video / movie adaptations, as well as there being many YouTube and cable shows with a barbarian main character.

Including a puppet / muppet show, of all things.

I suspect we (all of us creating new sword & sorcery content) will benefit from a new infusion of fans. I didn't create this series thinking it would become a huge hit. No, I created it because I like the genre and missed any new stories that I enjoyed.

Really, no characters I enjoyed.

Perhaps that is why I keep coming back to Skharr. He is a character in a world that is a bit removed from ours.

While I'm happy that we seem to be doing ok with the sales, I am beyond ecstatic to read your reviews (yes, I do peek from time to time). Like me, others care about this type of story.

There might not be a hundred thousand or a million of us right now, but just know that I'm one of them.

Book 07

You have just read the setup for Skharr DeathEater Book 07, *the Barbarian Princess*. Cassandra is a favorite character of mine (as is Sera, but for different reasons.)

I just got finished reading the last chapter on this story yesterday. I'm ready to go back and reread the whole unedited book once more.

I think you will like it... A lot.

'Til the next Skharr Book (or any of my other series with or without collaborators)!

Ad Aeternitatem,

Michael Anderle